Mary Logue has lived in
She has had stories and
zines and anthologies
American Poets Award.

MARY LOGUE

Red Lake of
the Heart

GRAFTON BOOKS

A Division of the Collins Publishing Group

LONDON GLASGOW
TORONTO SYDNEY AUCKLAND

Grafton Books
A Division of the Collins Publishing Group
8 Grafton Street, London W1X 3LA

A Grafton UK Paperback Original 1988

Published by arrangement with Dell Publishing
Co., Inc., New York, New York, USA

Copyright © Mary Logue 1987

ISBN 0-586-20107-6

Printed and bound in Great Britain by
Collins, Glasgow

Set in Times

With all my love, to my sisters

I've left the town where my sister was murdered. I've left the ripe lakes, fragrant in their blueness, their laughing, waving answer to the sky. I've met many people, made some friends, seen exotic sights, and felt pale to vivid emotions, yet the events of that summer have never left me. Everything I feel I measure against the love and hate I've felt for my sister, and I ask myself, will anything ever really compare?

It was not many years ago, but I was someone else then. This is someone else's story. It begins on a beach in midsummer. Two sisters are lying next to each other, one tan, the other turning a slow red in the hot sun.

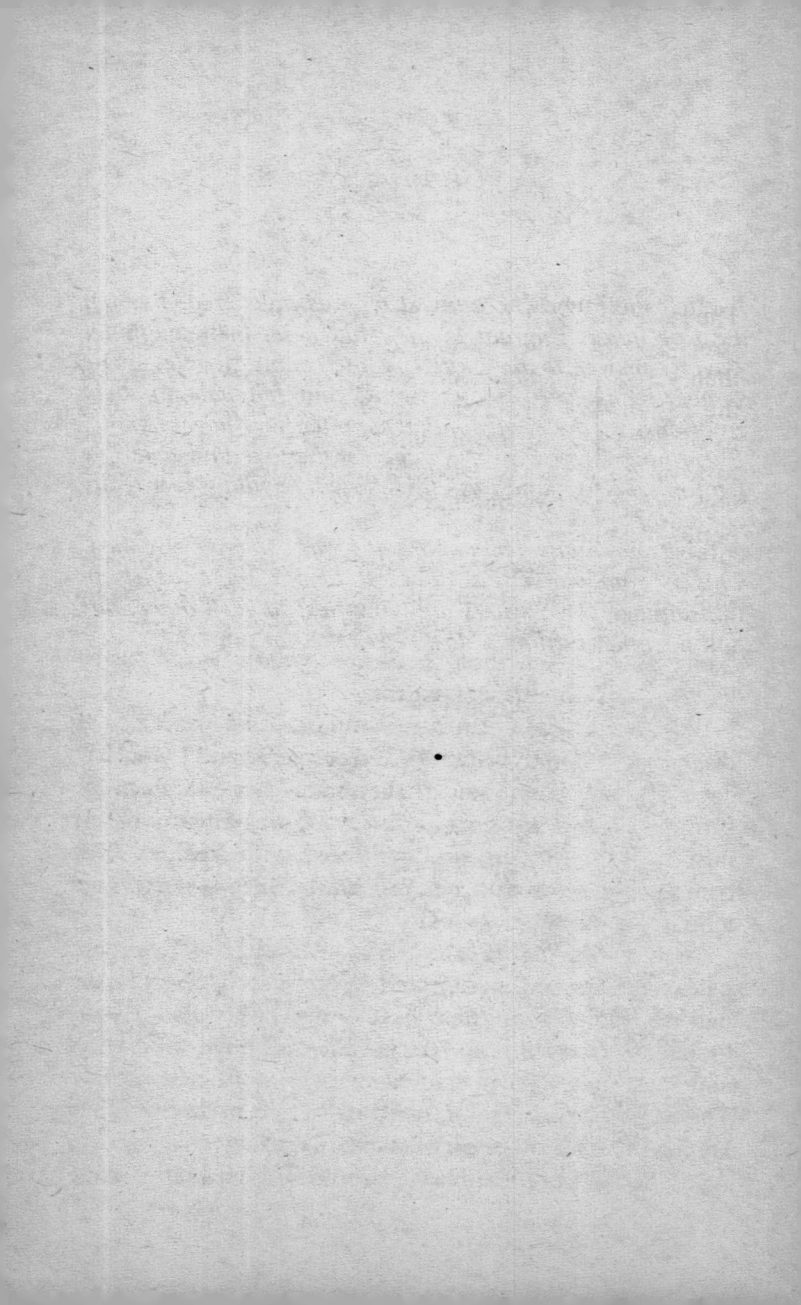

Chapter 1

The thin stripe of a bruise showed on Tricia's wrist as she stretched out on her towel. Amy saw it only for a second; then Tricia, either purposefully or unconsciously, pulled the arm in close to her side. Shaking her head, Amy tried to rid her mind of its buzzing thoughts. She was so used to worrying about her sister that she couldn't stop, even now that there wasn't much need. Tricia was so much better these days.

Amy closed her eyes, feeling the warmth of the sun sink into her skin. Relax, she told herself. For a moment Amy let her mind rise above them and see their two bodies laid out on their green and yellow beach towels like sleek fish on serving platters.

'I'd love to get a tan this summer. Like you. You're disgusting. I could lay out for a week solid and I wouldn't get that dark,' Tricia said as she shaded her eyes from the sun and looked down at her body. It was already lightly flushed from the sun and spattered with freckles. Her complexion went with her red hair, which was cut chin length and curled at the ends.

'You're like Mom and Dad. All three of you are paleskins. Maybe I'm adopted,' Amy joked. Even in the bathtub pictures of them as children Amy had always looked twice as dirty as Tricia. She had been thin, wiry, and tan where Tricia had been pale, soft, and plump. There was still the same contrast between them as they lay next to each other on the beach. Tricia was larger than Amy; her full, rounded body overflowed her bikini, while

Amy's one-piece suit was a snug fit over an athletic body. No one ever thought them sisters.

Amy leaned up on one arm and looked at Tricia. 'OK, you said you'd tell me at the beach. Shoot. How did the tryout go?'

'Well, I sang the songs that you and I picked out the other night. It went all right. It's just so hard for me to tell, I probably completely blew it.'

'Stop it, Tricia. Don't put yourself down. What did they say?'

'They had a couple more singers coming in. They said they'd let me know soon. I want the gig so bad. Maybe you could call Luke?'

Amy hadn't seen Luke in months and couldn't believe Tricia was suggesting she call him. Even if things had been all right between them she wouldn't do that. She hadn't been down to see the band he played in since they had broken up. 'Forget it. We're barely on speaking terms. His girlfriend, Angela, hates my guts. Anyway, you've gotta be professional about this. You're the best, Tricia. You know that.'

'Thanks, but I was really nervous. I haven't done this since,' she stopped, her face clouded over, then she went on, 'LA, since I was out there.'

Amy knew Tricia didn't like to talk about LA, so she asked her the question she'd been dying to ask. 'Did you really tell Danny it was over?'

'Yeah, and I'm serious this time. But he won't leave me alone. Calls every night. A couple times he's called real late, so now I'm unplugging my phone. He's always had a few drinks and he starts talking real sweet, like he's going to get someplace with me.'

Amy sat up to make a point. 'Don't let him get away with that crap, Trish. Hang up on him.'

'It's not so easy. We've been through a lot together.'

'More like he's put you through a lot.'

Tricia didn't say anything.

Amy stood up and looked around the beach, which was a haven for the leftover hippies and the artistic community of Minneapolis. People wore as little as they could get away with, occasionally nothing at all, which caused the police to patrol the beach on Cedar Lake several times a day. Everyone was crowded on to a small fringe of sandy beach circled with large oak trees and sprawling sumac bushes. Clusters of children were playing in the shallow water and a few heads were bobbing farther out, but for the most part people were scattered over the sand, listening to music, talking, and soaking in the sun.

Amy looked down at Tricia. Things were starting to go a little better for her. If only she could stay away from Danny. 'Do you still love him?'

'A little. It's like the opposite of how a pearl is formed. I've been thinking about this. Two years ago Danny gave me this pearl ring. It made me think about how the oyster made the pearl. Have you ever thought about it? For some reason I decided the pearl was like my love for Danny. White and round and valuable. Since then, all the crap that's gone down between us has eaten away at the pearl until all I've got left is a piece of grit.'

'God, you have been thinking. Did you tell that to Danny?'

'I thought about it, but I figured if I did he'd make me give him the ring back.'

Amy laughed, then announced, 'I'm going swimming. You ready for a dip?'

'Not yet. But I'm going to turn over, so could you oil my back?'

'Sure.' Amy searched in Tricia's satchel and found the coconut oil. Rubbing a palmful on Tricia's back, she could smell the heady odor of a sweetness so thick she could

11

almost taste it. As she massaged the oil into her sister's skin, Tricia let out a sigh of enjoyment.

While she was rubbing the small of her back, Amy noticed the purple bruise on the inside of Tricia's wrist again. It looked as if someone had grabbed her wrist and twisted it one way and the opposite way at the same time, and had been serious about it. Amy was going to ask her about the bruise, then stopped, remembering when she had picked Tricia up at the airport after she had returned from LA. It had been only a year ago.

Amy had stood watching the people leaving the airplane and then had seen Tricia. At first she wasn't able to accept that the women standing in front of her was her sister. The skin of her face was pulled tight as a stretched canvas and discoloured; on her cheekbones it had turned a golden-green, but around her eyes it was still freshly bruised purple with a hint of the blood vessels that had ruptured. Tricia had been so badly hurt that one of her eyes was swollen tightly shut.

Similar marks had circled her wrists, and when Amy asked her what had happened, Tricia said there had been a brawl at the club she was singing at and she had inadvertently stepped between two guys. She had been punched in the face and then had fallen and tried to break the fall with her arms, cracking her wrists hard on a table edge.

'LA was too tough for me,' she said. 'I couldn't cut it.'

Once they got home, their mother tried to get Tricia to go to a doctor, but she said she was fine, just needed some rest, and proceeded to drink Scotch until the bottle was empty, and then fell asleep on the couch. Amy didn't say anything to her mother because she didn't want to worry her, but the story seemed odd to her, especially because the marks on her wrists were so much alike.

Just as Amy was gathering up courage to ask her about

12

this new bruise, putting out a finger to touch it, Tricia turned her hand over and slipped it under her head. Amy's hand hovered in the air for a moment, then it went back to kneading the muscles that curved over Tricia's shoulders.

'How's that?' Amy asked, thinking to herself: forget the past, Tricia is so much better now, she hasn't had a drink in a month. If Tricia wants to put it all behind her, then I should too.

Tricia grunted, halfway asleep. Amy gave Tricia's back a final pat and ran down to the edge of the water. It was a perfect summer day. The sun was doubly bright, caught both in the endless blue of the sky and the darker blue of the lake. Amy stepped gingerly into the water to avoid the rocks lodged on the bottom and to test the temperature. It still had a slight nip to it, so she eased into it very slowly, a step at a time.

Once the water was up past her waist, she dived into the lake and swam underwater with her eyes open. The murky blue-green acted as a filter when she flipped upside down and stared through the aquamarine glaze at the sun. It was a trick she had learned as a child, to stare at the impossible light through a watery lens. She surfaced and treaded water, trying to let no disturbances mar the surface.

It was so peaceful. The beach looked an ocean away. There were no problems out here. She gave a kick with her legs and floated on her back. She sucked in a lungful of air to stay afloat. It caused a ringing in her ears. Closing her eyes, she thought if a pearl were love for Tricia, water was love for her. She envisioned falling in love to be like falling into a lake. A huge splash at first, a shock, and then a warm liquid embrace.

Suddenly a hand covered Amy's face, pressing her head down, and she was gulping in water. She tried to grab at

13

the hand, then twisted away and came up spluttering. Tricia was in the water near her, laughing. Amy dived underwater, grabbed one of Tricia's feet and pulled her under, but released her almost immediately. They surfaced together and began splashing each other. The water sprayed between them, with ghosts of rainbows dancing in it.

'You have to set up today at work, don't you?' Amy asked Tricia when she sat down on the towel next to her.

'Yeah.'

'Well, it's almost three-thirty. We should get going.'

'Cool out for another minute or two. I want to dry off a little before we go.' Tricia rubbed her feet with the edge of the towel, brushing off the sand. 'Oh, I've been meaning to ask you, what's the deal with that fry cook, Chuck? He's been really giving me the creeps lately. Is it just me or does he suggest illegal sex acts to all the waitresses?'

'Yugh. You do bring it out in the men. I'd suggest you just ignore him. Pretend you don't speak English.' Amy lay back down on her towel, even though she thought they should go. If only she didn't feel so responsible for Tricia. She supposed it had to do with being two years older than her. But, in a way, she was responsible. Two months ago, when Tricia had been fired from her last waitressing job because of drinking, Amy helped her get a new one working at the restaurant where she worked. It was only a burger joint, but it was a pleasant place to work, and it was good for Tricia because it didn't serve drinks.

So far, Tricia had only been late to work once, but that one time Amy had heard about it from Dot, their manager. In fact, Dot had called her up at home and asked her to come in for Tricia. Just as Amy was getting into

14

her uniform Dot called back and said Tricia had turned up. Amy never mentioned the incident to Tricia. There were many things she never talked to Tricia about, as if by never talking about them they hadn't happened, when instead they grew in her mind. But now she could let go of them all if Tricia stayed sober and was responsible for herself.

'Come on, let's go. I've got a dance class today, so if you want a lift, come on.' Amy started picking up all their stuff. She slipped into her jeans and put on her T-shirt. Tricia grabbed her clothes and towel in a bundle and they left the beach.

'Don't stop, that's Danny's car,' Tricia said to Amy as they approached her apartment.

'What do you mean, don't stop? You have to go to work, sweetheart.' Even as she said that, Amy drove farther down the block and then parked.

'Let's go to your house. I'll borrow your uniform and go to work from there. I don't want to hassle this.'

'You can't let him run your life.'

'I just don't want to see him. You don't know what he can be like sometimes.'

'Listen, I'm going in. You can stay in the car if you want to, but I'm going to tell him to leave you alone.' Amy got out of the car and Tricia reluctantly followed. When they got to the front door of the building, Amy paused for a second to see if Tricia would take the lead, but when she didn't Amy started walking up the stairs.

The door of Tricia's duplex was standing wide open. Amy went in first and saw Danny stretched out on the couch. He was smoking a cigarette and flipping an ivory-handled knife up in the air catching it. He smiled and she was surprised, as always, by how young he looked. He was her age, twenty-five, but, dressed in jean cutoffs, barefoot, his blue eyes washed with light, he seemed like a teenager, one who was playing hooky from school. There was always a catch to his smile, as if he were covering up for something.

'What are you doing here?' she asked him.

He put down the knife and stretched. 'Waiting for my baby. How are you doing, Amy? Looks like you got a little sun today.'

Tricia walked in behind Amy. 'Get your fucking feet off the couch.'

'Hi, sweetie. You're looking like a lobster. Sun doesn't like you as much as it likes Amy.' He tapped the cigarette ash carelessly on to the floor. 'By the way, some guy called you.'

'Danny, would you stay out of my life? What guy?'

'What am I, your secretary?'

'Come on. Did he leave a message?'

'Said his name was Hank.'

'Oh, one of the guys in the band,' Tricia told Amy.

'You know, I think we have some things to talk about.' Danny spoke with as much of a drawl as a native Minnesotan could get away with. As he was ready to launch into a little speech, he sat up, took a drag on his cigarette, put it out in the ashtray, and then smiled up at the two women. 'I mean really talk about. Things you haven't taken into consideration. And we don't need to go into them in front of Amy, but I was hoping to take you to dinner at some nice place and talk over old times and times to come.'

Tricia hardly listened to his speech. She threw down her beach gear, walked into her bedroom, and came back out with her uniform. 'If you don't leave, I'm calling the police.'

'For a woman in your position, you're awfully eager to call the police.'

16

'Shut up. I'll call you tomorrow and we can talk, but I don't have time for this shit now, Danny. I've gotta go to work.'

'So you've still got a job,' he sneered, then asked, 'How long do you think you'll last at this place?'

'Maybe I won't need to waitress anymore. I might be singing in a band pretty soon.'

Danny laughed, shaking his head. 'You just don't learn, do you? Didn't LA teach you anything?'

Tricia shouted at him, 'Shut up.'

Amy couldn't stand it anymore. 'Danny, why don't you leave?'

'Because your sister and I have some things to discuss. I might ask you the same question.'

'Listen, Danny, I can't talk now.' Tricia spoke more calmly. 'I'm sorry. If you go now I promise I'll see you tomorrow.'

Danny stood up. He had hair so white that Tricia and Amy's mother called him a towhead. He pushed it away from his face. 'OK. A date for tomorrow night, right?'

'OK. Just go.'

He walked up to Tricia to kiss her, but she pushed him away. 'Get out of here, Danny.'

Amy saw anger flicker across his face, then he put on a toothy smile. 'Wear something nice tomorrow night. We'll go to Lancelot's.' He turned and left.

'How could you promise him that?' Amy didn't understand Tricia. Danny not only didn't act like he would go away, he seemed menacing to her.

'Just to get him out of here.' Tricia stripped off her clothes. 'Do you see lines on me?' Her full rear end was snowy white, set off by the red banner of her back.

'Yup. You got burnt.'

'I have to get burnt to get any color at all.'

Amy blurted out, 'So what happened to your wrist? I noticed a bruise there.'

Tricia looked down at her wrist and then felt it, as if taking her pulse. After a moment she said, 'You know those big trays at work, the ones we use when we have to serve a four top? One of them fell on my wrist the other day. It really hurt at the time, but then I forgot all about it.'

Amy was relieved the bruise was the result of something so mundane. She almost couldn't believe she had had trouble asking about it. 'That happened to me once too. Those things are so awkward.' Amy turned to go, then turned back and asked, 'Who's Hank?'

'I thought you might know him. Guess he came after you and Luke broke up. He's the keyboard player in the band. Maybe they've made a decision.'

'Are you going to call him back?'

'Yeah, but not right now. I gotta get to work.'

Amy couldn't stop herself from warning her. 'Tricia, for God's sake, get your key back from Danny. He's just trouble.'

Tricia smiled fondly at Amy and then gave her a light tap on the shoulder. 'You mean for your sake. Don't you worry your pretty little head. I can take care of that guy. You better get going or you'll be late for your dance class, and if I know Todd, he'll give you hell.'

Amy was late for her dance class. She stood for a second at the doorway watching two lines of dancers doing their warm-ups. It still excited her to see people moving in unison. She whipped off her T-shirt and jeans and pulled on a pair of tights over her damp swimming suit. Then she sneaked into the second line of dancers. Todd, the instructor, nodded at her and went on leading the exercises.

Bending down low, she put her palms to the floor, then her wrists. She had been trying to dance at least a couple hours every day because the Bellington Dance Studio was holding auditions for its company in a couple of weeks. She was almost too old to make a career of it and if she didn't get in this year she would give up dancing, or the thought of dancing professionally. Maybe she would go back and finish school and dance would become just a hobby for her. But these auditions were important to her; she would always know she had tried.

She liked Todd's teaching. He was the one who had encouraged her to think of joining the company. She hadn't started dancing until she was nineteen, when she had taken a course at the University. It had been a revelation.

When she and Tricia were young they had never taken tap dancing or ballet. The only time she had had any dance instruction had been in seventh-grade gym and then she had been holding the sweating hand of a boy who talked to her about car engines. In high school she had always liked to dance to rock and roll, but this dancing was different, it was serious. She listened carefully to the instructor and then told her body what to do and it did it. It moved through the air, it jumped, it skipped, for short moments it soared. She knew it was as close to flying as she'd ever get. At night she would dream of floating up to the ceiling and having to hand-over-hand her way down by grabbing a ladder tacked to the wall.

She took the next three dance courses offered at the University, then her instructor encouraged her to go outside the University. 'We can't really teach you much more here. These classes are only designed to fulfill the Phys. Ed. requirements.'

The first class she had taken at the Bellington Dance Studio had been Todd's. That was three years ago. After

19

the last class he took her aside and told her that even if she lacked grace as a dancer, she had a dancer's body. Somehow, even though she realized he meant it as a compliment, she resented his saying that. The next semester she doubled up her classes, purposefully avoiding taking one with him. In the summer, when she finally rejoined his class, he had whistled approvingly as she moved across the floor in the first run. Afterward, he took out for coffee and told her she had something.

Todd and she had become friends. At first, she had assumed he was gay because he was a dancer. Then she had felt sure he was gay when he didn't make a move on her. By the time she found out he wasn't gay, they were fast friends.

She liked to watch Todd move. He looked like a sailor to her, black hair cut very short, piercing blue eyes, and rather large ears. He was a big man, much larger than most male dancers. There was an awkwardness about him that he was able to translate into fluid movement. A catch in his dancing that made her hold her breath, waiting for him to do something wrong, but he never did.

Todd was showing the class a patterned run across the floor as a drummer beat out the syncopated rhythm. When it was Amy's turn to do the run, she started strong and then halfway across the floor she lost the beat. Todd grabbed her hand as she ended her run and showed her the step again over to the side of the room. He did it with her and she felt the beat as she saw his body dip next to hers.

In her next run across the floor she did it right and caught him smiling at her. Throwing her head back, she took a deep breath. It was so exhilarating when her body figured out something that her mind couldn't.

After class Amy stayed and talked to Todd. She was having some problems remaining open through her pelvic area because she was very tightly strung there. Todd asked her to show him. Sitting down, she spread her legs as wide as she could. There were dancers who could easily spread their legs so wide that they formed a straight line. Her legs definitely were in a V shape.

'OK, when you're home alone watching TV . . .' he began.

'Yes.'

'Watch it with your legs spread out like that. It will give you something else to do.'

She laughed at his suggestion. Bending down, she touched her forehead to the floor. Sweat and grease had polished the wooden boards to a dark amber glow.

'And what are you doing Friday night?' he asked.

'Probably watching TV.' She popped up out of her stretch.

'Don't take this thing too far. Let's go out. Let's go on the prowl together.'

'I have to work tomorrow during the day, and Tricia might want to do something.'

He squatted down alongside her. 'How's she doing?'

'Good, I think. We went swimming today. She still hasn't had a drink. I didn't even have to ask her. She volunteered the info herself. I'm just holding my breath.'

'Well, I hope she can stick with it. You've been through the mill with her. When she was in LA and you hadn't heard from her for six months, I thought you were going to lose it.'

'I know. It was two years ago they went out to LA. Remember? Supposedly Danny had some big singing gig lined up for her. You know, since they've been back, it seems like he has a hold on her. Since then her drinking really escalated.' Amy thought of Tricia's drinking bouts. After a drink or two Tricia would begin to lose control of her movements, as if she had given them up to some

21

twisted puppeteer who took pleasure in making her head roll about her shoulders and her arms knock over drinks. But what happened to Tricia's eyes after a few more drinks was what scared Amy the most. They lost their color, the silky blueness of the iris disappeared, and they became dead eyes, seeing nothing and giving back nothing in return. Amy hoped she would never see those eyes again.

Todd was staring at her, waiting, so she smiled and said, 'And there's more good news. She tried out for a band. Unfortunately it happens to be Luke's, but aside from that, it's a really good step for her. And, finally, she's trying to break up with Danny. I should put it more positively. She is breaking up with him.'

'Great.'

'Yeah, but he was over there today, waiting for her when we got to her apartment. It give me the creeps. What if I hadn't been there and it had been one o'clock in the morning?'

'You're going to have to let her handle it, Amy. You can't be with her all the time.'

'Right. I am trying. What were we talking about?'

'Friday night. Going out dancing. Sound good?'

'Sure.'

'What time do you get done with work?'

'Six.'

'Let's meet here at seven-thirty.' Todd held on to her shoulders and, using her as a practice bar, shook out one leg and then the other. 'Forget about Tricia for a while. She's a big girl. She'll be all right.'

The night sky was luminous, capturing a melon color from the streetlights. The warm air trapped heat, light, and odor. Amy's downstairs neighbor had planted giant marigolds all along the walkway and they gave off a pungent smell, harshly sweet like an overripe peach. Amy was sitting on the front steps, waiting for the night air to cool down. But there was no breeze and the impregnated air settled around her. Unsticking her T-shirt from her skin, she blew down the front of it.

The night felt like it was rubbing up against her. It had been three months since her last affair, which had unfortunately been a one-nighter. Sometimes she thought she was too intense for most men. It hadn't been true with Luke, but she was coming to see that he was a rare kind of man.

She wondered if Danny and Tricia would stay separated this time. The last time they had broken up had been three months earlier, on Amy's birthday. They'd brought over a magnum of champagne to celebrate. Amy had told Tricia she didn't want to be around her anymore when she drank, but somehow she couldn't tell them to leave. They were a little drunk, but seemed so pleased with themselves at their surprise. At first they amused Amy. Their drunkenness was blumbling and sweet. But once the champagne was gone, Danny insisted they take the party to a bar where she could get a free drink.

'No, it's her birthday. She gets to choose what she wants to do. Those are the rules.' Tricia stepped between them.

'What do you mean, those are the rules?' Danny asked.

'In our family those are the rules. You get to pick what you want Mom to fix you for dinner and you don't have to do the dishes. Right, Ame?'

Amy nodded in agreement. 'Right, Trish.'

'So what do you want to do?' Tricia asked her. She went to put her glass down on the kitchen counter and missed. It shattered on the floor.

Danny bent down and started to pick it up.

'Don't do that,' Tricia yelled. 'I broke it, I'll pick it up.'

23

She grabbed a piece from his hand and cut herself. The red blood pooled into the palm of her hand and she dipped a finger in it as if to see if it were real.

Amy made her sit down in a chair and went to get a washcloth and some Band-Aids. Danny continued to pick up the pieces of glass. As Amy cleaned off the wounded hand, Tricia looked down at Danny and said, 'I hate it when you make me bleed.'

Danny threw the pieces of glass away in the wastepaper basket. 'You don't know what you want, you dumb bitch. You can just stay here with your sister and grow old. I'm leaving.'

As he was going out the door, Tricia informed him that if he left she never wanted to see him again. He threw the keys to her apartment at her. She threw them back, but he had already closed the door so they bounced off it and fell to the floor.

'Well, at least we got rid of him,' Tricia said.

'You two make me sick.'

'It's not me, Amy. It's his fault. It's all his fault.'

'Why is it all his fault, Tricia?'

'Because he looks at me a certain way. Voodoo. Well, it's like that.'

'What are you talking about?'

'If you'd listen to me once in a while.'

'I thought I did listen to you.'

'Between the words, Amy.' Tricia started laughing. 'You hate me when I'm drunk.'

'I don't like it. You're right about that.'

'Well I'm sure drunk now.'

Then Tricia had smiled a sweet, crooked smile and fallen backward on the couch, passing out. After taking off her shoes and covering her with a blanket, Amy left her there. She did the dishes, took a book to bed, but ended up feeling so sorry for herself that she cried on it.

Two days later, Danny and Tricia were back together again, after he made Tricia admit it was her fault she'd cut her hand. But their relationship definitely seemed to be deteriorating.

Amy decided to walk down to the Burger Delight and see if Tricia were still there. The restaurant was only four blocks away, on the main street of her small neighborhood, the West Bank, a rather run-down area of houses and shops across the Mississippi River from the University.

Amy felt comfortable walking down the backstreets alone. She nodded at a man coming her way, the day bartender at the 500 Bar. There had been a fire there one night a few years back that put the bar out of commission for almost a year. The next day a sign had appeared in the café across the street, 500 BURNED DOWN, 600 HOMELESS.

After walking past a movie theater, two bars, a leather store, and the Bellington Dance Studio, she reached the Burger Delight. She thought of how much like a small town this area was, located less than a mile away from downtown Minneapolis. In the late sixties the West Bank had been the center of hippiedom and drugs. Even though it was ten years later, people still thought of it in those terms. Amy had lived on the West Bank off and on for five years.

When she walked into the Burger Delight she shivered with pleasure at the wave of air-conditioned air. It looked like business was slow. Only three of the seven booths were full, and they were normally in high demand. But maybe the late show hadn't let out yet. She walked back to the kitchen to see who was on tonight. Ginger, a waitress with unnervingly black hair, banged the door open with her hip, carrying two cheeseburger platters.

25

'Hey, Amy.'

'Hey, Ginger. Tricia around?'

'I think she left. Ask Dot. She's out back.'

Amy walked through to the kitchen and said hello to Chuck, who threw a limp french fry at her, then motioned her over to the counter.

'You know what that sister of yours is?' he asked.

Amy had worked with cooks like Chuck before. He made a point of staring at her chest when she was reaching up to pick up an order. He told dirty jokes as he finished putting a garnish on a plate. She was sure it didn't help that he worked over vats of frying oil all day long, but his hair was long and stringy and his face scarred with acne. She tried to keep her distance and even managed to feel sorry for him, but she knew she didn't want to hear what he had to say about Tricia. 'Chuck, keep your perverted thoughts to yourself.'

'She's going to get what she deserves one of these days.'

'Stick your finger in the fryer,' Amy said, and walked away. Tricia had been right, he did have it in for her for some reason. She pushed open the back door and saw Dot smoking a cigarette, looking at the skyline of downtown Minneapolis.

'Not too busy, huh?'

Dot turned. 'Hi, there, Amy. Nope. Not busy at all.'

'Where's Tricia?'

Dot paused for a second and squinted her eyes at Amy as if to see her better. 'Tricia left a little early tonight. Some guy came down to get her.'

'Shit.' Amy let the door slam behind her. Even though she knew the answer, she asked, 'What guy?'

'Tall, blond, goodlooking. Is that her boyfriend?'

'God knows. As of this afternoon he wasn't, but maybe he is again.'

'What's the matter with him?' Under the back-door

26

light, threads of gray shone in Dot's blunt-cut hair. She raked her hand through it.

'More like, what's right.'

'She's a tough one, Amy. Not like you.' Dot dropped her cigarette and crushed it out with her white Earth shoes.

'I just don't get it. Today she told me she's trying to get rid of that guy.'

'That's sure not the way it looked tonight. She seemed real excited to see him.'

'I give up.'

'OK, big sis.' When Dot smiled, a dimple poked into her cheek.

'You're right. Enough. I'm going home. I'll see you tomorrow.'

As Amy walked back through the fallen night, the air was denser, with crickets chirping in frustrating evenness. She knew she was afraid for Tricia. Dot had said tonight that Tricia was tough. Amy didn't think so. Her sister's grip on life was strong, but her wrists were slender and fragile. Her bones were thin. Her skin was delicate; it bruised easily. Tricia carried secrets that seemed terrible in their unspokenness.

Trees circle the lake. The trees make shadows deep along the edges, like an outline. When we stand in the water, with it lapping at our ankles, we can look down and see the lace of the tree leaves above our heads reflected and two girls in bathing suits – one with long red hair caught back in a ponytail and the other, taller, thinner, with straight brown hair bleaching blond. We are serious, studying the water. The two wavering images are just as intent, staring at us. I look over at Tricia and say in a whisper, 'That's them.'

Chapter 2

Amy sat stretched out on the rug of her bedroom, drinking iced tea for breakfast and reading the morning paper. She tried to turn the pages of the paper with her toes. After she'd managed to do a page or two, the paper wrinkled so badly she decided it wasn't worth it, even if it was good practice for dance.

Since she had started to dance, she had become much more aware of every movement her body made. She didn't talk about it with anyone. It seemed as private and intimate a thought as one she might have about sex. Three or four times a day she would feel the alignment of her body, the curve of her back, the bend of her wrists. She would capture the sense of her bones in motion.

The phone rang and Amy knew who it was before answering it. Only her mother, Edna, dared call her before nine in the morning. Since Edna had been up since seven, she thought everyone should have had a good start on the day. Amy answered the phone. 'Good morning.'

'You're up?' her mother asked.

'Up and at 'em, as Dad would say.'

'Have you talked to Tricia lately?'

Amy understood her mother's concern about Tricia, but it still bothered her when she was expected to give a report on her sister's condition before anything else. 'She's still not drinking, Mom, if that's what you want to know. You could call her and find out for yourself.'

'I hate to ask her about it, Amy. God, dare we hope?' Edna's voice sounded full of it.

'Maybe. She's also in the process of breaking up with Danny.'

'I'll believe that when it's been a month or two. But at least she's got a job. If she can just stay sober, I'm sure everything will be all right.' After a pause she asked hesitantly, 'Has she said anything about going back to school?'

'She hasn't volunteered anything and I don't ask.' Tired of the questions, Amy told her mother the answer to one she hadn't asked. 'But she is trying to get a job as a singer again.'

'Oh, Lord, I hoped she had given that up. She's intelligent and she could do so much more than just wriggle around onstage.'

'Mom, that's essentially what I do when I dance.'

'That's different, Amy. You've studied dance for many years. It's an art.'

'I think singing is an art too.'

'Now, if it were opera, maybe.'

Amy didn't want to argue anymore and she knew the only way to stop was to give in. 'Yeah, you're right.'

'So how's your dancing going?'

'Real well. I'm trying to work out every day for a couple hours. Today I don't have any classes, but two other dancers and I have reserved time at the studio.' Amy finished her iced tea and started making rings on the newspaper with it. 'I should go, Mom.'

'OK, check in from time to time.'

'Yeah, we'll come out on Sunday. Tell Dad we've requested chicken on the grill. Bye.' Amy lay back on the rug and remembered growing up in Richfield, which was only a twenty-minute drive from downtown Minneapolis, but had been the country when she was a child.

On warm summer nights she and Tricia would hang blankets over the clothesline to form a tent and camp out.

30

Sometimes they'd let the boys know when they were going to be sleeping outside. Once they'd arranged a rendezvous with the Clarke brothers. Tricia and she stockpiled all the rotten vegetables from their father's garden and waited for them. The two unsuspecting boys whistled to announce their arrival and both received spoiled tomatoes exploding in their faces. The boys were driven off but toward early morning retaliated by spraying the girls with the garden hose while they were sleeping. Tricia tried to convince their father that it had rained during the night, Amy suggested it might be heavy dew that had drenched the blankets, but then they got the giggles and were sent to their room for the rest of the day. They were both so tired that they slept through most of it.

After browsing through the want ads, Amy tried to call Tricia but got no answer. She hoped Tricia was all right. If she was drinking again, almost anything could have happened to her. Amy felt a familiar fear run through her, as if her bones were freezing in the dead of winter and she had no way of protecting herself from the cold, and she didn't want to think about it. There was always the chance Tricia had landed in a detoxification unit again, and if she had it would be a couple more days before she would be released. It was hard for Amy to consider that possibility, for it would represent a huge step downward for Tricia when she was just beginning to climb out of the pit of her drinking.

Amy didn't know why she didn't really talk to her mother about Tricia, about the feeling she had that something even darker than drinking was a problem for Tricia. But sometimes, hearing her mother's voice on the phone made her feel as if she were twelve again, just learning about sex, just learning about her body, still

31

fighting with her sister and keeping secrets from everyone. In such a limited world there were no problems, only spats that would be over in an hour or so.

When she saw Dot standing in the door of the Burger Delight, Amy thought of circling the block and sneaking into the dance studio, but she wanted to know if Tricia had made it to work.

Dot squinted at her and said, 'Can you work?'

'No, I've got a rehearsal. Why?'

'Your sister didn't show up. We're short and it's busy.'

Amy's first impulse was to cover for Tricia, but she couldn't do that, she had her own responsibilities. Her second impulse was to skip rehearsal and find Tricia, no matter where she was, no matter what she was doing, just to reassure herself that her sister was all right. After looking up at the sky, which was blue as usual, she said calmly to Dot. 'Sorry, but I've got people waiting for me too.'

'That's it for her, then. She's out.'

Whether Dot was bluffing or not, Amy knew she couldn't work her sister's shift. So she agreed, 'That's the way it is, then,' and walked away.

They were working on a piece that Harriet, one of the lead dancers at the Studio, had choreographed, which was short but very energetic. The tentative title was 'The Day Before the Bomb.' It involved running and stamping, bursts of sounds, yelps, frenzied movements together, and then a splitting apart. Harriet and Mark, the third dancer, were about the same size as Amy, and they all danced like they were kids double-daring each other. It moved fast, then moved faster as they pushed it. Three minutes was all it lasted, but after going through it twice they took a time out and Amy felt her lungs heaving and pulling at

the sides of her chest. She █████████
up, like she wanted to spit out ████████
inside of her.

She walked slowly across the dance ██████
out the bank of windows over Cedar Avenue ████
she would see Tricia running to the restaurant. ████
would just show up now, she knew that Dot would ███
her back in a second. The Burger Delight was loose. Dot
was easygoing and understood how everyone had other
things that were more important in their lives than waitressing at a restaurant. She would not fire Tricia. She
would give her another chance. That's all Tricia needed,
one more chance. Then everything would be all right.

When Amy turned back to face the studio, she saw that
Todd had come in to watch. She wished he weren't there
or that he had come in while they were working out and
she hadn't noticed him. She still felt like she had to prove
something when he was around.

They went through the dance two more times, and each
time Amy had a better sense of the skewed rhythm of the
piece. When they finished the second time, they all tried
to look composed, as if being out of breath were a sin for
a dancer.

'It's coming, you guys. It's looking good.' Harriet
turned around and called to Todd, 'What d'you think?'

'Not bad.' He smiled at them. 'It made me want to
dance.'

While Amy was changing into street clothes, she
decided she couldn't check up on Tricia anymore. She
couldn't stop by the Burger Delight to see if she had made
it in or call her at home to find out why she hadn't.
Somehow Tricia's life had become more important than
her own. If Tricia was sober, if Tricia had a job, if Tricia
was happy, then Amy could breathe again, she could
dance, she could try to be happy. They were bound

years of her
                                          member a day

                                 ing up, bickering
                                 V show to watch,
                                 clothing and left it
                                 mal family dilemmas.
                            y each went through

                         ying constantly; any small
c   in skin and she would sob
for ho   gs. When Tricia's turn came,
she grew s   pixielike child, she blossomed
into a woman a   age and blamed this premature
aging on everyone in   r family. They could not possibly
understand her. Edna picked at her constantly, worried
about her, while Red ignored her, waiting for her to grow
out of it.

It was when Amy moved out to go to college that she
had begun to see Tricia's behavior more clearly. In high
school Tricia had had to deal with the sticky reputation
that Amy had left behind: smart, rebellious, but basically
a good girl, under it all a good girl. If Amy got in trouble,
it was for organizing a student rally. If Tricia got in
trouble, it was for smoking in the john. Their parents
supported Amy's infractions but condemned Tricia's.
Amy knew somehow their rebellion came from the same
place, wanting to get their parents' attention while defin-
ing themselves as different from them.

Instead of heading toward home when she left the
Dance Studio, Amy found herself walking down to the
Mississippi River, which cut through the University
campus. There were high bluffs on either side of the river,
with scrub oak trying to grow out of the eroding rock. But
below the Student Union on the east bank, there was a

flat parking lot and beyond that a grassy embankment. It was there that Amy flopped down and stared at the moving water and asked herself, as she had so often asked, what in all their growing up had led Tricia to drink the way she did? They had come from the same loving parents. What in their sibling rivalry had hurt Tricia so, Amy wondered, and was it her fault? Or was it just a disease like they said, a disease that some people caught and others didn't?

The first time Tricia had been drunk was when she was fifteen and a girlfriend had come over to visit. Tricia had described it to Amy later. They had dumped powdered Tang into a bottle of vodka. After drinking a whole bottle of this concoction, Tricia and her friend went for a walk in the field across the street. It was hot so they took all their clothes off and started running around. One of the neighbors saw them and called the police. When Amy came home, she found her mother and a policeman holding up a naked Tricia in the shower, trying to wash the vomit off her body before they put her to bed.

Tricia hadn't remembered anything when she woke up later that evening, but Amy hated it. She had hated seeing the naked, senseless body of her sister in the hands of a uniformed cop. When she tried to tell Tricia how horrible it had been, Tricia just laughed.

And so Tricia's drinking had started. A few months later she stole a bottle of their father's homemade date wine and got drunk at school. Amy had found her throwing up in her locker and cleaned her up in the lavatory and then walked her around until she sobered up enough to go home. She told her parents that Tricia had the flu and put her to bed.

When Tricia entered senior high school, she started hanging out with a whole new crowd of kids. She would skip out of school and drink Colt 45 with the seniors and

Amy would make up excuses for her, to both the school and their parents. Yet, at the time, it had seemed only a natural part of growing up. Tricia was finding her limit, just like all normal teenagers. Amy could remember drinking enough whiskey at a homecoming dance to blur a small portion of a fall night. It had been scary, and after that one incident she would recognize the danger signs and stop before she drank too much. But, after a while, Amy realized that Tricia liked the feeling of being out of control. She would brag to Amy of whole nights lost in a drunken stupor.

Still, up until a couple years ago the word *alcoholic* had never entered Amy's mind. Tricia was just a wild woman who liked drinking and drugs. It wasn't until they had lived together that Amy saw how dependent Tricia was on drinking, how she would go for a few days, sometimes even a week, without a drink, and then she would binge out and not come home for a day or two, often not remembering much of what had happened to her.

After a couple of incidents of Tricia bringing home strange men, Amy had decided to move out. She was tired of making excuses for her sister, didn't want to walk her around the block to sober her up, hated cleaning up after her, but the main thing she couldn't stand doing anymore was watching Tricia destroy herself.

As the sun dipped behind the rock outcropping of the river's west bank, Amy felt the chill of darker times to come. Unless Tricia kept her drinking under control, nothing in her life would be manageable. Still staring at the surface of the flowing water, Amy knew that in its depths it, too, was darkly polluted.

'What happened to you?' Amy asked when Tricia finally called. It was late in the evening, the night sky was a deep blue.

'I overslept.'

'What? Your shift didn't start until noon.' Amy caught herself before she asked Tricia if she had been drinking. Instead she asked, 'Have you talked to Dot?'

'No, I was wondering if you could call her and tell her that it was an emergency or something.'

'Forget it.'

'Listen, Ame. I can't lose that job. I can't count on this singing gig.'

'So you call. If you're going to lie, do it yourself. Don't ask me to do it.' Amy reached over and turned down the stereo. 'Call her right now. She'll still be at work. She'll understand.'

'OK.'

'Call me back.'

Tricia hung up the phone. Amy lay down on the rug by the phone. 'Good luck,' she said into the dead receiver, hoping that Tricia would be civil to Dot and give her a half-decent excuse.

Five minutes later Tricia called back. 'She fired me.'

'I can't believe that. She said that, but she didn't mean it. I know Dot.'

'What she said was I had a bad attitude.'

'What did you say to her?'

'I told her what she could do with her stupid restaurant.'

'Great. Did you tell her before or after she fired you?'

'After. What do you think, I'm an idiot?' Tricia blew up, then asked almost apologetically, 'Can we meet for coffee someplace?'

Tricia was sitting alone in a large red vinyl booth in Sunny's. She was the only person in the restaurant. Her red hair paled against the violet-red of the vinyl booth.

She had a cup of coffee in front of her and she was stirring it. Amy wanted to do something for her.

She sat down opposite Tricia. 'How can you drink coffee this late? Anytime after seven and I'm up all night.'

Tricia took a large gulp of coffee before answering. 'I don't have anything to get up for, so it doesn't matter how late I stay up. I'm reading *War and Peace* again. Remember that Russian Lit. class I was taking?'

'Before you went to LA?'

'Yeah. I never wrote my final paper. But I've got an idea for it now. Do you think I could still get credit?'

'Who knows? It's worth a try.'

A tight-faced waitress came over and handed them both menus without saying a word.

'You gonna eat something?' Amy asked.

'Maybe. I don't have much money.'

'My treat.'

Tricia lifted her head from the menu and smiled a closed-lipped smile. Maybe it came from being a waitress, Amy thought. Maybe we all learn to smile without showing too much.

'Thanks,' Tricia said. 'What're you going to have?'

'I think just some cottage cheese.'

'Yugh.'

'I have my audition soon and I have to watch what I eat.'

'I'm having fries.'

'Don't you get enough of them at work?' Amy wanted to pull the words back when she remembered too late that Tricia didn't work there anymore. Tricia wrinkled her face at the comment.

Amy leaned on the table and said, 'I forgot to ask you on the phone, did you talk to this Hank guy?'

'Yeah.'

'Well?'

'I guess it's good. They want me to come down and sit in. It doesn't mean I've got the gig. I think some other woman is going to sit in also.'

'That's great, Tricia. When?'

'Tomorrow.' Tricia looked at her and asked, 'Will you come?'

Amy had to stop herself from saying yes automatically to Tricia. She didn't want to go see Luke's band. It was too hard for her, brought back too many memories. 'I don't know.'

'Because of Luke?'

'Yeah, I guess.'

'Get over it, Amy. That was two years ago. You don't even have to talk to him.'

'I'll think about it. What are you going to wear?'

'Any chance I could borrow your silk blouse?'

The waitress came and took their order. Tricia pulled out a cigarette and lit it. She was careful in her movements. Amy had never smoked, but she liked to watch Tricia smoke. She did it elegantly. When she had her first drink or two, she drank them elegantly too. Until she got drunk. But even after she got drunk, she still managed to smoke with grace; she hung on to that somehow.

Tricia brushed her hair away from her face and Amy noticed a bruise on the side of her cheek.

'What happened to you now?' Amy asked, pointing at it.

Tricia's hand went up to the blue mark and covered it. 'Nothing.'

'Don't give me that "nothing." What's going on?'

'Couple has fight.' Tricia said it as if she were reading a headline in a paper, and not a front-page headline.

'How can you be so nonchalant? Did he hurt you?'

'Who?' Tricia's hand dropped away from her face.

'Danny.'

'Him?' Tricia's voice picked up on the question, then dropped down again. 'He hasn't got the balls. I'm the one who wore the balls in that relationship.'

'What did you fight about?' Amy asked.

'When we fight it's 'cause he wants to drink, and I'm trying not to. He wants to fuck, I don't. I don't want to do anything anymore. I kinda feel sorry for him. At least he's still trying.'

'How does it feel to not be drinking?'

'Feels like I can't think of anything else. Like a huge cake is sitting in front of me, lots of frosting, my name written across the top of it, it's my birthday and I'm only a year old and someone's trying to tell me not to put my hands in it.'

The waitress brought their order and set the french fries down between them. When Amy asked for a glass of water, the waitress sniffed but brought it.

'So what are you going to do?'

'What do you mean, what am I going to do?'

'I don't know, about money, about Danny, about drinking.'

'I need money. I don't need Danny or drinking.' Tricia picked up a french fry and speared it into the ketchup. 'That's all I know. I'll figure something out.'

They both began to eat. Amy thought the french fries looked a lot more appetizing than her bowl of watery cottage cheese.

'Todd and I are going out Friday night.'

'You two? I thought you were just best buds.'

'We are. We're going out looking for our true loves together. That way we can console each other when we don't find them.'

'Tell Todd he can stop by my place later if he has no luck. He's a hunk.'

'I talked to Mom today.'

'How's she?'

'Fine. Are you going to tell her?'

'What? About losing the job? She doesn't need to know for a while. That is, if you haven't told her already.'

'I haven't told her a thing. But you should reassure her that you're still not drinking. I know she'd like to hear that.'

'God, Ame. I don't like to talk about it. I'll jinx it. But, you know, I feel if I start drinking again, that'll be it.'

'What do you mean?'

'That'll be it for me.'

Amy didn't want to refute that statement. It might be better if Tricia believed it.

'We're still going out there Sunday, aren't we?' Tricia asked.

'Yeah, I told Mom we wanted grilled chicken.'

'And corn on the cob.'

'I remember when you had braces that one summer and Mom had to cut it off the cob for you.'

'Two summers,' Tricia corrected.

'You would crab about it, but you know, I was kind of jealous. Mom would put it in that blue bowl with a pat of butter on top. Sprinkle a little salt and pepper over it. She made it look so good. And you ended up with straight teeth while I still have this front tooth that sticks out.'

Tricia laughed. 'Yeah, but at least every time you went out to play hockey with the guys, Mom didn't remind you that you had two thousand dollars' worth of teeth in your mouth.'

'So are you going to get another job?'

'Guess so. And it won't be waitressing.'

'What? Computer programing?'

'Something that'll bring in some good money. I've got connections. You got a quarter? I want to play the jukebox.'

Amy fished out a quarter from the pocket of her shorts. Tricia walked across to the jukebox and selected a song.

'I can't believe you only get one song for a quarter. Remember when you got three?'

'We're getting old.'

The waitress came and cleared off their table. Tricia asked for more coffee. The jukebox played the song 'Three Times a Lady.'

'That was Danny's song for me when we were in LA.'

'Why in LA?'

'That's where I learned how to be a whore and a lady at the same time.'

Amy looked over at Tricia and smiled, but Tricia didn't smile back. Instead, she looked down and stirred her coffee.

Chapter 3

They sat in the parked car, silent, watching the neon sign, a cocktail glass with popping bubbles, blink on and off. It was a little after ten o'clock and the night sky was a deep blue-black color. Amy had backed her car up against a wire fence on the far side of the parking lot, away from the other cars closer to the club. Just a habit she had acquired working in bars, because drunk drivers tended to be bad drivers.

Amy knew Tricia was preparing herself to go into the bar and not drink, and still have the courage to get up and sing. As Tricia had put it earlier, 'This is the first time I'll sing in public without the smell of alcohol coming out with every note.' She had laughed, but Amy knew it was hard for her.

Amy remembered this club, the Times Bar. She remembered nights of sitting in the car, waiting until it was time, according to her own private code, to go in to watch Luke play in his band. While she was going out with Luke, she had come up with the rules of conduct for a band member's girlfriend.

Never go into the club during the first set. It made the night too long. Never walk in when the band was on a break, always wait until they were playing so you could find a table and get comfortable. Never start drinking until the last set. It made it too easy to get drunk. Avoid slow dancing with a stranger — with the whole band watching, it could be awkward. Always wait for the band member to come over to your table; don't go rushing up to him, as he often has business to take care of — adjust the sound, talk to the club owner, or greet visiting musicians.

She had tried not to forget that it was a job for Luke. She always acted as if she were having a good time, otherwise Luke might have wondered why she had bothered to come down. She never told him she came down to watch him up onstage. Sometimes his band would be booked for a month solid, seven nights a week, and it was the only way she got to see him at all. But it wasn't just that. She had fallen in love with him when he was up onstage and she liked to see him there. Dark and tall, he seemed mysterious and powerful. He rarely looked down into the audience, but seemed instead to be thinking of something far removed and would occasionally smile to himself.

When she had first met him she had had a lot of time to study him onstage. She had been waitressing at the bar he was playing at. She remembered when she first saw him she thought he was handsome in an odd sort of way. His nose was turned to one side and his mouth was full. His hands looked too big to play the saxophone, and yet they swept up and down the keys like it was the most natural thing in the world. He didn't kid around like the other band members did. Sometimes he would even read a book on the break. So she hadn't really talked to him, except to get him a glass of soda water when he asked her.

Then on a slow night Amy had seen a customer sitting in the far back booth of her section. She had walked back to ask him what he wanted and realized when she got close that it was Luke. He had his head down on the table and his arms wrapped protectively around it. She had leaned down and asked, 'Is there anything I can do to help you die?' He had told her later that he couldn't believe she had said that to him. He started laughing and raised his head up and said, 'Yeah, sit down and talk to me.' They had talked more and more each night until finally he had come home with her, to continue talking in bed.

Amy wondered what she would feel like seeing him onstage tonight. Since they had broken up she had never gone to a club to see the band, and she had missed the whole scene. She had missed the unwinding afterward, the end-of-the-night free drinks, the packing up of the instruments, walking out with the band. Sometimes the whole group would go out for enchiladas at Hot Tamales, or breakfast at Perkins; the guys would get goofy and she would be like the den mother. It had all vanished from her life when she stopped seeing Luke.

'How do I look?' Tricia asked, turning the rearview mirror toward her face and pressing her red lips together.

Amy leaned up against the car door and really looked at her sister. The lights from the parking lot hollowed her face, made it more theatrical. Her red hair was curled and soft around her face. Her eyes seemed bright. Amy admired Tricia's skill with makeup. When Tricia finished doing her face it looked natural, the makeup was part of her skin, but still highlighted her features – large eyes, high cheekbones – even made her thin lips look a little fuller.

'Very pulled together and slightly sexy,' Amy told her.

'You don't think I'm overdressed?'

Amy glanced at the low-cut, cream-colored silk blouse she had lent Tricia, which complemented the tawny gold skirt. 'As the singer, you're supposed to be the best-dressed woman in the club,' Amy assured her, then asked, 'How do I look?'

Tricia said immediately, 'Casual but chic.'

'God, really, that's always been my fashion goal.'

They both got out of the car and started walking across

the parking lot. Suddenly a dark blue car, almost invisible in the night air, came squealing over the pavement, aimed right at Tricia. Amy didn't have time to think, but grabbed Tricia's arm and pulled her back toward the safety of the parked car. The dark blue car skidded on the loose gravel and swung around, looking as if it would charge at them again. At the last second it screeched to a stop. Danny leaned out of the driver's seat, his voice thick with anger. 'I thought we had a date.'

Amy found herself laughing, nervous laughter, relieved that it was only Danny. But then she looked at his face again, outlined in the white light of the streetlamp. He was almost shaking with rage and his eyes were wild looking.

Tricia yelled back at him, 'I forgot I had something more important to do than listen to you whine.'

'Yeah, you seem to be forgetting a lot these days. There's a lot of things I could *make* you remember.'

'How did you find me?' Tricia asked.

'Saw Amy's car pulling away from the house with you in it. So I followed you. I can always find you, you know. I know you too well.' Danny opened the car door and looked as if he were going to come after Tricia. 'You're through, bitch. I mean it.'

Amy wished he weren't between them and the club, otherwise they could just make a run for it. She tried to pull Tricia back behind her, but Tricia just shook her hand off and walked toward Danny.

'Danny, get lost. I have more important things to think about.'

'Tricia, don't make him any madder,' Amy whispered to her sister, wishing she would shut up.

'Don't worry, Amy. I don't beat up chicks.' Danny slammed the door shut, then added, 'At least not when anyone else is around to see it.'

Danny spun the car around in the lot and then pealed out.

'What a bastard. He just loves to scare people,' Tricia commented.

'He's crazy,' Amy said.

'Bluff. That's all it is.'

'I don't know how you can be so sure.'

At the club's entrance Luke was talking to a waitress. The young girl was in a typical waitress pose, holding her tray on her hip, and laughing. Amy heard his answering deep laugh. She thought for a second of saying she had left something in the car. After all, this was not the way it was supposed to be; he should be up onstage where he belonged, where she could stare at him but not have to deal with him. But she knew she couldn't turn back now.

Luke looked up and saw them. Amy wanted to walk right by, but Tricia stopped and said hello.

'Hey, Trish,' Luke said, smiling. 'You ready to do it to us tonight?' Without waiting for an answer he turned and smiled at Amy – not saying anything, just smiling.

'Hello, Luke, aren't you going to even say hi to me?' Amy felt uncomfortable but didn't want him to know it.

'I'd like to do more than that,' he said quietly.

What does that mean? Amy wondered, then was embarrassed at even giving it a serious thought. Just his professional charm, so fucking charming he doesn't know when to quit. He thinks it's part of his job. 'Oh, really,' she said, then turned to Tricia, 'I'm going to go find us a table.'

As Amy walked across the dance floor, she looked up at the stage and saw with relief that the band was getting ready to play. That meant Luke wouldn't be able to come to their table, at least not for a set. Amy needed the time to get used to seeing him again.

She found a table midway between the stage and the back of the bar with a good view of the band. She watched Luke climb onstage and take his tenor saxophone out of its case. Pressing her hand down hard on the table, she thought to herself, it's been two years, I should be over it. Why can he still make me feel like I've stepped off the end of the earth and I'm falling through darkness?

Tricia sat down next to her and asked, 'How you doing?'

'Fine, how about you?'

'He can still shake you, can't he?'

Amy asked, 'Was it so obvious?'

'Not really. Except that you're hardly ever at a loss for words, so I knew he must be getting to you.'

'I don't want to talk about it.' Sometimes Amy hated it that Tricia knew her so well. 'Did he tell you when you would sing?'

'End of this set.'

'Good.'

'Not soon enough for me.'

'And the other woman?'

'Right before me.'

A waitress appeared next to them. 'What can I get you two ladies?'

After a moment's hesitation Tricia said, 'A ginger ale.'

'Soda water,' Amy said, then added, 'with a slice of lime, please.'

'You could have had a drink.' Tricia took out a cigarette.

'I know. But I didn't feel like one,' Amy said clearly, her voice coming out a little more forcefully than she had meant it to.

'Don't get grump with me,' Tricia said curtly. 'You're supposed to be here for support.'

Amy relaxed, hearing her sister's personal slang.

48

'Grump. You always did like to make up words. What did you used to call cute guys?'

'Kickers. Remember, because we'd kick each other whenever we saw a hunk.' Just then Tricia kicked her under the table.

Amy looked around, 'Where?'

'Onstage.'

Luke did look good. His brown hair was a little long. Amy used to cut it for him. He had slimmed down some and his pants fit him better than ever. Amy was about to say his name when Tricia said, 'Hank, the keyboard player.'

Turning her eyes to Hank onstage, Amy inspected him. In an all-American way he was good looking but not particularly Tricia's type. He was stocky with sandy-blond hair, which fell into his face when he leaned over to play. Then the band broke into a blues tune and Amy nodded to Tricia. 'He's not bad.'

Amy tapped her finger in time to the music and looked around the bar. The time motif was used extensively in the decor, old clocks lining the shelves above the liquor, red wallpaper with silver watches flying around on it. Even on the wall by the band there were rows of clocks – the simple round ones found in all school classrooms, but all set to different times. Amy glanced down at her watch. It was ten-thirty and the bar was filling up. There was not an empty table, and the dance floor, with the start of the second set, was crowded with people.

The Privates sounded good. This was about the third reincarnation of the group. Luke, Tom on drums, and Bobby on bass were the original backbone. They had been playing in a band together for about five years.

Luke was soloing. The horn flashed in the house lights, and he bent his body back as the music pulsed out of him. He didn't move much, actually he was rather subdued

49

onstage, but it made the slow rocking he did all the more mesmerizing. It was the same way he had moved in bed, slow and steady, Amy remembered, then pushed the thought out of her mind.

Tricia nudged her. 'They really sound good.'

Amy nodded. She loved to hear live music, and yet she hardly went out anymore. A tall, dark man came up and asked Tricia to dance, but she turned him down. Then he asked Amy and she thought, why not, everyone else is performing tonight. He slipped on to the dance floor in front of her and made room for her. Amy felt her body give in to the music, her feet catching the beat.

'My name's Tate, and you're a mighty fine dancer.'

'Thanks,' Amy said, and let her eyes stray for a moment to the stage. Luke had stopped playing; his horn was hanging from his neck and he was listening to the keyboard solo, but he was watching her. She closed her eyes and kept dancing. Sometimes it seemed like the only thing she knew how to do well.

When Amy sat back down at the table, Tricia held up her glass. 'Haven't seen you dance in a while, but you looked so graceful.'

'Just having fun.'

'And modest too.'

'Give me a break. It's your turn next, so you better watch what you say,' Amy teased her.

'Did I tell you what I was going to sing?'

'No.'

'Well, Hank learned the part for "Down So Low," so we're going to do that.'

'Great. You know I love that song.'

'Didn't you listen to it ad nauseam when you were breaking up with Luke?'

'That whole album.'

'It's odd how one song can make you remember so

clearly a period of your life. When I hear "I Want to Hold Your Hand" I can remember standing in the Rexall Drugstore, staring at a picture of Paul McCartney and wanting to marry him. I must have been ten.'

'Yeah, I was twelve with more mature tastes – I preferred John.'

While they were talking a blond-haired woman climbed up onto the stage. Amy pointed her out to Tricia. The woman was heavyset and wearing a red wraparound dress and had nails painted to match.

'She's a sight to make eyes sore,' Tricia whispered.

The blonde perched on the edge of a stool and sang an old Billie Holiday song in a thin, clear voice. She didn't move, except right at the end her hand rose up into the air.

Amy said, 'She's not bad.'

Tricia shrugged her shoulder. 'Perfect pitch but no soul. Just the opposite of me.'

'Oh, come on. You sing in tune.'

Luke thanked Tina, the blonde, and then called Tricia to the stage. Tricia stood, hoisted up the microphone, tapped it with a finger, and then turned to Hank. She snapped her fingers three times and then started to sing, low. Amy was always surprised that so much sound could come out of her sister's mouth. Her voice was like dark velvet, rich, thick, and mournful. It pulled you in to her. Amy felt the sound in her stomach as if a hand had been placed right over her belly and was pressing, not hard but constant. Closing her eyes, Amy sat back in her chair and listened, let the song flow over her like a wave breaking over her, and heard the pain in the voice and wondered where it came from. Was that why Tricia drank? To get the pain out. Maybe if she could just sing every night, she wouldn't need to get drunk anymore.

When the song ended the applause rained down and

51

Amy thought, she did it, she's got the gig. Tricia sang just the way a woman should: full and generous, holding nothing back, showing how much it all could hurt.

Tricia came back to the table with Hank and she introduced Amy to him by saying, 'This is my sister. She used to go out with Luke, but that was before your time.'

'That Luke, he sure can pick the woman,' he said, smiling at her.

'Why, thank you,' Amy said, and stood up to go to the ladies' room. 'Excuse me for a moment.' She sat back down when she saw Luke was coming over. Maybe it was time to stop being rude to him.

Luke smiled and said, 'Sounded good, Tricia. Thanks for sitting in. We'll let you know in the next day or two. The band will discuss it tonight.'

'I know where my vote'll go.' Hank put his hand on Tricia's arm.

'Thanks,' she said.

Luke sat down next to Amy and asked her if she wanted a drink.

'No, thanks. I'm fine.'

Tricia and Hank stood up and said they were going outside. Amy watched them walking away, wishing she had gone to the ladies' room when she had the chance.

'So how are you?' Luke asked.

'Pretty good. Dancing and working take up most of my time.'

'I wondered. I haven't seen you in an age.'

'How are you?'

His eyes dropped down to the table, then he shrugged. 'Fair. Things have been better, but I can't complain.'

Amy wanted to ask him what was wrong, but didn't feel she had the right.

'Tricia seems like she's doing all right. How's her drinking?' Luke asked.

'She's quit.'

'That's great. Remember the night we had to haul her home from a gig? We were getting ready to go and you didn't know where she was. Then you thought to look in the bathroom and she was passed out in the last stall. I had to come in and help you carry her out of there.'

'Oh, God, that was awful.'

'She was something else. Or I'll never forget the first night I stayed over and she brought two guys home with her. One for you and one for her. The one for you came walking into your room and found me already installed in your bed.'

'That was when she and I still lived together. I could have killed her. What did you think of me?'

'I did wonder, but you were pretty outraged, so I figured it didn't happen too often.'

'Well, I think she's going to stay sober this time. I really hope so.'

'Is she going to AA?'

'No, but she hasn't had a drink in a month, knock on wood.'

'We should have dinner sometime. You busy next week?'

Amy looked at him with surprise. Maybe he was just trying to be nice to her. 'Actually, I am. I've got my own audition coming up for the dance company.'

Luke stood up. 'Oh, well, good luck with it. Maybe I'll be seeing you down here again if Tricia starts singing with us.'

'I suppose you might.'

He walked away and she watched him head up to the stage and pick up his horn. He played a scale and then took the horn apart and started cleaning it.

Suddenly she was tired and wanted to go home. It was too hard going backward into her own life. She had loved

Luke so hard she didn't know how to talk to him casually, like a friend.

She went outside to find Tricia and Hank. They were leaning up against the wall of the building, talking.

'Trish, I feel like going.'

'So soon?'

'Yeah, I'm a little tired.'

Hank said to Tricia, 'Stay. I'll give you a lift home.'

Amy wanted Tricia to leave with her. She didn't want Tricia hanging out at a bar with a strange man, although Hank seemed pretty reliable. But Amy knew she couldn't stick around any longer. Seeing Luke again had been much harder than she had even imagined. It made her feel as if she was missing so much of life. She wished she had someone waiting at home for her.

'Yeah. Amy, you go on. I don't really feel like going yet. You know how hyper I get after I sing,' Tricia said. 'I'll talk to you tomorrow. What did Luke have to say?'

'We didn't talk about you, if that's what you want to know,' Amy said, then walked away, feeling resentful at Tricia for staying.

Behind her Hank called out, 'Did he mention that he just broke up with Angela?'

Amy stopped and looked at the moon, a blotch in an otherwise perfectly black night. 'No, he didn't mention that.'

Mother has freckles in the summer; they cover her shoulders and chest and the broad plain of her forehead. Dad wears a hat like a fishing hat, but he only uses it to pull down over his face when he sits in the lawn chair to take a little snooze. They let us walk down to the lake lot together, but we are not to go in the water unless an adult is there. We sit at the edge of the lake, building canals, bridges, dungeons, and castles, and the water comes to us.

The grown-ups play bridge and laugh downstairs. The noise of their party rises to us like spun glass and there is no way we can sleep. We sit at the foot of our beds, we have twin beds, and try to touch our toes together without falling off into the drowning water that flows between the two islands. The air is hot and we take off our pajama tops and talk of what lives in the water.

Chapter 4

Amy was pouring a cup of coffee for a customer when she saw Dot come in. It had been a slow afternoon. She had been left to cover the three-to-five shift, and had barely made eight dollars in tips. Not enough to buy the new leotard she needed. Distracted by her thoughts, she overflowed the cup and coffee spilled into the saucer. She hated a wet saucer, so she offered to get her customer a fresh cup.

'Don't bother.' The man lifted the cup off the saucer and slurped a mouthful of coffee out of it. The noise was enough to make Amy let him be.

She walked back into the kitchen, leaned against the counter, and watched Chuck. He was dipping uncooked potato fingers into the deep fryer and holding them while they sizzled golden, then covering them with salt and popping them into his mouth. When he saw Amy he plunked his coffee cup down on the counter and grunted, which meant he wanted more coffee with lots of sugar in it.

When she reached out to take the coffee cup, he grabbed her hand.

'I told you,' he said. 'I told you that she's going to get what she deserves.'

'Chuck, let go.' Yanking her hand away, she glared at him. She was starting to hate working with him. He watched her all the time she was in the kitchen.

'She's a slut. I know. And I know where she lives. I know where you live too,' Chuck mumbled.

Amy felt anger prickle along her arms, like when she

was in school and someone talked bad about her sister. She had gotten into many fights defending Tricia. 'Chuck, I don't want you to mention my sister again.'

Chuck looked at her and smiled, his mouth falling open. 'Did I say anybody's name?'

Amy flew out of the kitchen and ran into Dot, who was coming up from the basement carrying a pile of laundered napkins. 'You want to fold napkins?'

'Sure, nothing else to do.'

'I'm sorry about Tricia.'

Amy took the napkins from her and asked, 'What are you sorry about?' Amy hadn't meant it to sound mean, but it did.

'I guess she and I just didn't get along.'

'Sometimes she and I don't get along either. I thought you believed in sticking by your employees. God, if anybody should get fired it's that slimeball, Chuck.'

Amy walked away and sat at the booth closest to the kitchen. She watched her one customer slurp his coffee and read the paper. She folded the napkins in half, then again in half, and made a pile of the finished one. She was surprised Dot bothered with cloth napkins. Paper ones would have done the trick.

Dot came up to her and asked, 'Would you want to work a double tonight?'

Amy knew who was supposed to have worked. She decided not to say anything and let Dot figure it out for herself.

Dot picked up the pile of folded napkins. 'I suppose I have a lot of nerve asking.'

'I've got a date. Sorry.'

Her last customer got up and left. There was a quarter tucked under his coffee cup. Amy pocketed it and cleared his booth. It was time for her to go home.

* * *

57

The haze of the day had been burned from the sky, and it felt as if the night would be cooler. Amy had taken a shower and was letting the water evaporate off her body by standing in the window with a breeze blowing in. Unlike most people she liked to wash in the late afternoon, to take away the grime of working and separate the day from the night. Even from the second floor she could smell the cheap scent of the marigolds. She was looking forward to going out with Todd. They were going dancing and she loved to dance with him.

She checked her back in the mirror, as she was going to wear an open-backed sundress if she didn't have any tan marks. Her leotard had left a faint line, but she decided to wear the dress anyway. As she was going to the closet to find it, she heard the phone ring and ran to answer it. 'Hello?'

'Ame, listen, I have to talk to you.' It was Tricia, and she sounded like she was holding the phone away from her mouth.

Something was wrong. Amy could tell by Tricia's speech, which was thick and slurred. Not really wanting to know, she asked, 'What's going on?'

'It's just that, well, I'm freaked out.'

'Is Danny there?'

'No. I'm alone. Would you come over?'

'What's the matter?' Amy hated even asking the question. It meant she would go. Tricia would tell her the problem and she would rush over and try to solve it. It had happened too many times before for it to be any different this once. Did Tricia continue to create problems because she knew Amy was always there to help solve them?

'I've been drinking. Too much. I'm really feeling out of it. I'm afraid.' Her voice was thick with liquor.

Amy had known from the first sound of Tricia's voice

58

that she had been drinking, but still, to hear her admit it was a letdown. She closed her eyes for a moment, wanting to slam down the receiver, then said, 'You know, I was going out with Todd tonight.'

'Amy, I'm really scared.' There was a drop in Tricia's voice as if she were listening for something. Then she whispered, 'I have to talk to you. Things are getting too hard. I don't know what to do.'

'OK. Hold on. I'll be right over.'

She threw on a pair of shorts and a shirt. She'd have to stop by the Studio.

When she drove up to the Dance Studio, Todd was waiting out front. He waved at her. She pulled up to the curb next to him. He had a short-sleeved shirt and tie pants on and had slicked his hair back.

'I'm afraid I'm going to have to cancel our date.'

'You're standing me up?'

'It's Tricia, Todd.' Amy knew she sounded mad, and she hoped Todd wouldn't take offense. She was mad, but at Tricia.

'You mean she's drunk?' Todd leaned on the side of the car.

'Yes. I don't want to believe it, but she is. She called and wants me to come over and hold her hand.'

'I'll come with you,' he said, starting to go around the car.

The last thing she needed was for Todd to see Tricia at her worst. 'Todd, no. Thanks for the offer, but I think I'd better go by myself. I just can't leave her all alone. I'm really sorry. I was looking forward to tonight.'

'It's still early yet. I'll wait for you,' he suggested.

'It might take a couple hours to calm her down. I know I'm not going to feel like doing anything afterward. Listen, go out and have a good time for both of us, OK?'

'I won't have a good time, but I'll go out. Listen, I'm sorry she started drinking again. Tell her to shape up.' He sounded angry, then he half smiled and pushed himself away from the car. 'I'll call you in the morning.'

As Amy drove over to Tricia's house, she hoped Tricia wouldn't be so bad that she would have to go back into detox. Her first time had been three months ago. The police had picked Tricia up at three in the morning wandering the streets and had put her in the Hennepin County Detox Center. She had had to stay in the required seventy-two hours and, as a result, had lost her waitressing job at the Club, where she averaged a hundred dollars a night in tips. When Amy had gone to pick Tricia up, three winos had offered her money to buy them a bottle. Their voices shook and they smelled of sweat and vinegar. Tricia, pale and sober, walked past them as if they didn't exist.

Tricia had managed to stay sober for a while but three weeks later she had gone out to their parents' house and drunk a bottle of gin. Edna and Red had found her passed out in front of the TV set when they came home from playing bridge. They had propped her up between them in the car and brought her down to detox. After that stay she wouldn't talk to them for a month. They had considered committing her to a treatment center and Amy knew if it happened again, they would.

Amy watched the beer foam up as she poured it down the sink. She heard Tricia walk across the hardwood floor in the dining room. When the noise stopped she knew Tricia was standing in the kitchen doorway. As she reached for the last beer can, she felt a hand grab her wrist.

'What are you doing?' Tricia screamed at her.

'Let go.'

'You have no right.' Tricia went for the can and Amy knocked it to the floor. It rolled to hide under the table.

'I do. I'm your sister.'

'You're not. I disown you.' Tricia's eyes were clouded with anger.

'You can't.'

'I hate you. I hate your nose.'

'You hate my nose?'

Suddenly Tricia's face changed and her eyes cleared. 'Oh, my God, I'm creating a scene.' She walked out of the kitchen, holding the doorjamb. 'I'm creating a scene with my very own sister.'

Opening the refrigerator, Amy looked into the cold white emptiness. She turned and yelled, 'Have you had anything to eat?'

There was no answer, so she walked into the living room, where Tricia was lighting a cigarette. She maneuvered the cigarette toward her mouth in a long, flowing movement. After she had taken a quick little puff, she looked up at Amy.

'Yeah?' she asked.

'Have you eaten?'

'So what are you now, my mom?'

'There's nothing left in the fridge.'

'Snoop. Why don't you just leave? OK? Leave.' Tricia waved her cigarette.

'No. Listen, you're the one who asked me to come over here. What did you want to tell me, Trish?'

At the sound of her name Tricia's face softened and she looked as if she were on the verge of tears. 'Amy, I don't know. Why can't I be like you?'

'Isn't one of me bad enough?'

'You would never do some of the stuff I do.'

'Come on, Trish. Don't compare yourself to me. That's stupid.'

'That's what Mom and Dad always do. Why can't you get good grades like Amy? Amy doesn't use makeup. Amy is such a good girl. You're so fucking perfect, how can I compete with that?' Tricia was crying, tears welling in her eyes, then spilling down her face. 'You know, once Mom told me I was like Aunt Margaret. She wasn't even mad, she just said it. I think she's right.'

Amy was shocked that her mother would tell Tricia such a thing. Their aunt had died when she was forty-two. Amy barely remembered her. She had died of cirrhosis of the liver. 'You can't think like that. You're not like me and you're not like Aunt Margaret. You're just yourself. You're going to be all right. Take a deep breath.'

Tricia pulled her hair back off her face and said, 'Don't worry, I won't get hysterical. I took some downers.'

'Well, with that and the beer you should be crashing pretty soon.'

'No. I didn't want that to happen, so I took some speed too.'

'Lord.' Amy sat down on the couch and looked at Tricia. She looked so much older than twenty-three. Her skin seemed weary. When she tried to focus her eyes, her whole body wavered. Amy asked her, 'Where did you get the drugs?'

'A guy you don't know. Eddy. We have an understanding. He brings me drugs, and I do him a few favors.'

'So what brought this on?' Amy asked her, taking her by her limp shoulders and shaking her. 'Why did you start drinking again?'

'I just can't do anything right. I know I'm not going to get that singing gig with the band. My life is a mess. You wouldn't believe it.' Her breath stank, her eyes were slightly crossed, and her speech slurred. Amy let go of her shoulders. Tricia was in bad enough shape without having her sister whack her one.

'So you say.'

Tricia gave a short laugh. 'So I know.'

'Do you think you can solve something by drinking?'

'I have a lot of things to forget. I don't want to think about Danny anymore. I have to get away from him.'

'Then why are you drinking?'

'It makes me feel better. It makes me forget. Amy, I'm really afraid. Things are getting out of control. I thought I knew what I was doing. But now I feel like I'm in over my head.'

'What are you talking about?'

Tricia looked at her strangely, then got up from the couch. 'Do you want a beer?'

'I don't think there's any beer left.' Amy thought about trying to have a serious talk with Tricia about what was getting out of control, but she knew it would go nowhere. She would try to help Tricia straighten out, maybe even convince her of something, and the next day she would realize that Tricia didn't even remember the conversation. It wasn't worth it. It was never worth it to try to talk sense to a drunk. She'd just ride this binge out like she did all the others.

'Oh. No more beer, huh?' Tricia sat back down and lit another cigarette, although her first one was still burning in the ashtray. 'Do you like chicken wings? There's a great place that delivers chicken wings. Let's get some, OK?'

'Sounds good to me.'

'You order.' Tricia handed her a flyer with an advertisement for Charlie's Chicken Wings on it. 'I already tried once, but I couldn't get the right number.'

Amy dialed the number and ordered two baskets of chicken wings with fries. Tricia walked unsteadily across the floor and put on an album. She started to dance to the R and B tune and sing along with it. Her voice, husky with alcohol, sounded like a train whistle going off into the night on some lonely journey.

'I wanna go out dancing. You feel like it?' Tricia asked when the song was over.

'Let's wait for the chicken wings.'

'Yeah. I'm hungry.' Tricia went into her bedroom and came out carrying a half-empty gallon jug of red wine. 'Want some wine?'

'I'm not drinking anymore. Where'd you get that?'

'Hank brought it over last night. I made him leave so he wouldn't drink it all.'

'Last night? After the gig?'

Tricia screwed up her forehead. 'Yeah. What do you think of Hank? He grew up on a sheep farm. You know, I really want that job. Sometimes you just have to do certain things to get what you want.' Tricia reached for a dirty glass sitting on the coffee table. She then tried to lift the wine bottle and pour herself a glass of wine. She spilled some on the table.

Amy said, 'Why don't you let me do that?'

Tricia looked at her suspiciously. 'You'll dump it out.'

'No, I won't do that again.'

'Why don't you just leave?'

Amy grabbed the bottle out of Tricia's hand. 'Why don't you leave me alone? You're the one who called me. What am I – your witness? You want someone to see how bad off you are. Well, I'm not interested anymore. It's getting boring, Tricia. I hate it. It was great to see you sing the other night. That's the part of you I love. But this drinking bullshit makes me sick.'

'You don't understand at all. Here I am trying to tell you something and you won't even listen.' Tricia drank what wine she had managed to pour into her glass.

'What do you want to tell me? How sad your life is? Well, my life isn't a lot better, sweetheart. I don't have a boyfriend. I'm waitressing and earning zero money. I'm working my butt off dancing and I'm not even sure I'm getting anywhere. You're not the only one with problems.'

Tricia raised a hand as if to ward off the words. 'I want you to go now.'

'No way.'

'I'll call the police.'

'Go ahead.'

Tricia pulled the black phone off the floor and set it in her lap. She brought her face close to the dial and dialed 0. 'Operator. I want the number of the police. Nine one one. Thank you.' She hung up and started to dial. 'What was that again?'

'Nine one one,' Amy told her.

'Send the police. Thirty-eight forty Chicago Avenue. Number three. Thank you.' Tricia hung up and looked at Amy, her head rocking as if blown by a light breeze. 'You didn't think I'd do it.'

'Don't be so sure. I know you pretty well.'

'Then why am I like this?' Tricia held out her plump arms. She looked like a china doll, Amy thought, but something was cracking.

'I don't know. You don't seem to be able to get it together.'

'I lost my job.'

'I know.'

'You dumped out my beer. I can't believe you did that.'

Amy said nothing, but watched Tricia try to blink her eyes into focus. The two cigarettes had burned to ashen stubs. Tricia dropped the one she was holding to the floor. Then she got up and turned on the TV.

They were watching an 'I Love Lucy' rerun when the police knocked at the door. Tricia jumped up and opened it. 'Officers, this woman won't leave my apartment.'

The two policemen entered the apartment and stared at Amy.

Amy looked up at them, smiling. 'Hi, I'm Tricia's sister. She asked me come over here tonight. She's drunk and now she wants me to leave, which I have no intention of doing.'

The older, gray-headed officer took out a pad. 'She's your sister?'

'Yes.'

'She still has a legal right to ask you to leave.'

'Officer, she's intoxicated. She's had four cans of beer, some downers, a hit of speed, a glass or two of wine, and God knows, what all else.'

The two policemen looked at Tricia.

'I just want to be alone. Please make her go.'

'OK,' the gray-headed officer said, 'but she does have the right to take you down to detox. The shape you're in, that might not be a bad idea.'

'You can't do that,' Tricia screamed.

'Oh, yes, they can,' Amy said. 'I'll authorize them.'

'Make her leave.'

'Those are your choices. If she stays, you can stay. If she goes, you go to detox. We're not leaving you in this state. Your sister's only looking out for you.'

'She isn't. She just wants to be better than me.'

'It's your choice.'

'OK, she can stay.' She turned to Amy. 'I'll never talk to you again.'

There was a loud banging at the door. Amy noticed the younger officer's hand move to rest on the holster of his gun. Tricia walked to the door and opened it. A delivery boy was holding a large bag in his arms. He stared at the two policemen and said, 'Chicken wings. You order chicken wings?'

Tricia said, 'Yeah, in here. Just wait a second.' Tricia

reached between the couch cushions and pulled out a wad of money. She handed him a twenty, then put the money back in her hiding place.

As the police officers were leaving, the older cop said to Amy, 'Call us if she gets worse.'

'Do you want a glass of wine?' Tricia asked the delivery boy.

Amy winced and hoped the police hadn't heard her say that, since the delivery boy looked all of fifteen.

'No, thanks, ma'am,' he said, and smiled at the ten-dollar tip Tricia had given him.

Ricky was yelling at Lucy about buying a new dress. Amy and Tricia ate the chicken wings and watched the TV in silence until Tricia said, 'You know why I stay up so late? If I go to sleep, then I have to wake up.'

'Why don't you get some help? Go to treatment, Tricia.'

'Don't talk to me about that. You don't know what it's like to be locked up. Those people in there are crazy.' Tricia started digging around in the debris on the coffee table. 'Where are my cigarettes?' She got up and went into the bedroom.

Amy watched the end of the 'I Love Lucy' show and then turned the TV off, the black overwhelming the white. She felt completely drained; it all seemed so futile. Here it was the middle of the night and she was baby-sitting her twenty-three-year-old sister when she could have been dancing with Todd, having fun, maybe meeting a new man.

Tricia had not reappeared, so Amy went into the bedroom. Tricia, having not quite made it to the bed, lay sprawled in a pile of dirty clothes. Her red hair formed a halo around her white face with its open mouth. Amy bent down and listened to her breathe.

It was past one in the morning and Amy knew she

should go home. She squatted down on the floor and stared at Tricia. Looking at her sister, Amy asked herself, why can't I make her better? If I stayed with her, never letting her out of my sight, could I keep her from drinking, could I make her believe in herself? Amy put a hand on Tricia's shoulder and knew the answers to her own questions. She couldn't save Tricia from herself. She had tried once before when they lived together and had only started to sink with her.

Maybe she should have had her taken to detox. At least then, for three days, she'd be safe. Amy remembered her as a kid. Old women would stop Tricia on the street to touch her red hair, and she would wrinkle her nose at them.

Chapter 5

When Amy woke she was covered with a fine mesh of sweat and felt as if every ligament, muscle, and bone in her body had come undone. She didn't hurt. She just didn't feel like she could command her body to move.

Focusing her eyes on her alarm clock, she saw it wasn't even nine o'clock. Why had she awakened so early? She hadn't come home last night until after two and hadn't fallen asleep until much later. Then she heard someone calling her name, 'Amy.'

She grabbed a towel that was on the floor, wrapped it around herself, and went to the open window. Todd was standing in among the marigolds, waving at her. 'Hi,' she yelled at him. 'What's up?'

'Are you?' Todd asked.

'I guess so.'

'Wanta go have breakfast at the café?'

'Give me a second. I'll be right down.'

When Amy opened the front door, she found Todd sitting on her steps, depetaling one of the marigolds.

'Does she love you?' Amy laughingly asked as she saw the petals strewn on the cement steps.

Todd dropped the mutilated flower. 'I guess I'm just frustrated.'

'Why?'

'I got stood up last night.'

'You know that wasn't my fault.' They walked in silence to the Corner Café.

The café was busy for so early on a Saturday morning, but Amy figured that everyone was in there to escape the heat in the restaurant's air-conditioned comfort. She and Todd joined the line that snaked out from the counter.

'You taking a class today?' Todd asked her.

'No, but I wish I was.'

'Well, Dana had scheduled some time in the studio that she's not going to use. You want to do a workout with me?'

'Great.'

They ordered eggs and coffee and went to find themselves a table near the window. Todd took a sip of coffee and relaxed into the chair with a sigh. 'Coffee – I need it more than anything else in the morning. If I could shoot up the first cup, I would.'

'Addict,' Amy said, laughing at him.

'My only fault.'

Amy attacked her eggs. She was surprised at her appetite. 'God, it feels good in here. It's even making me hungry. I am sorry about last night. What did you end up doing?'

'Went and saw Willie and the Bees. I just hung out with friends most of the night. But right at the end I asked this pretty woman to dance. So we danced, but when the band quit she walked over and kissed the trumpet player. As usual, I left by myself. How was your night?'

'A nightmare.'

'What happened?' Todd asked.

'You won't believe it. Tricia called the police on me. But she was so gone that they took one look at her and said she was headed for detox if she threw me out. I stayed until she fell asleep.' Suddenly Amy wasn't hungry anymore. She felt as if she were back in Tricia's apartment, the smell of sour wine, old cigarettes; her sister's wandering eyes trying to land on something outside herself that was stable. Amy looked at Todd and said, 'I can't stand it that she's drinking again. I really don't know

70

if I can go through it anymore. I feel like I'm getting shredded up inside.'

Having cleaned off his plate, Todd reached across the table and grabbed a bite of her eggs on his fork. 'So stop. Why do you put up with that crap, anyway?'

'What can I do, Todd? Ignore her?'

'No, but you're too involved in her life. It's not healthy. If you'll come and take care of her whenever she's drunk or high, then it's like she can keep getting blasted. Like you're giving her permission.'

In her heart Amy knew there was truth in what he was saying, but she resisted it. 'So you know it all.'

'Maybe I see it 'cause she's not my sister. Tricia's funny and bright, but something's gone a little rotten in her.'

Amy pushed away her eggs. 'Maybe you're right, but don't say that, Todd. She's still my sister. You don't know what her life is like. I don't even know, really. She's just having some problems right now.'

'And you can't solve them, kiddo. You can't get me a girlfriend and you can't fix up Tricia's life. So cool out.'

'Get you a girlfriend? Now, that would be setting myself an impossible task.'

'Don't get nasty.'

'Don't tell me what to do.' Amy stabbed her eggs with a fork, then pulled it out slowly and set it down next to her plate. 'I'm sorry, but I guess I don't need you to tell me what I already know. I get mad at Tricia for her drinking, then she drinks more, then I get petrified something will happen to her and can't let her out of my sight. It's sick.'

'It'll be all right. Just give her some space.' Todd glanced around the café. 'Well, here we all are. You want to figure out who slept with whom last night? I see Walt and Geri are sharing a table. Weren't they divorced a year ago August?'

71

'Stop it. You're horrible.'

'Only trying to take your mind off your sister by gossiping. I really don't like to see how much you worry about her. Since Luke and you disbanded, she's been your primary fixation.'

'I don't want to talk about it anymore. When do you have studio time?'

'In an hour.'

Todd ran through a trial audition with Amy. First he had her do a series of warm-ups, throwing in one or two new exercises to check on the limberness of her legs. He pushed her hard, looking at her leg placement, poking her thighs, and correcting her posture.

Then he had her do selected runs across the floor, changing them each time to see how quickly she could follow his instructions. But they stopped before the most important part of the audition, which was the solo dance.

It could be done to any piece of music the dancers chose; the only requirement was that the dance be improvisational. The company wanted to have a glimpse at a dancer's inner choreography.

'So what are you going to be using for your improv piece?' Todd asked after they had gone through the runs.

'I'm still deciding,' Amy admitted.

Amy wasn't sure what she was going to dance to, and it was making her nervous. Everyone else she talked to had selected some music. Probably the selections would be mostly classical with some new music by Philip Glass or Steve Reich. She thought it might work in her favor to do something different, but she still hadn't come up with anything that inspired her.

'Well, you're looking good. If you do that well for the audition and you've got a strong improv piece, I'd say you're in.' Todd wiped the sweat off his forehead and continued to wipe upward so his hair stuck out from his face.

Amy sat down on the floor and rubbed her feet. 'God, Todd, I hope so. I don't know what I'm going to do if I don't make it.'

'Try again next year.'

'Forget it. I'll be twenty-six. That's too old to be studying dance and not actually dancing.'

'Why? Martha Graham danced her whole life.'

'I'm not fooling myself. I'm no Martha Graham. I need to be working on something, not taking classes. I love working on pieces. You know, I'd even like to try to choreograph.'

Todd touched her shoulder. 'Well, do a good job on your improv and I'd say your chances are more than good.'

Amy stood up and shook herself. Her arms and legs felt tight, as if she were trying to hold something inside herself and it was trying to get out. 'This isn't me being negative, Todd, but if I don't get into the company I think I might leave the Twin Cities. Really start over somehow. Do something totally different.'

'No more waitressing?'

'Man, I'm getting so tired of that. I feel the urge every day to accidentally drop something all over a business-man's suit.'

'Only businessmen?'

'Somehow they seem to get more than their fair share of my anger.'

'Where would you go?' Todd asked.

'The islands. Someplace where I could be totally sur-rounded by water.'

'Speaking of water, I'm ready for a swim. You want to come?'

'No, thanks. I promised myself I'd clean the house. It's really a pig sty. You wanta help?'

At home Amy put 'Down So Low' on the record player while she did the dishes. Listening to it reminded her of another time in her life, two years ago, when she and Luke were having problems. He was working so much she started to feel neglected. She would call him some nights late, after he should have been home from a gig, and he wouldn't be there. The next day he would tell her where he'd been: all-night parties, late-night swim, car broke down, but all she knew was he wasn't with her. And when he was with her, he was tired. Often too tired to make love. He would crawl into bed next to her and fall asleep and she would rub against him, wanting him to wake up, willing him to touch her, but he would breathe heavily through his mouth and pull away from her.

Then one night she went down to the club to see Luke and danced with a man, Rob, and they exchanged numbers. He called her a few nights later and invited her over to his place to listen to some new records. They drank wine and ended up making love on the floor in front of his stereo system. He said he didn't care about Luke. He just wanted to see her from time to time.

So for a few weeks she would go over to his house at odd hours and they would make love, barely talking to each other. One night he stopped by her apartment. It got late and there was a knock at the door. When Luke saw Rob, he told Amy he would talk to her in the morning and left. For the first time she and Rob spent the night together and she knew she had made a big mistake.

When she called Luke in the morning, he said he didn't want to see her for a while. She tried to explain, but she couldn't bring herself to tell him how much she had missed him, their lovemaking, how hungry she had been for someone to touch her.

Two weeks later they had talked again. Luke told her he was seeing someone else, a woman named Angela. Amy didn't tell him Rob wasn't serious about her, that now that they weren't sneaking around he wasn't even very interested in her. A month later she heard that Angela had moved in with Luke, and Amy tried to forget him. By that time Rob had stopped calling altogether.

Amy stacked the dishes to drip dry and went to take a bath. The album went on to the other old songs that reminded her of earlier times with Luke, their first year together when they had been so in love. She didn't blame Tricia for not knowing what to do about Danny. Sometimes, it seemed the pain of breaking up, the being alone, was unbearable. She knew it was one of the reasons she wasn't seeing anyone right now. Simply not wanting to start the process over again.

When the bathtub was as full as it could be with tepid water, she stepped into it, stretching out until only the tips of her toes and the rounded caps of her knees showed. She had found this slightly warm water was actually the most cooling temperature, with still a tinge of warmth to ease her muscles.

Todd was right about how protective she was of Tricia, but Amy wondered why she was. Had she gone right from worrying about Luke to taking care of Tricia? As if she needed someone to concentrate her energy on, so she didn't have to look at her own life so carefully. Maybe she should spend less time with Tricia and more time out and about where she might meet some nice guy. Go out with Todd, go out with other dancers from the Studio.

Maybe she should get drunk with Tricia. Show her that she wasn't the only bad girl in their family. When Amy thought of seeing Tricia drunk again, after a month of tiptoeing around her sobriety, she wanted to drop dish after dish on the floor and watch them explode into pieces of porcelain that no one could ever put back together again. It felt so hopeless. She resolved not to call Tricia for the rest of the day, although in the back of her mind she hoped that she would hear from her. They would be going out to see the folks tomorrow, that would be soon enough. She would go to the 500 Bar tonight and mingle.

'Todd, want to meet me at the 500 Bar for a drink later on?' Amy had the phone resting on her shoulder as she was painting her toes.

'I'm going out tonight.'

'What?' She almost dropped the receiver as she straightened up to hear what he was saying.

'I met someone down at the beach today. We're going to a movie.'

'I can't believe it. You're deserting me.'

'I wouldn't put it like that.'

'What's she like?' Amy felt left out.

'I'm not telling.'

'Do I know her?'

'I don't think so, she's not a dancer, she's a secretary in a law office.'

'Well, I'm going down to the 500 later on. Stop by there, the both of you, if you feel like it after the movie.'

'OK, maybe. But don't get smart with her. She doesn't know she's got to get your approval to go out with me.'

'I'll act surprised to see you. I'll even tell her I like what she's wearing. You know how charming I can be.'

Todd and his date never showed up at the bar. Amy went down around eleven and ended up almost closing the place. She knew most of the people in the bar by sight and quite a few by name. The West Bank was a tight community, and a lot of the dancers and musicians who worked at the Studio came to the 500. She was working on her third beer when Luke walked up and, without asking, bought her a shot of tequila.

'I didn't tell you the other night, but you're looking good,' he said as he handed her the shot-glassful.

'So are you.' She marveled that she was actually glad to see him. 'But why aren't you playing tonight?'

'A night off. Just like the normal people.'

She laughed. It had been one of their private jokes, wondering about the lives of the normal people – that part of society that owned houses, made car payments, had credit cards. 'So you're being a little normal tonight?'

'Only a little. I like your hair,' he said. 'That short cut suits you. I suppose it's the dancer look.'

'The modern dancer look.'

'Excuse me.'

She giggled and bolted the shot in one gulp. The bitter twist of the tequila made her smile. Medicine. Maybe that's why Tricia drank, to get better.

'So how are you and Angela doing?' The question slipped out of her mouth before she had a chance to think and stop it. Hank had told her that they were not together anymore, but she wanted to hear it from Luke.

'God, you know me as well as anyone, Amy. Don't know how you put up with me so long.' Luke smiled at her as if she were someone special, and she realized how much she missed him. 'Last few months she's done nothing but complain. Says I'm not paying enough attention to her. Wants me to be more responsible. I think mainly she's wanted me to be making more money. Well, anyway, last week she left me.'

Something pinged in Amy's heart. 'She did?'

'Yeah. I feel pretty bad about it, but I think she might

77

be right. I don't seem to have what it takes to make a relationship work.'

Amy stood still. She didn't know what to say. He did get so involved in his work, his music, that he had time for little else. But she remembered so many good times, the way he would sometimes wake her up in the morning by playing a ballad on the saxophone, or how after lovemaking he would beat out a rhythm on her back, sing in her ear, wake her in the night to tell her about a dream.

She had missed him so desperately when she finally knew it was over and he wasn't going to give her another chance that she had walked down to the bridge over the Mississippi and stared at the water that was leaving town. In her mind, she'd jumped down to it, her body free of her hopes and fears for a moment, until the water slapped her so hard she had reeled back from the imagined belly flop and pulled herself, literally, back together, back up out of the water, on to the bridge, and walked home, a few tears leaking from her eyes, but feeling somehow better. She had decided she could live without him.

'So how about you?' Luke asked. 'How's your dancing going? You said something about an audition.'

'Yeah, it's a week from today. I need to figure out my improv piece. I can't decide on the music.'

'You want a consultation?'

Amy laughed. She remembered a bit of music he had written for her. The repeating refrain sounded like wind over a prairie, a mixture of blues and country music. 'There is that one piece you wrote for me.'

'No, you need something new. You're a different person.' Luke leaned against the bar and looked around for a second.

'We decided to hire Tricia.'

'That's great. Does she know?'

'Not yet. Hank's going to tell her.'

'How's Todd?' Luke asked.

'Fine. He's teaching and working on a new dance himself.'

'Did I ever tell you about the time he came down to see me after you and I broke up?'

Amy shook her head no. Todd hadn't told her either.

'Well, he was mad at me and worried about you. Angela was there, so he made me go outside with him. At first I thought he was going to punch me out. Then we smoked a joint and he calmed down. He asked me to talk to you.'

'But you didn't.'

Luke looked at her and said, 'I was so hurt I couldn't think straight.'

And now he was standing with her in a bar, buying her a drink. They could talk until the bar closed, then he would ask if she wanted to go get some coffee, as it would still be far too early for him to think about bed. If she accepted they would talk another hour or two and then he would walk her home. She could invite him in and then he might touch her and she didn't know what she would do if he did.

Amy stared at Luke, such an intense man and she knew him so well. She wished she didn't know him at all and he was buying her a drink for the first time. He would be a wonderful man to have an affair with, but he was right, he didn't know how to last in a relationship.

'Oh, I see someone I should go say hi to. Thanks for the drink,' Amy said, and turned away from him. She didn't want to see how the evening might turn out with Luke; whether he stayed with her or not, she wouldn't come out of it a winner. Looking around the room for someone she did know, she saw a woman dancer from the studio, and walked over and sat down on a stool next her.

'Hey, Dara.'

79

Dara wore her stick-straight blond hair pulled back in a tight-knotted bun. She had originally studied ballet and didn't let anyone forget it. 'Hey, Amy. I saw you and Todd working out today. Are you teacher's pet or what?'

'He was just helping me out.' Amy wondered if he was going to show up at the bar, but looking around she didn't see him.

'I wouldn't mind private lessons from him.'

Amy had often been teased about her relationship with Todd and hadn't completely minded when people didn't understand they were just friends, but for some reason tonight it irritated her. She decided to change the subject. 'So what are you doing for your improv?'

They talked about the auditions for a while and then Amy saw Luke leave the bar. He left by himself. She had one more drink and felt her mind start to fizz a little from the alcohol. She set the unfinished tequila-and-grapefruit juice down on the bar, looked at the clock, which was set to bar time but still said it was almost a quarter to one, and said good-bye to Dara. The next time she'd see her would probably be on the dance floor when they auditioned.

Dara waved good-bye and then shouted, 'Break a leg.' Amy knew it was a traditional saying, but Dara sounded to her as if she actually meant it.

When Amy woke up in the morning she felt the tremors of a hangover, a phenomenon she hadn't felt in months. All she wanted to do was drink a huge glass of orange juice. She pulled herself out of bed and went to the phone to call Tricia. It was after ten and she knew their mother would have dinner ready at noon.

As Amy listened to the phone ring with no answer, she remembered the dream she had had the night before, a baby dream, the baby had been faceless, lying in a crib, but when Amy touched it, its face split wide open and became a huge mouth and it looked as if it were trying to talk or trying to breathe but she couldn't understand it or help it.

Even though she almost always remembered her dreams in the morning, she didn't really believe in analyzing them. They simply seemed to have their own reality. She hung up the still-ringing phone. Then, hugging her stomach, she walked into the kitchen to look for orange juice.

In the refrigerator all she saw was wilted lettuce, a row of smooth white eggs that made her nauseous, and a carton of milk, but no juice. She'd have to go out for it. She'd drive over toward Tricia's house and get some juice on the way. Tricia was probably there and was either not answering the phone or had disconnected it.

Amy bought a quart of juice at the 7–11 and drank half of it driving over to Tricia's place. The sun was glaring down on the street. She drove with one hand and drank with the other. She was looking forward to the day out at her folks, eating barbecued chicken and lying in the sun. For a second she wondered what Luke was doing on this Sunday. He had liked to come out to her parents' house and help her dad grill the chicken.

She parked the car in a wistful piece of shade in front of Tricia's apartment. Looking up at the windows of the apartment, Amy saw that nothing was stirring but guessed that Tricia was still sleeping. After running up the stairs she knocked on the door three times and waited. No sound. She banged on the door a couple more times and waited. Still nothing.

She cursed Tricia under her breath. Why, for a change, couldn't she be ready to go? Now, even when Amy did finally rouse her, it was going to take her an hour to get ready and then Mom would be mad at them when they got out to the house. She felt like leaving her. Just getting in her car and going without her. It was like Todd said. Because Tricia knew Amy would come and get her, she never had to get ready for anything.

Amy turned and went back outside. She sat down on the bottom step and watched the ants pulling huge pieces of leaf across the cement sidewalk. Sometimes she felt as if she had something huge tacked on to the back of her shoulder and she just couldn't throw it off. She couldn't do it, she couldn't leave Tricia. If she did, it would ruin her day and the folks would be disappointed. They wouldn't blame Amy but they would be upset and she would have no one to lie in the sun with.

She walked back up the stairs. It made her mad that she couldn't just leave Tricia. She wanted to yell at her. She looked at the door and kicked it. Then she tried the doorknob. The door opened.

For a second she felt paralyzed with fear, but then she laughed at herself and said out loud, 'Tricia?'

In the morning Dad leaves for work before we are up, but Mom still drifts in bed when we tiptoe downstairs to make our breakfast. I show Tricia how to put a few cornflakes in the bottom of a bowl, a splash of milk, and swirl it around so it looks like we have eaten. Then we take handfuls of cereal and stuff them in the pockets of our shorts. We walk down to the beach. No one is there. The water is quiet. We walk out to the end of the dock and drop in some of the cereal. A flake lies on the surface for an instant like a curled leaf and then a fish sneaks up from underneath and snaps it up. 'Those are the messengers,' I tell Tricia. 'They carry all the food down to them.'

Chapter 6

The sun shone in the front windows and made a cross-hatched pattern on the wood floor. The curtains fluttered in the wind and the room was filled with light and soft, moving air. Amy was glad to see that Tricia had straightened up the apartment. The coffee table was cleared off; only a pack of cigarettes and an ashtray sat on it. Tricia must be feeling all right if she had enough energy to clean up, Amy decided.

Amy walked quickly through the living room to see if Tricia was up. Why else would the front door be left unlocked? Maybe she had gone out to get the Sunday paper. The hallway leading to the bedroom was dark, but a light had been left on in the bathroom. Amy reached in to turn the light off and noticed that the toilet seat was up. A man must have been in the apartment last night. She wondered if he were asleep in the bedroom.

The bedroom door was closed and Amy stood a moment before knocking. Tricia could be such a grouch when she first woke up. Amy remembered her complaining about Danny, saying one of the things she had hated when they had lived together was his singing in the morning. She said it was inhuman that such a sound could come out of anyone at that time of the day. And once when Dad had shouted down to wake them for school, 'Rise and shine, Miss Americas,' Tricia had chucked a shoe across the room, shattering the full-length mirror that hung on the wall.

Amy knocked on the bedroom door. No sound. Not even sheets rustling, a groan. Amy wished she had called

Tricia last night, just to know what she had been up to. Maybe she had met someone, maybe Danny or Hank was in the bedroom with her. Amy knew Tricia was in there, in the bedroom. Then a feeling grew, came down on her shoulders; something was wrong. Nothing seemed to add up. The front door shouldn't have been left unlocked. Unless Tricia had gotten really drunk again last night. Unless Tricia was in trouble. Amy knocked once more on the closed door and then walked into the room.

The scene inside the darkened bedroom was one that Amy would never forget, no matter how late she stayed up at night, no matter whose arms she was held in, no matter how many drinks she had had or how far from home she traveled. The image of Tricia's sagging body and limbs tied to the bedstead was printed in her mind. The stocking stuffed in her mouth and black scarf tied around her head to hold it in. The black leather straps at her wrists and ankles. In her left breast was an ivory-handled knife, plunged halfway up the blade. Only a thin ribbon of blood wound down Tricia's chest and pooled on her stomach. The white skin, a whole naked body of it, but lacking a glow. The faint sunburn lines. The red hair flowing over white pillows. The thin lips. The freckles. The dying freckles.

Amy felt her throat clutch for air, suck it in, and let it out, throw it out in a whimper. She knew what she had to do. She had to walk up and touch Tricia's wrist and throat. To make sure no blood was moving. To confirm what she already knew. She closed her eyes and walked forward.

The air in the room was still and silent. There was the smell of stale booze, but there was no sound of breathing. Amy lost the impulse to breathe. She wanted no air in her body. She wanted what she could not have, a pulse under her finger when she touched Tricia's fragile wrist. She pressed her first two fingers into the wrist as her mother had taught her to do and found nothing, a lack of anything so complete it made her weak and sick. She touched Tricia's neck and knew it was the last time she would ever touch her sister. Then she walked out of the room and gently closed the door.

Leaning up against the door, Amy wanted to be protecting Tricia from the world, but knew that she was only trying to understand what she had seen. Flashes of it would come to her and suddenly she knew that she had been robbed without knowing it and a huge part of her was gone. She opened her mouth and a scream came out. The sound was not from her. It was from the part of her that had been so completely Tricia's sister. Now, she was no one's sister and she had no sister. She put her hand over her mouth to stop the shrieking sound that was coming out of it and walked into the living room.

Sitting down on the old green velvet couch, Amy remembered Tricia buying it at the Salvation Army, proud of finding such a bargain. The two of them had moved it into the apartment themselves. It had been heavy and clumsy but they had maneuvered it up the stairs. The first thing Tricia had done when they had it placed in the corner of the living room was sprawl out on it full length and say she knew she was going to be spending a lot of time on it. Amy ran her hand across the rough old nap of the couch and felt tears run down her face.

Soon she would have to start doing things, open the apartment up to the unavoidable world. But for another moment or two she wanted to stare at the sunshine on the floor and keep her mind as blank as she could. She watched the floating motes. Motes, she loved that word. She had been so glad to learn that those little floating worlds that turned and twirled in stirred sunlight had a name. Maybe they were where souls lived after someone died. Maybe that's all the room a soul needed.

She was getting too close to those horrible thoughts. She looked down and saw *War and Peace* on the floor next to the couch. Tricia wasn't quite done reading it. Amy picked up the book and looked at the page number, 1189. She held the book tightly in her hands and thought *never*. Tricia would never finish the book. She wished somehow that Tricia had finished it, with so much left unfinished in her life.

Amy put the book on the coffee table and noticed the pack of cigarettes sitting there. They weren't the brand Tricia smoked. Tricia smoked regular cigarettes, Marlboro. She used to kid and say she was a cowgirl because of the brand. Amy's hand was trembling as she reached for the cigarettes. She stopped short of touching them, as she realized she shouldn't touch anything.

The image of the blood came to her again, the ribbon of it, and Amy thought of the time her dad had accidentally run over her kitten with the car. She had come out on to the front steps and had seen the kitten playing with a piece of red yarn, rolling over and over in the gravel, trying to unwrap itself from the bright stream of blood. When it stopped rolling, it lay perfectly still and Amy knew it would never move again.

She looked at the closed bedroom door and began to cry again. This time they were slow, relentless tears, the kind that felt as if they could continue forever, they came from so deep within herself. Someone had killed her sister. She knew she should call the police. Maybe they could find out who had done it. Amy needed to know why Tricia had been killed. Amy remembered Danny's face screaming at Tricia in the parking lot. It just didn't seem possible that anyone could have killed her sister. Only yesterday she had been alive.

Standing up, she looked around the living room. It was the last place Tricia would ever live. Be alive. Now, people had to know. She couldn't keep it to herself any longer. Her parents were waiting for them. Somehow she would have to tell them what had happened.

But when she got to the phone, she dialed Todd's number. She twisted the phone's long cord and listened to the faraway ring go unanswered. She willed him to answer the phone, then cursed him when he didn't. He had told her she worried too much. Well, he was wrong. She wanted to tell him how wrong he was and see if he could comfort her then. When he didn't answer she disconnected and punched in 911, remembering the number from Tricia's calling the police the other night. For once in her life Amy wished Tricia were lying, passed out drunk, in the other room.

Chapter 7

Amy stood by the front windows and watched the police cars arrive. They drifted up as if in a dream. They were quiet, no sirens on. It was Sunday morning. People were at church or sleeping in late. Two men in regular suits got out of an unmarked car, two uniformed policemen got out of a squad car parked behind them, and an ambulance came cruising up. They formed a procession up to the house. Amy walked to the door to let them in.

'She's back in the bedroom.' She pointed the way and stepped aside. The men who were wearing hats took them off. It's only respectful, Amy thought, in the presence of death. The men walked by her with their heads bowed.

A silver-haired man in a well-cut suit stopped and said, 'I'm sorry. Do you know what happened?' The rest of the men went back into the bedroom.

Amy sat on the edge of the couch, trying not to see what was going on in the bedroom. The silver-haired man stood near her. He repeated his question. 'Do you have any idea how it happened?'

'Yes, but I'm trying not to think about it. She was my only sister.' Amy pressed the palms of her hands into her eyes, not wanting to cry in front of him. But she hated the thought of what she had to do, of all the people she had to tell.

She heard the man walk back with the others. He only stayed in the bedroom a minute, then he came out and put a hand on her shoulder. 'I think you should get out of here. You want to go have a cup of coffee? I'd like to ask you some questions.'

She looked up at him. The first word she thought of to describe him was smooth, or suave. If she had passed him on the street, she would never have guessed he was a policeman. He looked more like a salesman, selling life insurance. That's what Tricia needed, life insurance, but he was too late. Amy suppressed a short laugh that would have turned into a wail. She continued to stare at him. There seemed to be no traces of his profession left on him. Except, looking at him a little longer, she noticed that his face seemed tired, as if he often didn't want to see what was in front of him. 'Yeah. I'd like to get out of here.'

Amy stood up. She didn't want to stay in the apartment any longer, but she didn't want to leave Tricia alone with all these men. Then, with an odd sense of relief, she realized that no one could ever hurt Tricia again. Wherever she was, she was safe.

When they were outside, she pointed across the street to Fred's Diner. 'We could go there.'

All of a sudden the ordinariness of what Amy was about to do struck her. It seemed like every day her sister was murdered and she would have to find her and then go have coffee with a policeman. The street looked impossibly wide to cross. Like a river, it would grab her feet if she stepped into it and then sweep her away. She couldn't walk across the street. Her knees started to quiver. They wanted to go in opposite directions. The policeman was ahead of her, halfway to the other side of the street. She knew she had to sit down. He looked back at her. She sat down on the curb.

'Are you all right?' he asked.

'I'm afraid.' Amy felt the world turning quietly around her. She had never been so sensitive to its ongoing motion. She grabbed the curb so she wouldn't fall off. If

90

only Tricia would just come back for a while. So they could go have coffee and she could tell her some things.

Amy was panicking. She couldn't remember the last time she had told Tricia she loved her. It was too long ago. Tricia would never remember; she would never know how much. More than the world was full of people, more than the days of her short life.

She felt a hand on her shoulder and flinched away from it. Then somebody said to her, 'Can you stand up?'

'Of course,' Amy said.

The silver-haired man gave her a hand and she stood up.

She looked at him and said, 'I just don't want to be doing this.'

He said, 'I know.'

In the diner there were two customers sitting at the counter and a waitress reading the Sunday paper. Amy and the detective took a booth next to the window. From where they were sitting they could see the front of the apartment building.

The silver-haired man held out his hand and said, 'I'm Towne, Andrew Towne. I'm a detective in the homicide division. And you're the deceased's sister?'

'Yes, her name is Tricia. I'm Amy Curtis.' It was difficult to even say her name, it stuck in her throat like a thin bone that didn't want to go up or down. She swallowed hard. Amy wondered if she could have stopped all this from happening. She should have called Tricia yesterday. It might have changed everything. Maybe then her sister would still be alive. Amy felt tears pressing at the back of her eyes.

The waitress came up with menus, but Detective Towne brushed them away. 'I think we'd both just like a cup of coffee.' After she had left, he turned to Amy and asked, 'How many in your family, Miss Curtis?'

Amy sucked in her breath. She had to answer his questions. 'You can call me Amy. Just me and my sister and our parents.'

'Where do your parents live?'

'Out in Richfield.'

'Do they know yet?'

Amy felt tears peppering her eyes. She tried to swallow them and said, 'I couldn't call them. I tried but I couldn't say it over the phone. It just wouldn't be right. I have to go out there and tell them. When we're done talking, I'll go out there.'

'Fine. I understand.' Towne stared down at his hands as if giving her time to compose herself.

The waitress brought them two cups of black coffee in white coffee cups. Amy put her hands around it to feel the heat.

'How did you happen to find her this morning?' Towne asked her.

'We were supposed to go out to my folks'. I tried to call her but there was no answer. That's not that unusual. She's a heavy sleeper and she sometimes unplugs the phone. So I drove over. The door was open when I got there. That's how I found her.'

'Did you touch anything when you went in?'

'I guess so. I had to touch the doorknob. I can't remember what else. Oh, I touched her. Her wrist and her neck. That's it. Then I sat on the couch. Then I dialed the phone.'

'Do you know where she was last night?' Towne took out a small notebook and began writing in it.

'No, not really. We didn't talk yesterday. She might have been out at a bar.' Amy stopped a moment. She felt as if she were taking a test, that there were right and wrong answers to the questions he was asking her. She had to cut through this feeling and let him know she could be of some help to him. 'There's a few things you should know about my sister. She's an alcoholic.'

'How old was she?'

Amy closed her eyes when she heard him use the past tense. She bent her head down and took a sip of coffee. The dark brew ate into her stomach. 'She was twenty-three. I'm twenty-five. She's had a serious drinking problem for about five years.'

'What's your relationship with your sister?'

Amy froze. They were sisters, didn't that explain everything? It seemed that she had loved Tricia more than anyone in the world. Now her sister was gone and a smooth-talking policeman wanted to know what they had been to each other. 'She was my sister.'

Towne cleared his throat, then said, 'I understand that. How were the two of you getting along?'

The implications of his questions hit Amy like a slap in the face. He was wondering if she could have had anything to do with Tricia's death. She hadn't thought things could get any worse, but they were. She needed him to understand. 'I loved my sister. I only wanted good for her. She was having problems and I was trying to help her out. I would have done anything for her. Does that make sense to you?'

'Sure.' His face was relatively unlined, except for two lines that creased up from his eyebrows. 'What did she do for a living?'

'She was a waitress. But she just lost her job. A couple nights ago she tried out to be the vocalist of a band. She's been singing on and off for a few years.'

'Did she make it?'

'I think so. But I don't think she knew.' The idea that

Tricia would never know she had succeeded made Amy want to put her head down on the table and cry. Her life had just started getting better, turning around, and now it was stopped, completely over.

'Did she have a boyfriend?'

Amy didn't think of Danny as Tricia's boyfriend – their relationship had gone much beyond friendship and degenerated into need, greed, and fear. Danny had been so able to bring out the worst in Tricia and then seemed to enjoy doing it. He hadn't wanted her to succeed at anything, and now Tricia was dead. Amy brought out the thought that had been hovering in the back of her mind: maybe Danny killed her. 'That was his knife.'

'Whose?'

'Danny's. She was in the process of breaking up with him. Danny and she had been going out off and on for about four years. They did a lot of drinking together. She wanted to stop drinking and she wanted to stop seeing him.' Amy needed to be calm when she said what she had to say about Danny; she wanted this policeman to believe her. 'He wasn't very happy about breaking up with her. He didn't want to. He threatened her several times when I was around.'

'What do you mean by threatened?'

'I think he slapped her around, and then two nights ago he said she was through.'

'She was through? With what?'

'He didn't really explain. He was yelling at her in a parking lot. But I didn't like the way he said it. Tricia kind of shrugged it off.'

Towne looked down at his coffee and then across the table at Amy. He stared at her with light blue eyes that looked incongruous in his colorless face. 'Now I'm going to ask you some hard questions. But I want you to remember we need the answers. Was your sister involved

94

in S and M? Did she and her boyfriend play around with bondage?'

Amy knew that's what she had seen when she went into the room. Was that how much Tricia didn't believe in herself? Enough to let someone do what they wanted with her for pleasure, money; bruises worn as the medals of some strange need to be put down? Amy started to shake, cold with the glimpse of her sister's life. She was seeing again in her mind where that life had led, a room empty of breath, filled with death. Stagnant blood, not flowing anywhere.

Amy felt Towne waiting for an answer. She tried to remember the question. 'I don't know. Tricia and I were real close, but there were parts of her life I didn't talk about. She and Danny went to Los Angeles for a year, and I think she was involved in stuff out there that scared her. She called Mom and asked her to buy her a ticket to come home. She looked like she had been beaten up when she came home. Danny came back about a month later. She never said too much about it except that she was broke and homesick.'

'When was this?'

'About a year ago. Then she got a job working at the top of the IDS Building and lost that when she started drinking a lot.'

'You said she and this Danny were breaking up. Do you know how we can get in touch with him?'

'I don't know his address or anything, he just moved recently. He had been living with Tricia for a while. But his folks live in St Paul just off Summit and I'm sure they know how to get in touch with him. His last name is Swenson.'

'Was she seeing Danny at all?'

'Yes, I think so. He still had a key to the apartment. In fact, he was there the other day when Tricia and I got home from the beach, flipping a knife from hand to hand. He had let himself in. I told her to take the key back. I tried to warn her.' As she was answering Towne, Amy realized she knew where Danny might be that afternoon. His regular Sunday afternoon pastime was shooting pool down at a 3.2 joint. But, for some reason, she decided not to mention where Danny might be.

'What's Danny like?' Towne asked, looking at her intently.

'Danny? I don't know if I'm the right person to talk to. I think in many ways he fucked up my sister's life. He made her think she wasn't worth much. But at the same time he couldn't live without her.'

'But what did *you* think of Danny?'

Amy thought about Danny for a moment, saw him slouching on the couch, smoking a cigarette and carelessly flicking the ash on the floor. She wondered why dark hair was seen as a symbol of evil. To her, blond hair seemed more appropriate, nothing there, no color. 'He drank too much. He had trouble holding on to jobs. He was a few years older than Tricia, but he was very dependent on her. He wouldn't let go of her. But he had his moments. I feel like I don't know him anymore. I don't think I knew my sister. I will say this, it seemed like he loved her.'

'You know, the call a policeman dislikes answering the most is a domestic.' Towne looked up from his notes. 'People who love each other can do nasty things when they don't get their way.'

'Yes, I've heard that.'

'Did you notice anything unusual about the apartment when you got there?' Towne asked.

'It was cleaner than usual, and that pack of cigarettes sitting on the table isn't the brand that Tricia smokes.'

'Is it the brand that Danny smokes?'

'No. He smokes the same as Tricia. He taught her how

to smoke. He encouraged her to drink all the time. I think he liked to see her out of control. It gave him more of a hold on her.'

'Was Tricia seeing any other men?'

Amy remembered that Hank had been over the other night. And at times Tricia would mention some guy in passing. She had met well-to-do men at the IDS. Had it been just one man? Amy couldn't remember. It had been one of those things she hadn't wanted to know. 'She knew a lot of people. She didn't always tell me what she was doing, but I don't think she was faithful to Danny. She had just met the guys in the band she tried out for. I don't remember any other names, but I think she did see other men occasionally. If I remember anything I'll let you know.'

'Good. We'll want to check on everything. Any names. Anything.'

'What's going to happen next?' Amy looked at the apartment across the street. People coming home from church would stop and stare at the ambulance and the squad car, but then move on. She wanted to see something burst open, some kind of frenzied activity that would show what was going on.

'What do you mean?'

'What are you going to do to my sister?'

'We'll need to do an autopsy report. Determine cause of death.'

He said it so matter-of-factly. Amy wanted to scream at him. She wanted to ask him if anyone had ever died in his family, someone he loved. Or been murdered, had the life ripped away from them in the most evil act that humans could do to each other. She wondered if he'd felt the horror that vibrated in the bedroom where Tricia still was, the vacuum feeling of life being sucked away. For him was there nothing unusual about a beautiful young woman being killed?

Amy had to ask the next question. She had to be sure. 'Did she know she was dying?'

Towne looked at her as if judging her. Then he said, 'That's hard to say.'

'How long will the coroner's report take?'

'A day or so.'

'But someone definitely killed her.'

'He might not have meant to, but he did kill her.'

Amy looked down at her hands. They were white and bloodless, gripping the coffee cup. She said, more to herself than to the man sitting across from her, 'What am I going to tell my parents?'

They're like us and they're not. Their parents didn't want them, so they left them on the shore of the lake. The fish came and took them in. They breathe water like we breathe air. They have webbing between their toes. They swim all day long and at night sleep curled up in the seaweed at the bottom of the lake. But when the moon is full, they swim through the night, prowling and wanting to come out of the water. The silver light makes them miss the world they left. They're lonesome. We must help them. We have to give them presents and gifts and keep them happy. Otherwise, they will turn mean. We must watch out for them. They're so much like us.

Chapter 8

The Curtis home was on the top of a small hill, which made the driveway difficult to maneuver in the wintertime. But it was a bright, sunny day, and Amy remembered, as she pulled into the driveway, how she and Tricia used to roll down the hill when they were kids. They had a special way of doing it, a ritual. They would wrap their arms all the way around their bodies, trying to touch fingertips across their backs, then twist their ankles together, close their eyes, and roll. Then they would stand up and they would feel drunk, the earth plunging and pivoting around them.

Her family had moved to this neighborhood when Amy was five; she barely remembered the old neighborhood. Their shingled house was the same color it had been when they moved in – maroon with white trim. Every year Red painted a small section of it so he never had to do more than a few days' work on it. He would paint it in his old undershirts and baggy shorts and always drank beer and whistled.

Amy closed her eyes and tried to move back in time. She didn't want to walk into her parents' house and tell them the news. She wanted instead to be coming over so Red could fix a chair for her or so Edna could show her how to make a piecrust for the tenth time. She heard the wind blowing through the poplar trees. It was the sound that had sent her to sleep most of her life. She opened her car door and got out.

When Amy walked into her parents' house, they both looked up from the preparations of the barbecue and smiled at her. The sun was shining in through the kitchen window and church music was pouring out of the squat radio next to the sink. Her mother was slicing eggs and potatoes for potato salad. Her father was washing the grill. They stopped what they were doing when they saw her face.

'Got the fire going,' Red said to Amy.

Amy looked at her father and thought he had aged since the last time she saw him. Or else she hadn't really looked at him for a while. With the addition of white strands his hair was turning pink and moving off his forehead, so that he looked a little perplexed.

'Where's Tricia?' Edna asked. Her mother was wearing an orange dress. She often wore dresses on Sundays. Put one on for church and then left it on all day long. Amy didn't know what color her mother's hair was anymore. She had been dying it dark brown for years. Edna claimed it wasn't to hide the gray, just to give it some depth.

Amy walked through the kitchen and went to sit down at the table. A numbness was settling in her legs. She needed to be sitting down when she told them.

'Is she drunk?' Edna asked, running water over her hands. 'Didn't she come with you?'

'Mom and Dad. Come here and sit down.'

She knew they were hearing something in her voice, because they didn't ask any questions. They came and sat right down. Her mother's eyes widened. Her father wiped his hands on his jeans.

'Mom and Dad, I wish I didn't have to tell you this, but Tricia's dead. I just found her in her apartment. The police are there now.'

'No.' It came out involuntarily from Edna. She started to stand up, but then sank back down into her chair. 'Our Tricia? Are you sure she's dead?'

101

Amy could hear the hope fighting for life in her mother's voice. 'Yes, I'm sure. She's dead.'

Red clasped his hands and brought them to his face, closing his eyes. Edna looked wildly around and her mouth started to quiver.

'How?' Her father lifted his head up to ask that one-word question.

'They're not sure.' Amy thought of what she had seen and realized how much she wanted to protect her parents from Tricia's death. 'Someone killed her.'

'Oh, my God.' Edna started to slide off her chair. Red came around and grabbed her under the arms. 'Not my Tricia. Not my little girl. How can it have happened? I don't want it to be true.'

Red held her up as she began to sob. His face turned red and he sucked his cheeks in, but he didn't cry. Amy let her head fall to the table and felt the tears slide down her face. She hadn't cried as she was driving out. She was afraid she would never make it out to her parents' house if she let herself cry. But now the tears slipped out like they were oiled.

She heard the choir on the radio singing 'Glory to God,' and she wondered about the God who had taken her sister away. It wasn't the one she had been taught to believe in at church. The one from church told stories and held children's hands and put flowers on the altar. The one who had taken her sister away was the real one, the one who wasn't a father, who was a part of everything and knew all and let the world go on as it would. Amy hoped so much that wherever her sister was, she was all right.

If only it were yesterday. She would call Tricia and then go over to her apartment. She would never let her sister be alone again, but would stay with her always. If only she had called Tricia, maybe none of this would have happened. Now Amy knew she would never have another chance. It was all over.

Amy felt her mother's hands on the back of her neck and she stood up and fell into her arms. Her father put his arms around them both. This was the closest they would ever be, and the one they wanted to be hugging, the one they wanted to have their arms around, was not there.

'Now what do we do? What's happening?' her father asked. 'Where is she?'

'They've taken her away to do an autopsy. The detectives will call out here in a little while or I'll call them. They'll want to talk to you and Mom. They're going to try to find the person who did it.'

Red had his hands over his eyes, his head bent. He cleared his throat and said, 'I'm going to call the pastor.'

Both Amy and Edna sat still while he dialed. Amy didn't want the news to leave the room. With every new person that heard it, it became more real. It became more true. Her sister was dead. Tricia had died.

'Yes, Pastor Anderson. This is Red Curtis. We've just had a tragedy in our family. Our daughter, Tricia, has died.' As Amy heard her father's voice break, she knew this was how Red was making Tricia's death real for himself. 'Thank you, Pastor. Yes, we'll need to make some arrangements. I'm not sure when we'll want the funeral to be. Yes, say a prayer for her. Thank you.'

'Red, don't call anyone else for a while. Let's just sit here.' Edna turned to Amy. 'You hungry, dear?'

Amy knew her mother had to start doing something, so she said, 'Yes, Mom, I'd like a cup of coffee. Maybe a piece of toast too.'

Red stood up and picked up the grill from the sink and slammed it to the floor. He turned without looking at either of the two women and walked out of the house.

Edna watched him go, then bent down to pick up the grill. She looked up at Amy, 'What are we going to do? How are we going to stand it?'

The next few hours were a blur for Amy. Phone calls to friends and relatives. Amy tried to call Todd again, but he still wasn't home. Red and Edna talked to Detective Towne over the phone and he had arranged to come out to the house. Neighbor ladies came over with casseroles and kind words. Food appeared on the kitchen counter and Amy picked at it. She stood it for a while, then she went to her old bedroom and shut the door.

A yellow clear light filled the room. Her mother had made flowered curtains that neither she nor Tricia had appreciated. Edna loved frilly things, unlike either of her daughters. The room looked so clean, just the way their mother had wished they would have kept it. Every Sunday she made them straighten it up. After Amy got a record player for Christmas, they would put on fast-paced music and clean it to the beat of their favorite songs. Edna hated the music, but loved the results.

Amy and Tricia had slept in their parents' old double bed after they had bought one king-size. Every night she or Tricia would draw a line down the middle of the bed and make sure that the other person didn't have any part of her body over it. Amy crawled up on the bed and wished her sister were there to share it with her.

Sprawled on the bed, she remembered all the times she had fought with Tricia. As teenagers they had been approximately the same size and would borrow each other's clothes. Uncalled for, an image of Tricia, naked, head twisted in the strangest manner, rose up in Amy's mind and she fought it back.

The other night Tricia had hinted that she was doing something really bad, and now Amy was beginning to see what she had been referring to. If only she had asked her to explain, maybe she could have stopped it from happening. Sex, drugs . . . her sister had been in a bad way, and Amy wished she had talked to her about what was going on, instead of waiting for her to sober up.

Amy thought back to their first discussions about sex. How she, after seeing the sex filmstrip in sixth grade health class, had passed the information on to Tricia. To illustrate some of the points Amy had used clothespins, one designated male and the other female, and showed how they slid together, legs to head, the only logical way Amy had been able to see the man with his pointy little penis having access to the hole that was located between the woman's wooden limbs. Tricia had laughed but, always a quick learner, had moved on to try this position with her Barbie and Ken dolls.

Amy wondered what Tricia had been doing last night and with whom. She prayed that it hadn't hurt, that death had come as gently as it could, a moment of unknowing and then something new.

When they were in high school, they had spent many hours in bed, talking about boys. Tricia had been going out with a senior, who had been designated a hunk by all the senior girls. Tricia had been invited to the senior prom, while Amy had been invited out that night by the senior class president, but to go see a documentary on the Vietnam War. She had envied Tricia's frothy pink dress. Once she had tried to question Tricia about the rumors she had heard about her sister's loose morals. But Tricia had only laughed and asked if the senior class president was a good kisser. Amy had confessed that it was like embracing a Saint Bernard, and they had fallen off the bed, laughing.

Amy grabbed the ends of the patchwork quilt that was thrown over the bed, and even though it was a bright, hot

105

day, she pulled it over her head, blanked her mind of any thought, and fell asleep.

'Honey, the detective is here. Do you want to come out and talk to him with us?'

Waking up, Amy pushed away an awful nightmare, then knew it was real. Her sister was dead.

Somehow the house had been cleared of people. Detective Towne was sitting in the living room, speaking with her father. Towne was sitting on the new plaid couch and Red was standing, his fists clenched behind his back. Her mother had changed into a gray dress and Amy wondered if she thought it was a more appropriate color. Edna looked at him and asked if he was hungry.

Towne gave a half smile and said, 'Now that I think about it, I haven't stopped yet today for lunch.'

Amy went into the kitchen with her mother and helped her prepare a plate for him. There was the potato salad, red Jell-O salad with floating bits of canned fruit, cole-slaw, biscuits, sliced ham, and someone had even barbecued the chicken. She hoped it hadn't been her father.

When she handed the plate of food to Towne, he nodded. His dark silvery-gray hair, which had been so neatly combed back this morning, was falling forward over his forehead. It made him look less pulled together. She wondered how old he was, how long it had taken him to become a detective, how he felt about his job. She wondered if he had a family and kids, if he knew what she and her parents were feeling right now, if he allowed himself to think about it.

'Would you like to see some pictures of Tricia?' Edna asked Towne.

He nodded and put his plate aside, holding his hand out for the offered pictures.

'These were taken on her twenty-third birthday in May,' she said. 'We're all sitting at the kitchen counter.'

'Who's this?'

'That's Danny, her boyfriend.'

Amy wanted to shake her mother and tell her to stop it. She was talking to Towne as if he were Tricia's long lost godparent, instead of a cop investigating her daughter's death.

'I hear they were breaking up recently, though,' Towne said.

'That's what Amy told me also. I don't know if they were serious this time or not.'

There was silence in the room as Towne ate his food. Amy could feel all the unanswered questions swimming through the air and wondered how many of them would even get asked. She knew how hard this must be on her parents. Her mother always wanted everything to be all right and her father just wanted everything to be normal, to be routine. She wondered about herself and found a growing need to know the truth of what had happened. She, in her own way, had ignored the evil of Tricia's life for too long.

'So how did my daughter die?' Red asked.

'Sir, I'm not sure yet. We should know by tomorrow. There were no signs of struggle on her wrists and legs where she was bound, so she must have passed out. Amy told us that she had a problem with alcohol, so she might have been drunk. We'll know more after the autopsy.'

Amy watched her father's face and wished she had prepared him for the truth of Tricia's death. She was as bad as her mother, thinking that they didn't have to know.

Red stood up and walked to the picture window in the living room. A grove of birch trees and a large oak shaded the window in the summertime, filtering a soft green light into the living room. 'Do you have any leads on who did it?'

'We haven't talked to Danny yet. He's certainly a suspect. We'll try to find out where she was last night.'

'What about fingerprints?'

'We've dusted the bedroom and kitchen. There were two glasses in the sink. We'll just have to see what we can get.'

Red turned back and looked at the police. 'What can we do for you?'

'If you remember anything. Any names of friends of your daughter's. We'll be following any leads you can give us.'

'Amy will have to help you there. She knew all about Tricia's friends. My wife and I only saw her when she came out here. We only knew Danny.'

'I don't think he did it,' Edna said.

'Mom, don't say that. You don't know,' Amy said.

'There's a chance he didn't, Mrs Curtis, but he might know who did. We'll certainly know more once we've talked to him.'

'When will you be through with the body?' Red asked.

'I would hope by Tuesday.'

'May we go ahead with arrangements for a funeral, then?'

'Yes, of course.' Towne stood up to leave. 'If you have any questions or anything you'd like to let us know, Amy has the number.'

Amy walked him out to his car. She blinked as she went out the front door. It was still daytime and the sun was hot on her back.

Towne stopped by the car door and squinted at her. 'There was a bruise on the side of her face.'

'I know. But it wasn't from last night. She got that a couple nights ago.'

'What night?'

'Thursday.'

'How?'

'I'm not sure. She didn't really say, but I think it was Danny. I think they were fighting. She didn't seem too upset about it.'

'We're going to have to pull Danny in.'

Amy almost said she knew where he might be, but she kept her mouth closed. She realized she wanted to be the one to tell Danny. She wanted to see his face. So she told Towne, 'I'll write out a list of Tricia's friends tonight and I'll bring it by tomorrow. Will you be in your office tomorrow morning?' Amy asked.

'Yes,' Towne said. 'Do you know where we're located?'

'No.'

'The old courthouse building downtown.'

'Oh, yeah, there's always a swarm of police cars around it.'

Towne nodded, a hint of a smile in his eyes. 'That's the one. Just ask for homicide.' He got in the driver's seat of the steel-gray car. 'Don't go messing around, asking too many questions. Leave that to us. That's what we're paid to do.'

'Of course.' Amy stood away from the car. 'Oh, and another thing. Could you leave my parents out of this? I mean, contact me if there's any news or if you have any questions.'

Towne looked at her questioningly.

'They just don't need to be involved in this.'

'They already are,' he said, and started the car.

Chapter 9

In late afternoon the sky clouded up. Edna said it looked like a thunderstorm was coming on, and she walked slowly from room to room closing all the windows. Sitting in the kitchen, Amy could hear her mother's sandals click on the wood floor in the living room. Tricia gone, so little else changed. Both Edna and Red looked like they were carrying enormous weights, but they were still walking around. They had their routines set out here. Amy wanted to leave, but it seemed wrong to leave her parents at a time like this. They should be gathered around the kitchen table talking, but she didn't think they wanted to talk about it.

Amy peeked into the living room. Red was in there lying on the couch, as he often did now that he was retired. Edna was staring down at him as if she had never seen him before. They seemed so separate from each other. Small, isolated worlds that suffered all alone. Amy didn't think Red was sleeping. He just didn't like to talk as much as the rest of them did, so he retreated into a nap.

'Mom, I'm going to have to go into town.' Amy didn't want to leave her parents, but she felt as if she were suffocating. She needed to talk to a friend, she needed to talk to Todd.

'You're not staying here tonight?' Her mother stood in the kitchen doorway.

'I have some things I should do in town. I'll call you later on.'

'Amy, I know we can't stop our lives, but I was really hoping you'd stay here tonight.'

'I can't.' Amy knew she couldn't leave it at that. Her mother deserved more of an answer. 'It has to do with Tricia. I should go over to her place. Settle things with the landlord.'

'Oh, I didn't even think of that.' Edna pulled at her hands. 'Had she been drinking again, Amy?'

After the initial shock was over, Amy had known the questions would come. Maybe there was a part of her that did want to leave the house and not have to suffer her parents' grieving as well as her own. In the silence after the question Amy knew her mother had already guessed the answer, so she simply nodded her head.

'God damn it. Why? I just don't understand.' Edna stood in the middle of the dining room, her shoulders heaving. 'I don't understand any of this. How could someone do that? Why Tricia? Why?'

Amy walked up to her, put an arm around her, and led her to the kitchen table. 'You want some iced tea?'

Edna shook her head, then said, 'No. You know, what I'd like is some hot tea. I've been feeling chilly all day long.'

Amy put the familiar orange kettle on the stove. 'I'm not sure why she started again. I think things just got to be too much for her. I didn't tell you this, but she lost her waitressing job. But you know what's kind of funny? – well, not really funny, but anyway, the singing audition went well. I think she was going to get the gig.'

'My poor kid. Did you know that she was drinking? Before?'

'Yeah, I went over there one night and she was pretty drunk.'

'We should have put her in the treatment center. I

111

knew we should have done it. At least we'd still have her.'

'But we didn't. She really didn't want that, Mom. That doesn't mean we shouldn't have done it, but she made some choices. It's no one's fault.'

'She was my child.'

'So am I. And I don't think you're responsible for the way I turned out.' No one is responsible, Amy reassured herself. We just both needed attention. I got it by being good, sweet, and accommodating. Tricia tried to get her fair share by being a bad girl, causing trouble. And it worked; Edna and Red did lecture her, scream at her, withhold privileges. It was no one's fault. They were all just playing out their roles. It is so sad, Amy thought, so sad that we seem to have so little choice of our roles.

Amy went to look out the kitchen window and by habit looked at the thermometer attached to the side of the frame. It was eighty-five degrees out, and the leaves were hanging on the trees, not the slightest breeze stirring them. If a storm came it could be a bad one. The ominous stillness was a precursor of a tornado.

'But you're different.'

'Remember Aunt Margaret. She was an alcoholic. Whose fault was that, your mother's?'

'It wasn't the same.'

'Why, because Aunt Margaret died when she was forty-two of a poisoned liver and Tricia died when she was twenty-three of a poisoned life? I don't think that's much of a difference. People make those kinds of choices.' Amy remembered that Tricia had said once Edna had compared her to Aunt Margaret. What a role model to grow up with. Their aunt had been a wonderfully alive, crazy, dangerous woman, who wore incredibly sheer nylons and gave them tastes of exotic drinks, like daiquiris that had little pink parasols sticking out of them.

112

Amy took the whistling kettle off the stove, poured a cup of hot water, and dipped a tea bag in it until it turned as dark as the sky. 'Here. I just don't want you to blame yourself. What happened is bad enough without you suffering any more than you have to. I know Tricia loved you as much as I do. What more can a mother ask for?'

As Amy drove out of the neighborhood, the storm burst. The clouds had turned the sky a murky black. The wind tore through the trees and blew the slender white birches around as if they were strips of paper. Sheets of water fell from the sky, and the windshield wipers couldn't keep up with the rain. Amy hunched up close to the window and kept driving until she came to the turn before the freeway. Then she pulled off the road.

The rain was squeezing in through the top of the car window where it wouldn't shut tight anymore, and she was getting wet. She started to cry. She was crying for Tricia, but more than crying because Tricia had died, she was crying because she had been left behind. Somehow Tricia had escaped and maybe where she was she wouldn't miss anyone. But Amy felt stuck in the middle of her death. She knew she should try to let go of it and leave it to the police, but just as she could never quite let go of her sister while she was living, Amy knew she wouldn't be able to let go of this last mangled shred of her, a death that needed solving.

Wiping her face with an old napkin she found on the floor of the car, she wondered what she should do. She actually felt like driving around in the storm. She decided not to get on the freeway, but take the slow way home. There were stop signs every two blocks and she would roll to a stop and see no other cars coming. No one was walking in the pouring rain.

Driving through the suburban neighborhoods, she won-

dered how many of them had tragedy in their lives. She
had always known that people she loved would die, but
she thought they would die when they were old and, in
some way, done with living. Yet she read in the news-
papers that children were run over in the streets while
running after balls, that young businessmen had heart
attacks in elevators, so she knew no one was exempt.
Suddenly the world seemed so dangerous. She had this
feeling on the freeway sometimes, a moment of disbelief
that the horde of cars that were flying across the roads
didn't all crash into each other.

There was a small shopping center she was coming to,
one that everyone had used before the malls had popped
up, circling the town. The bar that she had thought Danny
might be at this afternoon was in the shopping center. She
turned in and pulled up in front of it and sat in the car.

The Round-Up was a 3.2-beer joint that had four pool
tables as its main attraction. Not a place that Danny liked
to go for 'serious drinking,' but on a Sunday afternoon he
and his buddies usually met there for a pool tournament.
Everyone put in five dollars and the winner walked away
with sixty.

Amy had dropped Tricia off there a few times after
they had been out at their folks'. She would sometimes
go in with her and have a beer, watching the men glide up
to the pool table, chalk up the tip of their pool cues while
checking out the shot. Then they'd call it in a low, rough
mumble. 'Corner pocket.'

Staring at the beer sign in the window, she knew she
could pull out of the parking lot. But she decided to go
in, to tell Danny and watch his face. It would tell her
something.

After scurrying through the last drops of the thunder
shower, she walked into the bar and was disappointed to
see that Danny wasn't there. In fact, the bar was almost

114

empty. She had missed the tournament, but she wanted to find out if he had been there.

When she sat down on a bar stool, the paunchy bartender lumbered over. 'What can I do for you?' He planted both his large paws on the bar.

'I'd like a charged water.'

'Nothing to go with that?'

'All you serve is beer, right?'

'Yeah, right.'

Amy looked around to see if she knew anyone. There were only two old guys sitting in one corner, drinking silently together, and a dark-haired man wearing a flannel shirt looked vaguely familiar, but she couldn't place him, unless it was just that she had seen him here before. Staring at a ghostly image of herself in the mirror that was behind the bar, she wondered where Danny was.

When the bartender set her drink down in front of her, she asked him if Danny had played in the tournament that day.

'You mean the tall, thin, blond guy?'

'Yeah.'

'I'm pretty sure he was here today.' He turned and yelled at the dark-haired man. 'Chuck, wasn't Danny boy here today?'

'Why? Somebody looking for me?'

The voice sounded defensive to Amy, and she twirled around on her bar stool to see Danny standing behind her. He had a pool cue in his hand and didn't look too happy to see her. Amy looked around to see if she could get by him. He took another step closer to her. She felt the icy hand of fear caress the back of her neck. He was standing right in front of her. 'What're you checking up on me for?'

'Danny's just a little sore 'cause he didn't win today.'

The dark-haired man had walked up and punched Danny in the arm. 'Came awful close, didn't you, Danny boy?'

Amy was afraid, but she just stood and stared at him, willing him to look her in the face.

Danny dropped his eyes and said, 'Get out of here, Amy. I know what you're going to say.'

She froze. Unable to move, she tried to say something, anything. Finally she blurted out, 'I was out at the folks' and just thought I'd stop by.'

Danny's face cleared. 'Well, that was nice of you.'

Amy didn't want to tell him about Tricia in front of all his buddies, yet she was afraid of being alone with him. She still didn't know about him. He had looked upset to see her. Maybe he thought she was going to tell him to leave Tricia alone.

'You want to go sit in a booth?' she asked him.

'Sure. Gus, give me a draft.'

They went and sat in one of the three booths at the far end of the bar. The only lighting was a Hamm's beer sign with a fake waterfall plummeting down the side of a cliff, FROM THE LAND OF SKY BLUE WATERS was written across the top of it. In the blue light Danny's face looked drawn and sallow. Amy decided to move slow.

'So how've you been?' she asked him.

'Looking for work. Your sister's thrown me for a loop. I hate it when she starts acting this way. She thinks she wants to break up, but she don't. She claims I'm interfering with the rest of her life. That's what she should get rid of. She just doesn't know what's good for her.'

'What do you want to happen?' Amy asked him.

'What do you mean?'

Amy took a deep breath. What she was about to ask him was cruel, but she did it anyway. 'What do you want to happen with you and Tricia?'

'God, Amy, you know we've been together for years.'

A half smile lit his face. 'Believe it or not, I want to get married. I want her to settle down. I know you think it's all my fault that she's so fucked up. But it's scary to me too.'

'I know.'

'She blames me for it. She thinks that if she left me everything would be all right, but it wouldn't. I want you to know that it isn't my fault, none of it is.'

'OK.'

'I'm worried about her, Amy. She's going to hurt herself.'

'Danny, I'm really sorry. I'm so sorry I have to tell you this. Tricia's dead. She was killed last night.'

Danny stared at her. Amy looked down. She had wanted to see his face but now that she had the chance she looked away. She heard him say, 'What are you saying? Is this a joke?'

'No.' She turned back to face him and found him wide eyed, still staring.

'Is this some kind of gag? Did she tell you to do this to me?' Danny looked frantic, then his face hardened. 'What a bitch.'

'No, Danny, it's no joke.' Amy wanted to get away, but she needed to tell Danny how it had happened. 'She was killed by someone last night in her apartment.'

'I tried to call her, but she wouldn't answer the phone. Why didn't she answer the phone?'

'I don't know.'

'Who did it? What happened to her?' Danny's voice took on the thin edge of incomprehension.

'Someone tied her up, gagged her, and stabbed her.' Amy stopped for a second. The image of Tricia lifeless and alone came to her so strongly that she couldn't see Danny or the bar they were sitting in. 'That's how I found her this morning. She was lying on her bed. I wanted her

117

to be sleeping, but she was dead. With your knife stuck in her chest. I thought maybe you'd know who did it.'

'God damn it.' Danny was struggling for control. He gripped the table. 'I warned her. I told her not to do that anymore.'

'Do what?'

'She did it for the money, sometimes. I hated it.'

'Did what, Danny?'

'It doesn't matter anymore. She's dead. It's all over.' He drained his beer.

'It does matter. Tell me what you're talking about. She's my sister. I have a right to know.'

'Maybe but you wouldn't want to know. You never really wanted to know what went on with Tricia. Always just a little too good for her. She admired you so much. She would never have wanted you to know what she was doing.' Danny was yelling at her.

'Danny, stop it.' She couldn't believe he was saying such things to her. He was the one who had ruined her sister. 'At least I loved her. Was she in trouble?'

'She was asking for it all the time. I think it did something for her. She was tricking a little out in California and then tried to quit when we got back here, but she said she missed it. She missed the danger. Said she knew she was alive when she was tricking.'

'Tricking. What do you mean exactly?'

'What do you want, a definition? Go look it up in the dictionary. I want you to get out of here.' Danny stood up.

'Listen, Danny, I'm sorry. Sit down. I wanted to tell you rather than the police. They want to talk to you. Tell them everything you know. We have to find out who did it. Do you understand?'

'Right, the police want to talk to me.' Danny spit out the word *police*. 'I'm their number-one suspect. I'm sure they'd love to talk to me, then stick me in jail for fifty years.'

'Where were you last night?'

'I was watching a football game on cable with Eddy.'

'So you have an alibi. You have nothing to worry about.' Amy tried to reassure him. She could see he was becoming frightened.

'Eddy doesn't like the police.'

'He doesn't have to like them. All he has to do is tell them you were with him.'

'He's a coke dealer.' Danny said it slowly, as if he were explaining something difficult to her. 'He don't deal with the police.'

'But this is different. They're not going to go digging up his life history. If he's a friend, I'm sure he'll stick up for you.'

'I'm glad you're sure. You can go talk to him. I'm going to get another drink. You want something?'

'No, thanks.'

Danny walked up to the bar. He stood for a second with his back to Amy, then he ran out of the bar. She sat in the booth stunned. What did that mean? He could have broken down and not wanted her to see, or he could be running away from something he had done.

Amy sat and watched the dark-haired guy play pool all by himself. She felt the four men in the bar were watching her. She didn't know what to do. She was afraid to leave the bar, but she didn't want to stay much longer. Maybe she had made a big mistake by telling Danny. She wondered if she would ever see him again.

*Mom sits in the shade. She's talking to a neighbor lady.
She looks out at us every so often and waves a hand. We
are in water up to my chest and Tricia's neck. We both
have precious stones we have found on the shore. They are
light colored so they are easily seen in the green-stirred
water. We take turns throwing them down to the bottom of
the lake and diving for them.*

*Tricia comes up sputtering, water and spit coming out of
her mouth, but a stone proudly shown in each hand. She
throws them up in the air. I watch them cut into the water,
noting the ripples and the distance between them. I suck in
a lungful of air and dive under, entering a world of slow
movement and filtered light. I pull the water through my
arms and do a wide frog-kick with my legs. Fish dart
between me and the bottom. The dirt rises up to meet me
as I spot the first stone nestled in some seaweed. Picking it
up, my lungs start to burn. I search the bottom and let out
a little air. No stone. My lungs are aching. I need to
breathe. Then I see the stone a stroke away. I pull down
and grab it, then push off the bottom and shoot up into the
sun and air.*

*When Mom says it's time to go home, we walk out to the
end of the dock and put both our stones down. The next
day they are gone. We know where.*

Chapter 10

When Todd opened the door and saw Amy standing there, he threw his arms around her and held her close. She sank into him and whimpered against his shoulder. Something was pushing against her ribs, wanting to come out with a roar. She couldn't hold it any longer. Her skin was cracking open and her tears were flowing like rivers from a spot deep inside where she had stored all her hopes for Tricia. Her whole body shook and Todd held her tighter. As the sobs ripped out of her, she was scared she wouldn't be able to stop crying. Swallowing, she tried to calm down a little until finally she was quieter. The tears diminished to a trickle. Todd patted her on the back and she sighed.

Pushing her away from him, but still holding her by the shoulders, he said, 'I heard about it on the news. I couldn't believe it. I hoped there was another Tricia Curtis.' He pulled her into the apartment and made her sit down on the couch. 'Can I get you something. Would you like something to drink?'

'God, now I know what Tricia felt. I would love to get completely out-of-my-mind drunk. So drunk I couldn't feel anything.' Amy wiped her face. She looked up at Todd and saw sadness in his eyes. Todd and Tricia had actually gotten along pretty well. Every so often the three of them had gone to a movie together, or met for dinner. Amy remembered once Tricia had been wearing high heels and Todd had taken her arm to help her across the street. It had seemed such a sweet gesture to her, almost old fashioned, and she had thought for a moment that they might be attracted to each other. But Todd had also seen Tricia's faults and was often critical of her.

'You want to split a beer with me?' Todd asked. 'Unfortunately, I only have one. It'll relax you a little. You feel as tight as a trap.'

'Please.'

Amy followed him into the kitchen. The far wall was all cupboards and painted Todd's favorite colors, yellow and aquamarine. He believed in being comfortable in the kitchen, so instead of the usual dinette set he had arranged two sagging easy chairs around a small coffee table. As a result the kitchen looked more like a living room or a den.

Todd poured the beer into two mugs, an inch of foam topping each glass. He handed her a mug and watched approvingly as she took a big gulp. 'So tell me, what happened?'

'What did you hear?'

'That Tricia was found dead this morning and that the case is under investigation. Cause of death uncertain.'

Amy thought for a second about the cause of death. Lack of air. Maybe too much to drink. Blood pooling on her stomach. 'I found her.'

'God, Amy. I'm so sorry.'

'It's my own fault. I should have called her yesterday. I could have stopped it from happening.'

'What?'

'She was having such a hard time. Losing her job and all. I should have talked to Dot and asked her to give her the job back. Then maybe she wouldn't have started drinking again. There's so much I could have done and I didn't do it. I didn't do anything.' Amy drank half her glass of beer in one swallow, the beer tasting sweet and bitter going down.

Todd rubbed his jaw. 'You're wrong, Amy. You're as

wrong as you can be. You're acting like you could have played God with your sister. I don't want to hear any more of that shit. You did all you could do. More than most people. Tricia chose the life she wanted to lead. It involved way too much drinking, and a very loose life-style. You couldn't stop that.'

'I don't know. I feel like it's my fault. It's all so unfair. Who would want to have murdered her?'

'She was murdered?' Todd shuddered as if he had been hit in the shoulder and Amy recognized the reaction.

'Bound, gagged, and stabbed with a knife. It looked like some kind of S-and-M scene. The detectives said they'd know more after the autopsy. Todd, they're doing an autopsy on Tricia. I just can't believe any of this. All day long I've been trying to wake up from this nightmare, pinching myself, and I keep hurting. I can sit here and taste the beer and hear you and yet feel totally unreal.'

'Horrible.' Todd drank from his mug. 'I can't believe it either.'

Amy finished her beer and looked around for some-thing else to drink. What she actually wanted was some hard liquor, a shot of something that would take her breath away. She knew Todd didn't keep anything like that in his house.

Todd touched her arm. 'I hate to ask you this, but do you have any idea who did it?'

Amy closed her eyes. They were sore from crying and she was sure they were all puffy. 'I have thought about it. It keeps coming back to me. The question. Who? Who? This is going to sound weird but, in a way, it seems unimportant. I mean, she's dead – what does it matter who did it? It won't make her alive again. But I do want to know. I want to know why it happened.'

'Do you suppose Danny did it?'

'Yeah, that's who the police are focusing on. He had a

123

key to her place. He had a reason. I told you about the other day when he was at her place. He was really angry with Tricia. I could see it in his hands, like he didn't know what to do with them.'

'So what will the police do, go to his house and haul him down for questioning?'

'If they can find him.' Amy stared at the black-and-white linoleum floor. 'I did something pretty stupid. I was near this bar he plays pool at and I went in and he was there, so I told him.'

Todd leaned back in his chair. 'You what?'

'Maybe it wasn't a coincidence, I don't know. I had a pretty strong feeling he would be there. The way I look at it, he either knew already or he would have found out soon enough. But think about it. If you had killed your girlfriend, would you go play pool the next day?'

'Maybe, if I didn't want anyone to suspect me.'

'I don't know, Todd. I don't like Danny at all, but he seemed genuinely upset.'

'Maybe he thought it would take longer for someone to find the body.'

'God, I never thought of that. He did tell me he was going to get a beer and then he turned and ran out of the bar.'

'Have you told the police?'

'Not yet. I suppose I should. Do you think they'll be upset?'

'How should I know? I can't believe you sometimes. Why did you want to talk to Danny? What were you thinking of?'

Amy didn't say anything. Instead she stood up and walked over to the cupboards and started to open and close doors as if she were looking for something. 'I can't explain it. I don't want to think anymore. Let's get out of

124

here. Go someplace. Todd, I think I need to get a real drink.'

  'You sure you want to go out?'

  She nodded.

  'OK. Where can we go on a Sunday night?'

Downtown Minneapolis was quiet. Only a few cars lined the wide streets. Amy could see the IDS Building pointing to a starry sky as soon as they turned off of Washington Avenue. It claimed to be the tallest building between Chicago and the West Coast and would probably hold that title for a while longer.

  The Foshay Tower, which had previously had that honor, looked shrunken in its old age. Amy remembered Red taking her and Tricia to look out of the grated windows at the top of the old structure. She had the feeling that if she took one more step or even one more breath she would fly out the window and float above the whole city, so she stood far away from the windows. Tricia was only six, but she stood as close as she could, asking their father to hold her up as she stared out over the city, scrambling in his arms as if she wanted to be set free in the blue and the building tops.

  When Tricia had worked at the top of the IDS, it had been fun to go up there for drinks. The city dazzled below like a bank of gems, and when it was very clear Amy would swear she could see Wisconsin more than thirty miles away.

  After they parked the car and started walking toward the steel-and-glass building, Amy realized he could be anywhere, the man who had killed her sister. A tall, whip-quick man, shadowy eyes, twisted hands, that's the way she pictured him. He could be anywhere. As they entered the atrium of the IDS Building she realized he might be

125

up there in the club right now, waiting to pick up another woman and she would never know. He could be anyone.

The Crystal Court of the IDS was empty in a way that it never was during the day, and it resounded sinisterly from their footsteps. The stores on the lower and upper levels were gated closed, and the darkness from outside seemed to press against all the levels of windows that towered above them. They walked through it and went to the elevator marked OBSERVATORY, which also stopped at the sixtieth floor, where the Club was.

She and Todd got into it alone and they were lifted upward in a stomach-queasing move. She reached out for Todd's hand, and he took it.

'I haven't even asked you how your date was.'

He grinned. 'It was all right.'

'You're smiling.'

'I said it was all right.'

'You like her?'

'Yeah. She's nice.'

'Are you going to see her again?'

'She's having me over for dinner tomorrow night.'

'Sounds good. When do I get to meet her?'

'We'll see.'

The door eased open and they entered the quietness of the sixtieth floor. There were mirrors opposite the door, and Amy stopped to brush her hair off her face. She was glad she had had it cut short. It never got mussed. She was wearing a short skirt, a light top, and heels. In the summer she knew she could get away with such dress at the Club. It wasn't that fancy, although she had insisted Todd put on long pants before they left his house.

They both looked all right. They could have just come from their sailboat on Lake Calhoun, who was to know? Did she look as if someone had just died in her family?

'What time did you hear about Tricia?'

126

'On the six o'clock news.'

A band was playing a jazz ballad when they walked into the Club, an old Billie Holiday tune. Amy remembered Tricia singing it when she'd dress her bed. Housecleaning of any sort always gave her the blues, she used to say.

Amy glanced around quickly and saw an old friend of Tricia's, Sandra, bent over a couple's table putting huge fruited drinks down in front of them. A tuxedoed man came up to seat them.

'Could you put us in Sandra's section?'

'Certainly.'

He led them to a table right next to a floor-to-ceiling window. Amy looked out over the city. It seemed to sparkle less than usual, but then on a Sunday night most shops and buildings were closed. She turned away from the window and saw Sandra approaching.

Tricia had called her 'Sandman.' Said she was as sweet and sleepy as they come. She did have pretty sandy-blond hair. It hung in her eyes as she leaned over to talk to them. 'Hey, there, Amy. Haven't seen you in an age. How's life and how's that crazy sister of yours? We miss her around here.'

Todd looked at Amy to see how she would handle the question.

'I don't really know how to say this, but Tricia was killed.' Only a few days before, Tricia and she had been stretched out on the sand together. If only there were a way to go back.

Sandra blanched. 'No, Amy. Don't tell me that. How did it happen?'

'The police aren't sure yet, but it looks like someone murdered her.'

'No. It's too awful. I'm so sorry. I'd been meaning to

127

give her a call. I can't believe it.' Sandra put down her tray and just stood there.

Amy looked out the window. The city was down below them, caught behind a pane of glass. Unreal. Floating above the city. She should probably say something to Sandra to try to make her feel better. 'I can't believe it either. She always liked you.'

'She was so great.' Sandra gave a little sob and then said, 'Excuse me for a second,' and went running out of the Club.

'Todd, is it wrong to be up here drinking?' Amy asked.

'Of course not.'

'It's how the Irish handle it. Death. They drink and tell stories and remember the person as hard as they can.' This was a good place to remember her. Tricia had liked working up here. She had felt important for a while.

Todd nodded and stared at the band. Then he slid his hand across the table and placed it over hers. 'How you doing?'

'Don't ask me yet. This is harder than I thought. I guess I didn't think. I just wanted to get out.'

When Sandra came back she was blowing her nose, but was otherwise in control. 'Sorry. I feel really bad about your sister.'

'How're things with you?'

'All right, I guess. So what can I get you tonight?'

'I'd like a Margarita,' Amy said, thinking of the swirl the tequila could put her mind in.

'Just a tap beer,' Todd added.

Sandra nodded and walked away. The uniform she was wearing was different from the one Tricia had worn when she worked here. Maybe it was the summer outfit. Short black taffeta skirt with only a tight-fitting vest on top. Lots of leg showing below.

When Sandra came back to the table, Todd excused

128

himself. Sandra set down the drinks and gave Amy a knowing look. 'New beau?'

'Old friend.'

'Too bad.'

'No. Actually, it's fine. He's a great friend. What's up with you? Are you seeing anyone?' Amy asked her.

'One of the bartenders and I have been hanging out after work. Pretty loose setup. No commitments, which is fine with me right now.'

'I know what you mean. But sometime I'd like to meet a guy who wanted more commitment than me. One who wanted to get serious.' Amy lifted her drink and took a sip. The Margarita was a little too sweet for her taste, but she didn't feel like complaining.

Sandra was still standing next to the table. She was fidgeting with her tip money.

'Do you want me to pay for these drinks right now?' Amy asked.

'It doesn't matter. I'd like to talk to you. Meet me in the bathroom in a few minutes.'

Amy watched Sandra walk up to the bar, put down her tray, and then leave the Club. When Todd came back, Amy told him she'd only be a moment and went to the ladies' room. Sandra was standing at one of the mirrors, putting on a bright orange lipstick. Amy stood behind her and talked to the reflection in the mirror.

'What's going on?'

'What do you think of this lipstick?'

Amy just stared at her in the mirror. Sandra nodded her head toward the stalls. Someone flushed a toilet.

An older woman came out of one of the stalls. She took out a comb and began to comb her hair, standing next to Sandra. Sandra turned and offered her lipstick to Amy.

'No, thanks.'

The older woman finished combing her hair and left.

Sandra turned around and leaned against the sink. 'I don't want anyone else to hear. Maybe I'm being overly dramatic, but it scared the shit out of me to hear about Tricia.' Sandra put her hands to her cheeks and closed her eyes.

'Why?' Amy asked.

'Because there's been a guy around here asking about her.' Sandra turned to the sink and started to wash her hands, even though she had done nothing to get them dirty.

'Who?'

Sandra wiped her hands on the roll of white towel and faced Amy again. 'I don't really know his name.'

'What do you know?'

'I know that he's no good. I told Tricia. I warned her to stay away from those kind of guys.'

'What kind of guys?'

Sandra's voice dropped both in pitch and volume. 'He didn't seem to know the limit, the line, the edge, where things had to stop. He went beyond it.'

'Why?'

'It wasn't a game for him. It was real. He wanted it all.'

'Sandra, exactly what are you talking about?'

'Sometimes she'd meet men up here. Or sometimes at another bar. You know, they'd buy her some drinks and then get kind of friendly. There was a woman who would set it up. I did it a few times. Tricia did too.'

'Do you remember this guy's name?'

'I'm not sure I ever heard it. We always called them nicknames. Weird ones. Like Merlin or Peter Pan.'

Chapter 11

The air in the still room was heavy. It felt like a thick, dusty curtain blowing across her face. She was breathing slowly, trying to keep the panic from rushing down her throat and blocking it. The dark turned darker still, the night was bottomless, and she couldn't breathe. She heard someone in the room. Footsteps were coming toward her. A presence was filling the room. Someone's hand was on her throat. She couldn't move her arms or legs. Someone was on top of her, pushing down. She was powerless. She had to open her mouth, widen her throat – so she could breathe, no, so she could scream.

When a thin wail broke from her lips, Amy sat bolt upright on the couch. Sweat was pouring from her body. The T-shirt she was sleeping in was soaked through. She could hear Todd's even breathing in her bedroom and was relieved that he was there. When they had left the IDS, he had insisted on coming over for the night. After some argument she had agreed, but only if he slept in her bed. She knew her couch was much too small for him. Not wanting to wake him up, she tiptoed across the living room to the kitchen, and closed the door behind her.

The illuminated clock on the wall said it was four in the morning. Looking out the window, she saw the faint liquid light of dawn on the horizon. The birds were twittering away. She decided to wait for daylight to come before going back to sleep.

Amy walked into the bathroom, turned on the light, and stared at herself in the mirror above the sink. Thin face, big eyes with shadow slivers underneath, and a cap

131

of dark hair to frame it all. Her sister was dead and she looked no different. Somehow that disgusted her. She wanted it written all over her face, tattooed across her forehead. The wound should show so that other people would have some visual measure of the pain she was feeling.

These were middle-of-the-night thoughts, she knew. She hoped they would wither and die in the morning light. All Amy wanted was to have Tricia back and she knew that could never be. It was simple and impossible. She stretched her hands out and pressed them against the surface of the mirror, covering her face's reflection. Gone.

Todd woke her up when he came into the kitchen to make some coffee. Amy had fallen asleep, slumped over in one of the folding chairs around her table. Her neck ached from resting on the chair back.

'Was my mouth open?' she asked him.

'I didn't notice.'

She rubbed her eyes. 'How could you not have noticed that? My throat feels all dried out, like someone's been vacuum-cleaning down there.'

'You look pretty awful. Why are you sleeping in the kitchen? I thought you were going to sleep on the couch.'

'I started out there, but I had bad dreams. I thought of waking you up, but it was way too early. I just didn't want to lie back down again.' She watched him walk across the kitchen. There was a bounce in his walk. He looked pretty good.

'This calls for some serious coffee. You're lucky you have the expert on hand. Now, if you just have the proper equipment.' Todd found her coffee tucked into the door of the refrigerator and smelled it before he packed the dark grounds into the top of an espresso pot. 'I'm telling you, what you need is a good hit of bean.'

132

'I'm not arguing.' She watched him move around her kitchen with the ease of a waiter, setting up their coffee cups and getting out the cream. 'Thanks for staying last night, Todd. You were right. I did need someone here.' For a moment she thought of Luke. Today she should call him and tell him what had happened.

Todd sat down in the other chair. He had on only a pair of shorts and his dark hair was sticking straight up in back. 'Listen, you know I'll be here for you whenever you need me. But I think you should go home. Let the police do what they do and spend some time with your folks. Why don't you stay out there, at least for a night or two?'

'Yeah, I think I will. For some reason I just couldn't stay there last night. It was too close, like the walls were moving in. When I was little, that house seemed so big, but now it's puny. And it reminds me of Tricia so much.'

'I suppose.'

'Last night when I woke up, I sat here at the table and thought about it all. I tried to figure out what has happened. Tricia always could come up with these great metaphors for her feelings, and I realized it felt like I was missing a limb. I keep reaching out to touch it and it's not there. I only hit air. It's such a shock. Out of the blue I'll think, oh, I should call Tricia and tell her what's going on, talk to her about her own death.' Amy touched her face and it was wet. 'I miss her so much, Todd. I don't know what to do.'

'I'm so sorry.' Todd stood above her and, reaching down, began to massage her shoulders. He didn't say anything more, but his fingers eased away some of the tension in her shoulders. The espresso pot let out a burbling noise and Todd took it off the stove.

'Maybe you'd like your coffee iced this morning, madam?'

'Yes, please.'

133

He put away the coffee cups and packed two tall glasses with ice cubes and then slowly poured the coffee over them. 'Milk, sugar?'

She nodded.

'What are you going to do today?'

'I was trying to tell you before I started bawling that last night I made a list for the police of Tricia's friends, especially the guys. Everyone at Burger Delight, like that horrible Chuck. He's been making lewd remarks about Tricia. All the guys in the band. I didn't tell you, but one of them, Hank, brought her home the other night and I know he stayed for a while. Then there's this drug dealer she mentioned the other night when she was so out of it – Eddy. I'm going to tell them about Sandra too. Do you think I should? She seemed so scared last night.'

'Maybe don't make a big deal out of it, but mention her.'

'Yeah.'

'Well, that should help them.'

'This is too weird, Todd.'

After drinking four glasses of coffee Todd sprang to his feet, realizing he had a class to teach in ten minutes. He kissed her on the top of her head and left her sitting at the kitchen table. Looking out the window, she saw the day was bright and still. Nothing moving. The tree leaves hung limply from the branches. The green seemed dusty. She heard a kid screaming for his dog, at least she hoped it was his dog, with a name like Bonkers. She was sitting so quietly, she could almost feel air resting on her shoulders. It was time she did something.

First, she knew, she should call her parents. She had left rather abruptly last night. She picked up the phone and dialed their number. It rang twice; then someone picked up the phone but didn't say anything for about three seconds. Amy knew it was her father. He always did that, waited for a few moments before saying hello. Maybe he was preparing himself. 'Hello.'

'Hi, Dad. How are things out there?'

'All right. The pastor came over. Could you find out when they're going to release her body?'

Amy felt her stomach clench. 'Yes, I will. I'm going down to talk to the police soon. Is Mom there?'

'Yeah. Are you coming home?'

'After I'm done talking to the police.'

'Good,' he said.

'Hi, honey,' her mother said. Her voice sounded monotone.

'How are you doing, Mom?'

'Not so good.'

Amy sighed. 'I know what you mean.'

'I didn't sleep too well last night. Your father got up twice. I'd hear him go in and sit at the kitchen counter. I don't know what he was doing. So I'd lie awake in bed and wait for him to come back. You coming out today?'

'Yes, that's why I called. I'll be out soon. Is there anything you need?'

'No, but did I tell you Molly's coming? She's driving straight through.'

The police were housed downtown in the old county court building, which looked like a fort built to defend the city from anything that happened along. It was built out of enormous, rough-cut slabs of granite and had a copper spire with a clock tower. She used the clock to tell time from points all over the city, but she had never had a reason to go into the building before.

When she walked in the main entrance, the cool of the marble floors and walls wafted over her. The building's sturdiness reassured her. There was an atrium in the

135

middle of the building that went up several floors. A marble statue of the Father of Waters sitting on top of an alligator and a tortoise presided over the space.

An old woman was sitting at a table behind the statue with a sign saying INFORMATION, and Amy asked her the way to the homicide division. She looked Amy over, then pointed up the stairs to the second floor. 'Turn to your left, then take a right. You'll see the sign.'

Amy walked through the door marked HOMICIDE and then up to a counter that cut off the rest of the room. Behind the counter were office cubicles with people walking in and out of them. It reminded her of a beehive. The woman behind the counter looked up from the crossword puzzle she was doing. 'Yes?'

'I'd like to see Detective Towne.'

'What's your name?'

'Amy – Amy Curtis.'

The woman looked at her sharply, and Amy could see that she recognized the name. 'Please wait a minute.' She turned and pushed a button on an intercom. 'Amy Curtis's here. OK.' She turned back to Amy and said, 'He'll be right out.'

When Towne came out to get her, she was surprised to see him dressed in a polo shirt and light summer slacks. He looked as if he was on his way to the country club, except for the black pistol growing under his armpit. She wondered if going to the scene of a crime demanded a suit or if that just happened to be what he was wearing on Sunday. 'You want to follow me? We can go to my office.'

Amy followed him through the honeycomb of offices. After a couple turns she lost track of where they were until they came to his office, tucked away in a corner. He offered her a chair, and when she looked at his desk she saw a photograph of Tricia's room with Tricia absent from the bed. She looked away from it and Towne turned it over.

'How are you doing today?' he asked.

'Just all right. Do you know anything more?'

'We should be getting some of the lab-test results back today. Toxicology is checking to see what drugs or alcohol she had in her. The autopsy should be done by tomorrow.'

'My dad wanted to know when we could have the body.'

'I would say by Wednesday.'

'OK, I'll tell him.' Amy sat up straight in her chair and cleared her throat. 'All right. I have some information to give you.'

He sat down and pulled out a pad of paper and a pencil. 'What's that?'

'A couple things. I went to the Club in the IDS last night. I don't think I told you, but Tricia used to work there. She got fired because she went on a bad binge one day and didn't make it in for work. I ran into this waitress that used to work with Tricia, they were pretty good friends. Her name's Sandra, and she still works there. She told me some guy had been coming around lately, asking for Tricia. She said that Tricia had gone out with him a couple times. She also said he was kinky.'

'Who is this guy? What does she know about him?'

'She couldn't remember his name, or not his real name, but she told me his nickname might be something like Peter Pan.'

'Would she be able to recognize him?'

'I'm sure she would, but I don't imagine he's in your files. I suppose he's well off – you know the kind of men that drink up there.'

'What's her name?'

'Sandra. I don't know her last name. If you talk to her, go easy on her. I think she's real scared.'

'Maybe under hypnosis we can get her to remember the real name.'

'You do that kind of stuff?'

'Yes, it's pretty effective for names and numbers. I'll get in touch with her.'

Amy found herself staring at his face. He had cut himself shaving, a small nick right below his left ear. She wondered what his hours were, if there were ever such a thing as a normal schedule for him. He looked as if he had just gotten up, his hair still slightly damp from a shower.

'Well, we haven't been able to get in touch with Danny. He never went home last night. You have any idea where he might be?'

Amy felt cold sitting still in Towne's office. She was dressed only in shorts, sandals, and a T-shirt, and the air-conditioning was working well. She rubbed her shoulders and then said, 'I saw him last night. I happened to remember that he sometimes played pool on Sundays at this one bar that was on my way home, so I stopped off there. He said he didn't know anything about Tricia, that he had tried to call her the other night and that he was with someone watching a football game.'

'We'll have to verify all that. Did he say where he was going to be?'

Amy remembered him running out of the bar. He hadn't told her anything about where he would be. 'No, but if he gets in touch with me, I'll let you know right away.'

Towne stood up and walked over to a file cabinet and pulled out a file. 'I wish you hadn't spoken to him. I guess there's not too much we can do about it now. It sounds as if you might have spooked him. Unless he's got another girlfriend, he should have gone home last night. I've got a guy staking out his place today, so maybe he'll show up. I suppose you told him we wanted to talk to him.'

'I did mention that.'

Towne sat down with the file in front of him. 'We need to check his fingerprints. We've got a good set of prints off a glass that was in the sink and a bottle that was sitting next to the bed. There was also a partial on the toilet seat.' He looked down at her hands. 'We're going to need to get a set of prints from you also. Could you do that before you leave?'

'Of course. If those prints do turn out to be Danny's, that might not mean that much, because he was there a lot. With Tricia you don't know how long that stuff had been sitting there.'

'You said she had just cleaned.'

'Well, it looked like it, but she still could have left dishes and things around.'

'OK.'

'I have a funny feeling about Danny. He does seem like the logical suspect. Maybe it's because I know him . . . even if I don't care for him too much, I just can't believe anyone I know could do something like that. I just don't know about him.'

'Why?'

She was surprised he was taking her comments seriously. In fact, she was surprised he was acting as normal as he was. Maybe she had seen too many movies, read too many books. She had expected him to give her the third degree about talking to Sandra, to distrust everything she said, but he seemed to believe her and be interested in her ideas.

'I've known Danny for as long as he's gone with Tricia. They've had their ups and downs, but I don't think he could have killed her.' Amy remembered the knife and the blood. Danny's angry face, screaming at them in the parking lot, came back to her. 'They did fight a lot, but it was more verbally. Thinking back on it, I see now that he might have been trying to get Tricia to stop what she was doing.' She remembered how Danny had looked last night, the disbelief on his face.

'He's all we've got right now.' Towne said it a little defensively, closing the file. 'We need to talk to him.'

'Are you done with Tricia's apartment?'

'Yes. Speaking of which, among her belongings we found some photos. I could identify most of the people, but who is this?' He held up a black-and-white photograph of a young woman with long dark hair. She was standing in front of a school building. Her face was thin, her eyes large, and her mouth determined. She looked as if she had her whole life ahead of her.

'That's Tricia when she was seventeen.' Amy took the picture from him and remembered how pretty Tricia had been. Even in six years the drinking had taken its toll. Tricia had still been attractive, but she had put on weight and her face would look puffy in the morning, her eyes dull and listless.

'I'm sorry.'

'You couldn't help it. She looked different when you saw her.' Amy put the picture in her purse. Suddenly she wanted Towne to understand about Tricia. She wanted him to like her. He probably thought she was just a tramp, a drunken, confused woman who had asked for what she got. But that was not the truth. Tricia just had never known what to ask for, and, more importantly, she had never thought she was worth anything. 'She was really a great sister. Funny and smart.'

'Yes?'

Amy couldn't believe she was saying this to him, but

she continued, 'I just think it's important you know a little about her. She didn't deserve what happened to her. Not at all.'

'Amy, we're going to do everything we can do to find out who did this. We have a pretty good record here. Seventy-five percent of the homicides committed in this city are solved.'

Not wanting to say anything else stupid, Amy stood up to go. She just didn't want her sister's case to be part of the twenty-five percent. 'Am I allowed to go to her apartment?'

'Yeah, and if you come across anything let us know. Here are the keys.' He opened an envelope and gave them to her. 'Before you go, could you look at this? We found a list of telephone numbers next to the phone. Could you look over the names and tell us who these people are?'

'Yes. In fact, I made up this list last night. I'll compare the two.' Amy identified all the telephone numbers. For as many people as Tricia had known, there weren't that many numbers. She handed Towne her list.

'What do the stars next to Chuck, Eddy, and Hank mean?' he asked.

'Oh, I forgot I did that. I guess those are three guys I think you should be sure to check out. Chuck is the cook at work, and he's been saying awful things about Tricia lately. Also he told me he knew where she lived. Hank's the keyboard player in the band I was telling you about. I know he brought her home one night. And Eddy – well, he's her drug dealer. Also I think he's the guy Danny was supposed to be with the other night.'

'OK, we'll check them out. Thanks for this list.'

Amy looked at him. 'Anything I can do to help you, just let me know.'

'You've been a big help. Why don't you just take it easy?' Towne said to her as he put the file away.

As she walked out of his office, Amy thought to herself, because she was my sister, that's why.

Tricia is in my bed, shaking. She has had a nightmare. I whisper the words my mother told me, 'It's just a dream. Everything's all right,' and smooth her hair back from her face. In the sliver of moonlight I see her wide eyes. She says, 'It was them, Amy. They were coming to get me.' I tell her it was only a dream, but the next day she doesn't want to go into the lake. I splash some water on her as she sits on the shore and she cries.

Chapter 12

Clutching the keys to Tricia's apartment in her hand, Amy stood out in front of the duplex on the sidewalk. As she squinted her eyes up at the front windows, the building seemed to grow. She thought she saw something move inside and then decided it was only a curtain blowing in the breeze.

Todd had offered to come with her, but Amy had wanted to go alone the first time. She didn't want to talk about what she was feeling, rather just feel it and get it over with. She also needed to look hard at the apartment and see if she could find something the police had overlooked or hadn't known was important. Maybe the fact that she knew Tricia better than anyone else would help.

Walking up to the front door of the building, Amy felt uneasy that it wasn't a security building. Anyone could walk into these old buildings. Someone might have been waiting for Tricia that night, hiding behind the staircase. Amy walked around and looked behind the stairs. There were a few dried leaves back there, but nothing else. When she checked Tricia's mailbox, she found a flyer for a car wash and the *Reader's Digest* sweepstakes envelope, declaring Tricia Curtis a possible winner, all she had to do was send in the enclosed envelope to find out if she had won.

Amy tried the apartment door a couple times to be sure it was locked. It wouldn't open, but she knew the lock was just a simple one that could be sprung with a credit card. She pulled out the key, with a police identification tag on it, and slowly opened the door.

The first thing she noticed when she walked into the living room was the talcum powder. Everything was coated with it, the TV set, the bookshelves, the door. There were traces of powder scattered all over the room, making the room seem dirty, or dusty as if it hadn't been lived in in a long while. Amy guessed the police had used it to find fingerprints. She sat down on the couch. Remembering the money roll Tricia had stashed there, she felt under the cushions but found nothing. She hoped Tricia had spent it all and tried not to think of what her sister might have done to earn it. Something that killed her in the end.

She wondered if Tricia's presence was still lingering in the room and if it could help her figure anything out. She shut her eyes and imagined Tricia, her legs curled under her on the couch, cigarette smoke twisting up into the still air. 'Where are you, Tricia? What happened to you?' At the sound of the questions Tricia melted away and went spiraling up with the smoke. Amy opened her eyes and the room was empty.

In order to find out what had happened to her sister, she had to keep an open mind, take all the facts in. She couldn't shut anything out just because she didn't want to see it. It could be that Danny murdered Tricia. Amy knew she had to think of it as a possibility rather than avoid it. She didn't want it to be true, but then she didn't want her sister to be dead. The idea that her sister had been in love with a man who might have killed her seemed to make Tricia's life even more futile.

Coming up the stairs to Tricia's apartment, the thought had occurred to Amy that it might have been a total stranger who had killed her. Tricia could have gone out the other night, gotten drunk, picked up some weirdo, brought him home, and he could have murdered her. The police might never find him. It might also be that some one of the men Tricia had met down at the IDS club had located her and come over the other night; maybe this 'Peter Pan' guy killed her on a lark. Or because he didn't know when to stop. Amy wondered what Tricia had been doing with those men. In some strange way she wanted to take a few steps into the world that Tricia had lived and died in.

Amy stood up to do the work she had come to do. Break up Tricia's household. Most of the furniture they could donate back to the Salvation Army. Red had said he would help her move out anything she wanted with a truck. There were a few things Amy wanted to keep.

Walking toward the bedroom, Amy wished the police hadn't closed the door. She didn't want to open it again. It was too much the same as the last time. A sunny day. A terrible stillness. Amy stopped in front of the door and stared at it. Just a wood door with a small glass doorknob. Tricia had liked that doorknob. She claimed it was one hundred years old. Tricia had only been twenty-three, not one quarter as old as the doorknob. Amy reached out and touched it. It felt cool in her fingers, almost slippery, like a fish, a glass fish. She took a deep breath and turned it. It creaked as if it had its own small voice and was screaming a tiny wispy scream.

With her foot she pushed open the door to the bedroom. The room was only dark and dirty. No ghosts. Turning on the overhead light to dispel the darkness, she stepped into the room. The vinegar smell was still there. She began to gag. Moving quickly, she opened the window near the bed and raised the screen. Sticking her head out, she took in a few deep breaths. Her stomach calmed. Turning back to the room, she looked around and said, 'Fuck.' There was no stopping and there was no

146

going back. She had said she'd do this by herself and now she was stuck. Alone. Get rid of the bedclothes, she decided, and so she reached down and stripped the flowered sheets from the mattress, stuffing them into a pillowcase. Those would be thrown away. She rolled up the rug and pushed it into the hallway.

Dragging a suitcase out of the closet, she looked up at the shirts and dresses hanging like lifeless thin bodies and realized that almost all of Tricia's clothes would fit into the small suitcase. Amy picked up the two waitress uniforms that were on the floor of the closet, probably exactly where Tricia had stepped out of them. They were too soiled to salvage.

Sliding all the hangers together, she noticed a top she had never seen before way at the back of the closet, certainly one she had never seen Tricia wear. It was a black leather corset. Instead of fastening up the back, it zipped up the front. Amy took it off the hanger and held it in her hand. The leather felt as smooth as a face. She turned to the full-length mirror standing up against the wall and held it up to her body. It looked as if it might fit her. It must have been awfully tight on Tricia. Her breasts would have risen above it like white frosting on chocolate cupcakes. Men would have reached out to finger them.

Amy folded it up and stuffed it into her purse. Maybe this was the clue she'd been looking for. Not so much a clue that would lead her to Tricia's murderer as a hint at what Tricia had been getting into, a life that could lead to a murder.

Among the pile of clothes she saw a cashmere sweater she had given her sister for Christmas. It was turquoise blue, and when Tricia had tried it on, she had looked so elegant. She had turned to Amy and said, 'Where will I ever wear this? I never go anyplace fancy enough.'

When Tricia had come back from LA she had only the

clothes she was wearing. Edna and Amy had gone through their closets and given her hand-me-downs, which were still the majority of the clothes in the closet. An old smock of her mother's, a purple turtleneck of Amy's, even an old plaid wool shirt of Red's. Amy threw most of them away. She didn't want them back and she was sure her parents wouldn't either.

On the nightstand next to the bed Tricia had a large bowl that she kept her jewelry in. There was nothing of any real value in it. Just trinkets she had picked up over the years. Amy held a pair of gaudy, dangling earrings in her hand and decided to keep them for herself, something festive to remember Tricia by. Again she turned to the mirror and put them on. Not her style, but dramatic. Swinging her head back and forth, she watched them dance near her chin. She smiled. Sorting out the rest of the jewelry, she selected a plain jade bracelet for her mother, who loved to play with them, and a silver chain for Aunt Molly, who didn't wear jewelry as a rule. All that was left in the bowl were unmatched earrings and a tangled mess of necklaces that Amy threw away.

In the drawer of the nightstand she found the Bible Red had given Tricia on her eighth birthday. On the inside cover Tricia had written her name ten times, each time varying the way she wrote the capital *T*. Sometimes it was a cross, or a swooping boat with a mast, or fancy with the ends curling up. Amy put the book in the pile of things to keep. Her dad might like to have that.

When Amy was finished with the bedroom, she put the suitcase next to the front door and brought two bags of clothes down to the garbage cans out back. Before shutting the door of the room, she looked in one last time. It seemed so empty. A slant of sun hit the end of the old mattress, which was sitting on the floor. Amy knew the most intimate part of her work had been done.

148

When she opened the refrigerator, she found two cans of beer the sole occupants. Without thinking she popped the tops off both of them and upended them into the sink. Then she turned to the cupboards and started emptying them. She found a couple boxes outside the back door and used them to pack the dishes. Just as she was putting the last of the dishes into a cardboard box, there was a knock at the front door. Amy dropped a plate and it broke as it hit the floor, pieces of it scuttling across the floor like fish trying to swim out of water.

Standing quietly, she waited to hear if there would be another knock. When she heard nothing, she walked quietly through the living room, toward the door. She got to within a few yards of it and heard a scratching noise. A piece of paper was being shoved under the door. At first she had been afraid to know who was knocking, now she needed to know. Amy ran to the door and yanked it open.

A man was bent over in front of the door. Amy let out a small cry. When he straightened up, Luke smiled at her. 'You scared me, too,' he said. 'I didn't think anyone was home.'

'What are you doing here?' she asked.

'Just leaving a message for Tricia. I've been trying to call, but she hasn't been answering the phone and we've got a rehearsal today. I wanted to be sure she knew about it. I told Hank to tell her, but I haven't been able to get in touch with him either. So I decided to come over and leave a message. I thought maybe she hadn't paid her phone bill or something.'

Amy wished Luke would stop talking. When he finally did, she asked, 'You haven't heard the news lately?'

'No, I've been kind of laying low, these last few days. Actually, since I saw you the other night.'

'Come on in.' He followed her in and she shut the door.

She sat down on the edge of the coffee table and looked up at him. 'I was going to call you today. I guess I thought you would have heard. Tricia was killed that night. She was murdered here. I found her the next morning.'

'No.' Luke blinked hard and set his jaw. 'Do they know who did it?'

'Not really.' Amy could tell he was trying not to cry. Seeing him so close to tears put her over the edge and she began to cry, her shoulders shaking. He stepped close to her and wrapped his arms around her head. Her arms went naturally around his legs and she burrowed her head into his thigh. She felt his hand stroking her hair. She wished she could stay this way for a while, held by a man who had meant so much to her. Then he bent down and kissed the back of her neck and she pulled away.

'I need a Kleenex.' She got up and walked into the bathroom. Don't even bother to look at yourself in the mirror, she thought, it'll only make you feel worse. Of course, there were no Kleenex, so she had to settle for toilet paper.

When she came out of the bathroom, Luke was sitting on the couch, smoking. 'It was so great to see her the other night, singing and looking good. I can't believe it. I can't believe she's dead.'

'I know.'

'God, Amy, how are you doing?'

'I'm numb. Just doing what I have to.'

'Is there anything I can do? What are you doing at her place anyway?' he asked her.

Standing across the room from him, she wondered the same thing. She tucked her T-shirt into the waist of her shorts. It had come undone while she had lugged the clothes down to the garbage. 'Just trying to straighten things up. Throwing things away. It's pretty awful work.'

'Do you need any help?'

150

'Actually, I could use some. There's a mattress in her room I'd like to get out of here.'

'OK, let's do it.' Stubbing out the cigarette, he stood up.

Without waiting for her, he walked into the bedroom and hoisted the mattress up on its side. He grabbed hold of one of the handles and started moving it toward the door. 'Could you get the door for me?' he asked.

Amy ran ahead of him and made sure the bedroom door, then the kitchen door, and finally the back door, were all open wide enough. 'I better help you down the stairs.'

'OK.' He leaned the mattress against the stair railing and whipped his shirt off over his head. His shoulders were wet with sweat and his chest was covered with dark hair – like a horse, she thought – it had always reminded her of the way horses' hair has grain, swirling one way, then the other. She had liked to run her hand across it. He wiped under his arms with his shirt, then hung it over the railing. 'You better take the back. I'll grab the front. Have you got hold of it?'

She told him she did. He lifted the front of the mattress to his shoulder, which made it almost level with her carrying it at her waist. She was tempted to tip it over the railing and just let it fall, but she knew the neighbors wouldn't appreciate it crushing their flowers. When they got it down to the ground, Luke helped her arrange it in among the garbage cans.

'Do you want a glass of water?' she asked him when they had climbed back to the top of the stairs.

'Sure,' he said, and sat down on the top step. She went inside and unpacked two glasses, let the water run until it was cold, and filled the glasses. When she came out, Luke had wrapped his shirt around his neck. 'I like this hot weather,' he said.

151

'So when was Hank supposed to have gotten in touch with Tricia?' Amy handed him both glasses and sat down next to him. The wood step burned the back of her thigh. She moved forward a little so her shorts protected her leg.

'I thought he was going to talk to her Saturday night.'

'I wonder if he did. I wonder if he knows something. What's he like?'

'He acts like a kid. But he's almost thirty years old. He's been playing with the band for a couple months. I like him. He's not super smart, but he's real musical. He can play anything he hears. One of those.'

'Does he have a girlfriend?'

'Not that I know of.'

'This is kind of a personal question, but you know he drove Tricia home the other night after the gig. Did he say anything to you about that night?'

Luke thought for a bit before he answered. 'Let's see. It was the next night that we met and pretty much decided we wanted to ask Tricia to join the group. He was all in favor. What did he say about her? He might have said she was well built. But anyone could have seen that. You don't think he had anything to do with what happened to Tricia. I can't see it. I really can't. He seems like a good guy.'

'I'm not saying anything. Just wondering. Where do you think he is right now?'

'Well, he isn't from the Twin Cities. He's from Willmar. Maybe he went home for Sunday dinner. He goes back there a lot.'

'Shit. I can't believe I'm even asking you questions. Can't seem to help it. I just want to know what happened to her.'

Luke put his arm around her waist. 'That makes sense.'

Amy sat very still. He wasn't doing anything but

152

touching her. The sun was beating down on the top of her head. She felt slightly dizzy.

Not looking at her, Luke said, 'I'd just like to hold you in my arms, make you feel a little better.'

She squeezed her glass tightly in both hands. 'I have to go out to my folks'.'

Luke didn't say anything. They sat next to each other on the steps and both finished their water. Luke handed her his glass and she took it. He took his arm away from her waist. She stood up and he did too.

'Tell your mom and dad how sorry I am. I always liked Tricia. I know how important she was to you. Amy, I'm really sorry.' He went down the back stairs and disappeared around the corner of the house.

Chapter 13

When Amy pulled into the driveway of her parents' house, she saw her aunt's Volkswagen Rabbit parked there. Then Aunt Molly appeared in the doorway, wearing a lime-green sweatshirt and jeans with blue lizard-skin cowboy boots. Amy was glad to see her round, solid face.

'Hey, Amy, come give your old aunt a hug.'

They hugged, and Amy smelled her outdoor smell, like newly harvested hay, not sweet but alive.

'It should never have happened. I thought Trish was going to make it. I thought she was getting better.'

Amy said, 'I thought she was too. And then she started drinking again.'

When they walked into the kitchen, Amy didn't see her parents anywhere. 'Where's Mom and Dad?'

'They went to the funeral home to make some arrangements. I said I'd stick around here and wait for you.'

'How are they doing?'

'They're going to be all right. They've got each other.'

Amy thought of Aunt Molly living by herself in her trailer home near Rapid City. Her husband had left her five years ago for a waitress he had met on a business trip. 'How's everything with you?'

They sat down at the kitchen counter, where Aunt Molly had a glass of iced tea half drunk.

Aunt Molly put her hand over Amy's and said, 'Sweetie, I'm fine. You live through it. When you're in it, you don't know how you'll ever do it, but somehow one day you wake up and you're on the other side. When your uncle left me for his lollapalooza, no slur on the waitressing profession in general mind you, just this one little floozy in particular, I thought of climbing up Mount Rushmore, staring deeply into Lincoln's eyes, and then jumping. But it seemed like a lot of work. So instead I went out and got a job so I had a reason to get up every morning. But he was only a husband, and I'm seeing that his place can be filled. Tricia was your sister. You'll never have another one. I'm so sorry.'

'I know. I still have trouble believing it. I think she's playing a joke on us.'

'So what exactly happened? I think your folks told me the diluted version.' Aunt Molly chipped pink polish off her nails.

'The police aren't sure yet.'

'What do they think happened?'

'It's not good.'

'It doesn't need to be good. I loved Tricia too. She told me one time when she was about five years old that if she didn't already have a mama, she'd like to have me for one. What happened to her?'

'It looks like she was killed. Some guy was over there and tied her up. He gagged her and stabbed her with a knife.' Amy said it fast to get it over with.

'Poor kid. Who the hell was she running around with, anyway? She didn't know how much she was worth. Do they know who did it?'

'The police have got some leads, they think. None of the test results have come in, you know, the autopsy and all that. I've been trying to help them as much as I can.' Amy said, then on impulse added, 'I really want to know why it happened.'

'You just don't worry your parents. They've lost one daughter.'

'I won't.'

'I got right in my car after your mom called me.

Probably should have flown. Just wanted to be here, the moment I heard, and it still took me nearly twelve hours to get here. Driving across the lonesome land at night, it made me wonder what it's all about. You love someone and they leave you, or they die.'

'Makes me feel like not loving anyone ever again.'

'That's a solution, or else love so many people that you could never run out.'

Amy laughed. 'God, if I didn't know you better, I'd say you were a Pollyanna.'

'Never. Not me.' Aunt Molly held out her chipped fingernails and said, 'These things look like the Badlands or, would you believe, the Badhands?'

'Have a little respect, Aunt Molly.' Still laughing, Amy wiped her hand across the wet spot her aunt's glass had left on the counter, then asked, 'Does this remind you of when Aunt Margaret died?'

'What?'

'You know, drinking and dying young?'

'I suppose. I hadn't thought of it.'

'Was Tricia much like Aunt Margaret? I don't really remember her that well. I was about ten when she died.'

'What kind of question is that? Are you trying to figure this out, or what? Margaret was a very frivolous, unhappy woman. Tricia seemed to me like she had a little more going for her. For one thing, she was smart. Although I'm not sure it helps to be smart. Then you really know how goofed up everything is.'

'Yeah, I am trying to figure it out. Why did you turn out the way you did and Mom turn out the way she did and Aunt Margaret have the drinking problem? What makes it happen?'

'You know, one thing that was the same about Tricia and Margaret they were both the second child. It might be a hard place to be in the family. I don't know, I was the baby and I liked that. But Margaret was always competing with Edna.'

'That's what it was like with Tricia and me,' Amy said, nodding. 'I remember our piano lessons, we started taking them at the same time and of course I was better, because I was two years older, but I wasn't a lot better. I'd put her down. I'd make fun of her. Just to keep my advantage. What a horrible sister I was.'

'No, that's the way it works. One time Edna persuaded Margaret to chop off her ponytail just because Edna was jealous of her long hair. Lordy, was our mama mad about that.'

'Aunt Molly, I think Tricia was getting into some real trouble.'

'What do you mean? Drugs?'

'Drugs and sex.'

'Well, don't tell your mother. She doesn't need to know this. Was Tricia doing more than sleeping around?'

'Maybe. I found a black corset in the back of her closet today when I was cleaning it out.'

'I had a black corset once.'

'Back when it was in style.'

'Listen, Amy, just 'cause you don't even need to wear a bra. What do you know about lingerie styles?'

'The police said the way she was murdered, it looked like an S-and-M scene.'

They both fell silent as they heard a car pull up in the driveway.

Edna and Red were dressed soberly. Amy couldn't remember the last time she had seen her mother with a hat on. She had even applied a smeary film of lipstick. Her father had on a pair of dark slacks and a clean white shirt with a dark tie blotting the front of it. They nodded their heads and sat down at the kitchen counter.

'The funeral's going to be on Wednesday. Just a short

157

memorial service,' Edna said, and then started to cry. 'I'm going to lie down for a while.' She walked down the hallway to her bedroom.

Red looked at Amy. 'You going to stay here tonight?'

'Yeah. I cleaned up Tricia's place today, so I'll stay here tonight.'

'Your mom would like that.'

'OK, Dad.'

Dinner that night was subdued. They didn't turn the ceiling light on over the dining room table, instead just let the natural end-of-the-day sunlight filter in through the curtains. It felt strange to eat out in the dining room. Usually Edna and Red ate at the counter. It was more cosy with just the two of them. But since Aunt Molly was here, they sat at the big table and passed around the beef and tomato hot dish a neighbor lady had brought over. When you're sad, eat, that's how Minnesotans dealt with grief, Amy thought, yet did find the overcooked pasta reassuring.

The problem was that one on one they could talk about how they felt about Tricia's death, but assembled all together they had to pretend that everything was all right, make small talk, not really say anything.

Amy finally pushed away her plate of food, half finished.

'Honey, don't leave that good food there.'

'I can't eat any more, Mom. It's too hot to eat this kind of stuff anyway.'

'You are such a picky eater.' Edna reached for the plate.

Aunt Molly put her hand and stopped her from taking it. 'Let it be, Edna. A little wasted food isn't a tragedy. Neither you nor I need to eat any extra either.'

158

Remembering the jewelry she had taken from Tricia's, Amy stood up to get it. 'I'll be right back.'

Finding her purse where her mother had put it on her bed, she took out the jewelry and picked up the Bible. She handed them around at the table.

Aunt Molly broke the silence first by saying, 'Thanks, Amy. Would you help me put it on?'

Edna held the bracelet in her lap and stared out the window, while Red just laid his hand on the Bible, like he was swearing to something. They all sat there for a while and then Edna started taking the dishes off the table. The phone rang in the kitchen and Aunt Molly answered it.

'Amy, it's for you.'

For a second Amy wondered if it could be Luke. He knew the number out here and he also knew she was out at her folks'. Then she decided it was probably Todd, checking on her.

'Hello.'

'Yeah, Amy.'

Amy froze. It was Danny. 'Where are you?'

'Never mind. I gotta talk to you.'

'Fine. When? Where?' She wouldn't mess it up this time. She would let the police know.

'I can't make it tonight. Let's say tomorrow afternoon, three o'clock, at the houseboat under the railroad bridge. Just you alone, Amy. I gotta talk to you.'

'OK, I'll see you then.' He hung up before she could say anything else. She twisted the phone cord and then untwisted it as she thought about meeting Danny. She didn't like it. What could he have to say to her that could be so important? And she didn't like the meeting place, it was the most deserted place he could have chosen and still have it be in the city. Maybe he had killed Tricia and

159

he wanted to be sure Amy could never testify against him. She would have to be very careful.

When she walked back into the dining room they all looked questioningly at her. 'Just a friend calling to say he was sorry to hear about Tricia.'

'That's nice,' Edna said.

Red cleared his throat and stood up, saying to Amy, 'Come down in the basement. There's something I want to give you.'

She followed him down the stairs to his workshop. All his tools hung from the wall like dulled medals. When she had been a kid, she had loved to sit and watch him build furniture. The sawdust piled on the floor and it was her and Tricia's job to clean it up afterward. He would let them build doll furniture out of the scraps.

Next to the workshop was his gun cabinet. He had built it himself and it housed two .22 rifles and three small handguns. At one time or another she had shot all of them. He opened it and reached in for a small gun she knew well, a Ruger Mark II. She had learned to shoot on it.

'You girls would have inherited these guns anyway. I want you to have this one now. You remember how to use it?'

'Of course.' As she took the gun from her father, she thought how glad she was she knew how to use it. She was starting to feel it might not be a bad idea to have a gun around, especially if Danny wanted to see her.

Automatically Amy checked to see if the gun were loaded. She knew it wouldn't be, her father never kept a loaded gun in the house, but she did it out of habit. The second commandment of gun safety was – as soon as you pick up any firearm, immediately open the action and inspect the chamber. Before either Tricia or she was allowed to handle the guns they had to pass their junior marksmen course. They had been the only girls in the class and had been thrilled with all the attention they received.

Amy turned away from her father and, holding the gun in both hands, took her shooting stance. It had a nice solid weight to it. She remembered going plinking with Red and Tricia. Edna thought it was horrible. Maybe she wouldn't have minded so much if one of them had been a son. But Tricia and Amy had loved it. Going out to a gravel pit and setting up tin cans and bottles on a fence, then mowing them down.

When their father wasn't looking, Tricia and Amy would click the barrels of their guns together like two of the three musketeers. At that young age, if they weren't fighting, they were best friends and had many times sworn allegiance to one another, 'One for two, and two for one.' The thought of that promise affected Amy, and the gun started shaking in her hands.

'Wish I had given you each one sooner.'

'It wouldn't have done her any good, Dad.'

He turned the matching handgun over in his hand, the one that would have been Tricia's. 'I wish I'd have done something.'

Some money is missing from Mom's purse and she sits Tricia and me down at opposite ends of the couch. Tricia's legs stick straight out in front of her and she wiggles her bare feet back and forth. 'Now, you girls are going to sit there until one of you tells me who did it.' 'Mom, are you sure you didn't lose it or spend it?' I ask. 'That's enough out of you, Amy.' She leaves the room. Tricia and I look at each other, then we start to laugh. Mom, hearing the noise, comes back into the room. 'Stop that, this is serious. I didn't raise my children to be thieves.' She leaves again. Tricia reaches into her pocket and pulls out a five-dollar bill. Then she edges off the couch and goes into the kitchen. I follow her. She holds the money out to Mom and she says, 'I took it. I wanted to give it to them.' I kick her and Mom raps me on the head and Tricia runs out into the backyard.

Chapter 14

Driving into Minneapolis the next morning, Amy remembered she was supposed to work that night. She would have to stop off and tell Dot that she wouldn't be able to make it. Since she had promised to meet Danny, there was no way she could work the shift. Last night she had tried to call Towne from the phone in the basement so no one would overhear her talking to him, but she hadn't been able to get in touch with him. The woman at the desk assured her he would get her message. Amy hadn't wanted to wait around at her parents' in the morning, so she hadn't talked to him yet.

It was half an hour before the Burger Delight opened. Dot would be there already, setting up, drinking coffee, folding napkins, overseeing the crew that had dragged in. It would be a good time to talk to her. She wouldn't have had enough coffee to be crotchety. Amy hoped she would give her the whole week off.

Amy swung off the freeway on to Cedar Avenue and then parked down the block from the Burger Delight. The morning air already had a hint of sullenness to it. She walked around to the back door, which was propped open with a broom handle. Chuck turned around to look at her but, after a glance at her face, turned back to his work. Amy stood and watched him for a second. With a long knife he was chopping up onions. Suddenly he turned with the knife still in his hand. 'What are you looking at?'

'You.'

He stepped closer to the counter. His voice dropped

into a hoarse whisper. 'You leave me alone, Amy. Don't you think anything about me. Don't look at me like that.'

Just as she pushed through the swinging door, she heard him say something. 'What?' She turned around.

'I said I don't know anything about your sister.' He said it as if he were barking out an order for more coffee, and she had no desire to hear any more. She pushed open the door.

Dot was sitting, facing away from her, with a napkin in her hand, but she was staring out the window. Amy sneaked up on her and then swung into the other side of the booth.

'Good morning, Dot.'

'Amy.' Dot's voice held real concern.

'I came by to tell you I quit.' Amy surprised herself. She hadn't planned to quit, just take some time off, but she realized she was angry at Dot for having fired Tricia. Maybe if she wouldn't have fired her, Tricia wouldn't be dead now.

'Let's talk about this.'

'I'm the one who thinks we should talk. I think there's a few things you better explain to me.' She stopped, not wanting to go on, not liking how her own voice sounded.

'You want a cup of coffee?'

The casual offer touched Amy. She leaned against the back of the booth and said yes.

Dot got up and poured her a cup of coffee, then set it down with exaggerated carefulness. 'I'm listening.'

'God damn it, don't be so understanding.'

'You don't think I feel like shit? I fire a decent waitress 'cause she gets on the rag with me and two days later I find out she's dead.'

Amy couldn't help herself. The words came out of a place deep inside, a place that still had some feeling, 'It's not your fault. I don't blame you for firing her. I just want to understand what was going on.'

'What do you mean?'

'Was there anything going on with her that you didn't tell me about?'

'God, Ame, you've worked here a long time. She was your sister. I didn't want to talk to you about Tricia. She wasn't a bad kid. The thing that bothered me was when these guys would come around. And not to eat here. To see her. I just didn't like it. She didn't do anything horrible until that one night.'

'What one night?'

'You know the night you came down here, looking for her . . .' Dot looked up at the ceiling, then straight at Amy.

'Yeah?'

'And I told you that it was slow and so I let her go.'

'Uh-huh.'

'Well, I didn't let her go.' Dot picked up the napkin and started stretching it out between her two hands. 'She just left. A guy came in here, talked to her for a minute, and then she just walked out with him. She tried to tell me later it was an emergency. But what can be so urgent she doesn't have time to walk back and tell me she's got to go.'

Something made Amy wonder if she were right in assuming it was Danny. 'What did he look like?'

'I told you that night. Tall, blond, good looking.'

'Had you ever seen him before?'

'No, he wasn't a guy who had been in before. At least, not while I was here.'

'Did you ever meet Danny, Tricia's boyfriend?'

'No. He called her a lot, but he never stopped down.'

'Well, it does sound like it was Danny. Why didn't you tell me that she walked out on you?'

'I guess I felt it was between me and Tricia. You had done enough for her. But when she didn't come in for work that next day, that was it. I'd had enough. Too undependable.' Dot took a sip of coffee, then said, 'I'm sorry, Amy. I really am.'

'You know she was murdered.'

'God, Amy, how horrible.' Dot twisted the napkin in her hands until it looked like a wick for a large candle. 'I don't know what to say. The news said that she had been found dead in her apartment, but that the cause was still uncertain.'

'I'm not going to be able to work my shift this week.'

'Don't worry about it. You've got a job here whenever you want it back.'

When Amy walked into the darkened hallway that led to the stairs of her duplex apartment, she winced. It was the dark. It seemed to breathe. She turned on the overhead light and ran up the stairs. Inside the apartment the phone was ringing. Impatient, she dug through her purse for keys, then dumped the contents out on the floor. The gun fell out with everything else and she picked it up, then fished the keys out of the jumble of ratty Kleenex and gum wrappers.

Pausing for a second, she heard the phone ring again. Her purse and its contents were still strewn all over the hallway, so she quickly picked them up. She fumbled with the lock, opened the door, ran through to the living room, and into the kitchen. Lifting up the receiver, she put it to her ear and heard the click of disconnection.

'Shit,' she said, slamming down the receiver. It probably was Towne.

She dialed the number of the police station downtown and asked to speak to Towne. When he came on the line, he said he had tried to call and asked her what was up. She told him about her planned meeting with Danny.

'A houseboat by the river?'

'Yes. Do you know where Cedar Square West is? It's just down from there. Actually, it's right below the railroad tracks that go over the river.'

'I know where you mean now. It's pretty deserted down there.'

'It is. I don't think anyone's living in the houseboat anymore.'

'OK, here's what we'll do. You're supposed to meet him about three? Rather than meeting you beforehand, we'll just watch for you down there. Just in case he's watching your house, he'll see you walk over to the river alone. I'll have a couple plainclothes cops positioned down there, out of sight. But go ahead and talk to him. Let's find out what he wants before we nab him.'

Amy couldn't read him; she didn't know if Towne was glad she had called with the information, or if he still blamed her in the first place for their problems locating Danny. She hung up, feeling oddly disappointed. At the same time that she wanted to help the police catch Danny, she felt like a traitor and she didn't feel like Towne was giving her any support.

When Amy walked into her bedroom to change her clothes, she was surprised to see her bed was unmade. Then she remembered that Todd had been the last person to sleep in it. The rumpled sheets reminded her of that morning, Tricia's bed. She hated the sight of it. As if someone else had come in and messed up everything. Bedsheets and bodies. She hated the need for sleep, the need for other people. No one should ever drink coffee again or have a normal conversation. Todd would never be able to understand. No one could understand what this

167

felt like. She didn't want them in her life anymore. No one. She grabbed the top sheet and ripped it off the bed.

There was something aching in her muscles, something that needed to be tested. Amy pounded the pillow as if it had the face of a man with lips and lying words. No heart, he could have no heart for what he had done. She felt her fists sink into the feathered flesh and clenched her teeth for a final blow. Then she threw the pillow across the room, envisioning a lifeless body hitting the wall and sliding to the floor. She tore the bottom sheet off and then yanked the mattress off the bedstead.

When nothing resisted her, she felt her shoulders shaking and slid to the floor, leaning her head against the skewed mattress. Her hands were locked into fists, and as she opened them slowly she wondered if they had any real power. Or if they were only capable of pretend fighting against shadow opponents and would become wilted rags against any real trouble. She curled up into a ball and waited for the shaking to stop.

As she lay flat against the floor, she heard the phone ring, but this time she didn't run to answer it.

'Hello,' she said clearly after she had let it ring for the third time.

'Is Amy there?' It was Todd.

'This is she.'

'Ame, that you?'

'Yeah. Who'd you think it was – Tricia?'

No answer from Todd. She had shocked him.

'I'm cracking up a little bit over here.' Amy tried to make a joke out of it.

'Want me to come over?' he asked.

'You don't need to see this.'

'What if I want to?'

'You don't want to. Nobody does unless they have to go through it.'

168

He paused, she imagined, thinking of the tack he should take with her. 'How were the police?'

'The police were fine. They've got a job to do. They're happy.'

'OK, knock off the tough-girl routine. So crack up. Why don't you go and have a good cry and I'll talk to you later.'

'Why didn't you make the bed?' As soon as the question came out she realized how idiotic it was.

'What? I didn't think of it.'

'I'm sorry. It just gave me the creeps to go into my bedroom and find it all messed up.'

'Do you want me to come over and make it? Actually I was calling to see if you wanted to work out.'

'Todd, it's the furthest thing from my mind right now. I really can't think about dancing or the audition. Maybe I won't even try out.' As she said the words, she didn't want to believe them. Tricia's death had already caused so much harm. A part of her knew she had to start fighting for what was important to herself.

'Amy, do you need some company tonight?'

'No, if you want to go on a date with your sweetie pie, you can.'

Todd didn't say anything for a moment, then he spit out, 'Thanks.'

'I'm sorry. A million times I'm sorry. I don't know where all this is coming from. I'm glad you're seeing someone. I'm just a little fucked up. I'll call you later if I need company. I promise.'

'Good. I'll see you.'

'OK, bye.' As soon as she hung up, she wished she had asked Todd to come over. She didn't want to wait alone for her rendezvous with Danny. Thinking about their conversation, she realized she was upset about his seeing this other woman. The timing was bad. She didn't want him getting involved with someone else when she needed his support so badly. There was no one else she could talk to like him. His having a girlfriend made her more aware of her own aloneness. She thought of Luke and wondered what might have happened between them at Tricia's if she hadn't pulled back.

She went into the living room and took her pants off. Then, dressed in only a T-shirt and underpants, she placed her feet so they formed a straight line. First position. Slowly, she bent her knees and felt her upper thigh muscles catch and hold her body as she lowered it. When she reached the place of the most tension, she held it for a second and then started back up. She tried to glide up as if her body were slightly lighter than air and it was moving up on its own. Floating up until it was only the balls of her feet and her toes that tied her to the ground. She repeated this movement five times and then went on to second position.

Her arms held a ball. She lifted it up and watched it float away. She started her stretches. One leg forward and then the other. The sweat was rising, surfacing on her skin like beads of oil on water. She glistened. Bending, she touched the floor with her fingertips, lowered to her knuckles, open-palmed it with her hand, then carefully brought her face to her knees. She was doubled up like a piece of paper folded in half. She held the position until she needed to breathe and then she rose, inch by inch, up into the air.

After the warm-up exercises Amy didn't have the energy to do anything more. Dancing seemed like another world. A world she wanted to live in again; she hoped she would get the chance. But for now she had to worry about the police and Danny. Flexing her legs, she felt the tops of her thighs. She would wear tennis shoes and run if she had to. She was pretty sure she could outrun Danny.

What if he saw the police and realized a trap had been laid and tried to take her as hostage? Stop it, she said, shaking her body out. Nothing's going to happen.

Sitting down on what remained of her bed, she thought of her parents. She needed to watch out for them – they didn't have to know what she was doing, meeting Danny, but they must have the sense that something was being done about Tricia, especially her father. There was no way she was going to let them blame themselves for what had happened to their daughter. Amy knew if it was anyone's fault, it was Tricia's. She was just coming to see that.

Amy felt anger shoot through her as she thought about Tricia. Why had she been so careless with herself? Why had she let this happen? Amy felt the loss of her sister still plummeting within herself, like a stone that's been dropped into a deep well and hasn't yet hit the water, Amy knew she hadn't yet felt all the ripples of Tricia's death; she knew she was still tensed up at the top of the well, listening.

Remembering the bag of clothes she had taken from Tricia's, she went and pulled out the black leather top. It seemed so sinister to her. Dead animal skin. She looked it over and found a little pocket in the inside. Inside the pocket was a calling card, with the name Suzanne on it.

Before she could change her mind, Amy decided to call her. Just a woman's name, maybe it meant nothing, but she had to try. She might be the woman Sandra had mentioned, the woman who arranged things. Amy heard the phone ring twice and then someone answered. There was a pause before a woman's silky voice came on, saying. 'This is Suzanne. I'm so glad you called. I'd like to know in what ways I can be of service to you. Please leave a message and I'll get back to you at the first convenient moment. Don't hang up, now. Leave your name and number. Bye-bye.'

Amy was so intent on listening to the voice that when the beep sounded and it was time for her to leave a message, she blanked. She had to leave a name but it mustn't be her real name. 'Hi. This is Emma Fox. I'd like to talk to you. Please call me back,' After leaving her telephone number, she quietly hung up the phone.

She didn't know what she would say to the woman when she called back, but she would think of something. Suzanne's message had a note of insinuation in it. She would follow that, she would be vague. She would let Suzanne suggest why she had called her. Maybe it was a false lead, maybe it led down an empty dirty alley into a woman's life she didn't even want to know, but she needed to take it. It might be the road Tricia had traveled. Amy had to know.

Chapter 15

Amy didn't like it at all. Not any of it. Here she was sitting in her car on a hot summer day that was turning windy and cloudy, down by the river, waiting. It was ten minutes past three and she felt ready to jump out of her skin. The leaves of the cottonwood trees were slashing in the wind. The river was flowing by.

She had no idea where the police were or where Danny was. Finally she decided it was too hot to stay in the car. Maybe Danny had meant to meet on the riverboat. She was pretty sure no one lived there anymore. She got out of her car and picked her way down to the riverbank. An old deserted garden was blooming, its edges blurred with weeds.

To get onto the riverboat she had to walk across a two-board bridge that was secured on both ends. It creaked and swayed but seemed stable. A small metal walkway ran all the way around the edge of the boat. She stepped on to that and walked toward the back of the boat. It's called the stern, she thought.

There was a small sunning deck with a towel stretched over the railing. The towel looked as if it had been there for a while, faded by the sun and streaked by the rain. She walked over to the railing and stared at the water. The river was moving slowly by, carrying bits of debris with it, leaves, branches, paper cups. Sheltering her eyes with her hand, she stared up at the railroad bridge. Someone was up there. She couldn't tell if it was Danny or not. The sun was too bright behind the person; all she could see was a tall shape, leaning on the railing of the bridge.

Looking at her watch, she saw it was now nearly three-thirty. There seemed no evidence of anyone on the boat. Then she heard footsteps on the metal walkway. Without thinking she stepped around to the other side of the boat, just out of sight of the deck. A man came around the side of the boat, and by peeking up over the window that looked into the boat, she could see his back. It wasn't Danny. And it wasn't Towne. This man was tall and thin, with dark hair. She held her breath. What if Danny had sent someone to meet her? Maybe he was in on something with Eddy. Maybe the thin man was Eddy.

She didn't know where the police were hiding and decided that if the man on the deck had a knife or a gun, it wouldn't matter if the police were only just up on the shore. They would be too late. She was so glad she had worn her tennis shoes. Quietly, as if performing some intricate dance, she started to tiptoe down the other walkway. She heard the man walk across the deck and look at the water. Just as she reached the forward deck, he turned and saw her. Pushing a lounge chair out of her way, she ran across the deck and reached the makeshift bridge.

As she jumped on to it, her foot went between the two boards and she screamed with pain as both sides of her leg were scraped and bleeding. She caught herself on her hands and tried to pull her leg out.

Now the man was on the front deck and she started screaming for help. Her leg was wedged tightly between the boards and she watched the blood run down it and into the water swirling below her. The shadow of a man standing right over her was reflected in the water and she yelled, 'Towne.'

174

The thin man grabbed her under the arms and said, 'It's all right. I'm a cop. I'm with Towne.'

She started to shake and looking up, saw the figure on the bridge run over to the east bank of the river. It might have been Danny.

Sitting in the back seat of Towne's car, Amy stared at her leg. It was going to be all right. Nothing was broken, but it looked awful, two long strips of red from her ankle to her knee. It was bruised, but she could bend it and walk on it. Hopefully she would be able to dance on it. That was what was important. She had to audition. Now she realized how much she wanted to audition.

Towne was wearing a white dress shirt, but it was no longer dressy. The sleeves were rolled up and the collar unbuttoned. A tie hung loosely from the collar, the knot of it almost undone. His jacket was thrown over the back of the car seat.

'You sure you don't want to swing by the hospital? It would be on us,' he said. There was actually some concern in his voice, and it surprised Amy.

'No, I'm fine. I can tell it's all right.' Even though it sounded funny, she went ahead and said, 'I can tell what's going on with my body. I'm a dancer.'

It seemed to reassure him and he stood up. 'Well, I'm real sorry he didn't show up. I have a feeling he won't call you again, but I might be wrong. I wonder what spooked him.'

'I saw someone on the bridge. I think it might have been him.'

'If it was, he won't call for sure. He probably saw the whole setup.' Towne looked up at the bridge and followed the length of it across the river. Then he said under his breath, 'Shit.'

'How's it going?' she asked.

He wiped his face. 'I'm bushed. Running around and getting nowhere. Witnesses who won't talk or won't allow themselves to be found. We just got the coroner's report back.'

Amy just looked at him, waiting for something heavy to be placed in her lap.

'Well, Amy, your sister died by choking on a gag that had been stuffed too far into her mouth. And she was intoxicated at the time of death. The percentage of alcohol in her brain was .05.' Towne said it all clearly, then went on. 'We'll be releasing the news of how she was killed to the papers pretty soon, so I wanted to tell you first. We'll hold back the fact that she was tied up and simply say that she was strangled. We need a way to sort out the murderer from the weirdos that call. But it'll be pretty graphic.'

She knew he wasn't telling her everything, so she had to ask, 'What about sex? Can you tell if she had had intercourse?'

'Yes, we can, and yes, she did.'

'So what about the knife?'

'That was done after. She must have trusted this person, because she did let them tie her up. There were hardly any marks on her body, so she must not have struggled.'

Amy bit her lower lip and tears ran down her face. She couldn't say anything, but she wished they were near a bathroom, not down by the river.

Towne said, 'I'll get you some Kleenex.' He climbed into the front seat and she covered her eyes and cried.

Now I know how she was killed, Amy thought. How much more do I need to know? She remembered the body of her sister as she lay on her deathbed. It would soon be a picture that thousands of people could conjure up. There was a difference between outside knowledge and inside knowledge. All she had known about her sister and had worried about for so long was becoming outside knowledge. Other people would know it too. Even in death Amy wanted to protect Tricia from those people. They would not have understood her if they had met her while she was alive, and they would never begin to understand her now. Amy needed to know what had happened to Tricia and why she had been killed.

Towne rummaged around in the front seat for a few moments; then he turned around and faced her. In his hand was a slightly wrinkled yet unused handkerchief, which he handed to Amy. She didn't ask where it had come from.

'Have you told my parents yet?' Amy managed to ask after blowing her nose a few times.

'No, I thought I'd let you.'

'Thanks.' Amy touched her leg. It was throbbing, measuring the beats of her heart. She looked over at Towne to see if he had any more to tell her.

He was staring at the river and started talking without looking at her. 'I woke up in the middle of the night last night. And it wasn't from a bad dream. I sat up in bed and wondered if we would be able to find the guy, you know, the guy who killed her.' He wiped at his face again. 'Listen, let's get out of here. I don't know why I told you all this down here. Let's go get a cup of coffee. First I better get rid of the rest of these guys.' He went over and talked to the men in a dark gray car that was parked a ways up the road.

When they walked into the dark interior of the Little Wagon, there were only two other customers, two old men standing up at the bar who looked as if they had made a career out of sampling the different forms of alcohol. Amy looked at them and wondered if Tricia would have reached that point of stupefication if she had lived long enough.

Towne motioned her to a booth along the side wall. The sides of the booth were over her head and made it seem like she was sitting down in a railroad compartment. She laughed involuntarily when she thought of the bar's name.

Towne gave her a half smile and asked, 'Have you ever been here before?'

'No, but I like it.'

'What would you like?'

'I'll just have coffee.'

They sat in silence for a moment, then Towne sighed and said, 'I just wish Danny had shown up. It's looking pretty bad for him that he's not around. I think he's our guy.'

When the waiter came, Amy was surprised to hear Towne order a seven-seven. She just ordered coffee. The waiter nodded, and returned with them in a moment. Towne paid for both of them.

Towne held his drink in his hands, but didn't take a sip. Instead he addressed Amy again. 'You know, a lot of people think we've got all these tricks we use to find who's the murderer. Like it's a whodunit or something. We go around gathering up little cryptic facts and then bring all the suspects together in one room and ask them some pointed questions and pull the murderer out of a hat. It isn't like that. We just use common sense. I hate to tell you this, but it's looking like Danny is our number-one suspect, and I think you know that. His fingerprints are all over the place. On the glasses in the sink. The only other sets are Tricia's and yours. He had a motive. We need to find that guy.'

'What about everyone else? Did you talk to Sandra?'

Suddenly thirsty, Towne took a huge gulp of his drink.

178

'That's another thing I need to talk to you about. She denied everything. She said she didn't know what you're talking about. That you had come up Sunday night and threatened her in the bathroom, but she didn't tell you anything because there was nothing to tell.'

'Why would she say that?' Amy said, then remembered Sandra's face, the fear written on it. She was so young and scared. Dealing with the police was probably just too much for her.

Towne nodded. 'I don't know. I thought you might.'

'Where did you try to talk to her? You didn't go down to where she worked, did you?'

'No, we went over to her house. I always try to talk to people face to face. I want to see their eyes when I talk to them. I think you might be right, she's lying about something. But it still gives me nothing to go on.'

'I think she was probably petrified.'

A man walked in and slipped into the booth next to Towne. He tipped his hat at Amy but kept it on. His suit coat looked as though it had been used to wipe his brow, which was sweaty and wrinkled. 'Nothing,' he said to Towne. 'Hasn't shown up at his parents' and hasn't come near his own apartment.'

'Amy thinks he might have been up on the bridge, watching us.'

'Great.' The cop did wipe his face with the sleeve of his jacket and then asked Amy, 'Do you think he'd skip town?'

Amy remembered Danny running from the bar; she wondered how far he'd go before he'd stop and think about what he was doing. 'Maybe, but I have a feeling he'd come back.'

'Let's keep somebody staked out at his place,' Towne said to the man, who nodded and then got up and left, without another word.

'Did you find anything out about Chuck, the cook who worked with Tricia, or Hank, the keyboard player?' Amy asked.

'Yeah, Hank's fine. Country kid. Doesn't have any kind of record. But Chuck is a bit of a nut. Has been in and out of detox. Ended up in a halfway house, then got kicked out because he started a bed on fire.'

'Did he fall asleep while he was smoking?'

'No, it wasn't his bed. It appears he might have started it on purpose. But they couldn't prove it. All they could do was throw him out of the place. I sent someone down to talk to him. Don't really expect too much. Like I said, I think our best bet is Danny.'

'There's someone else you should check up on, a friend of Tricia's,' Amy said.

Towne looked at her for a second. She wondered if he trusted her. 'Sure,' he said.

'Well, she's someone I remember Tricia talking about from time to time. Once she made some kind of joke that this person, Suzanne, could handle a whole roomful of the Knights of Columbus. I found her number in one of Tricia's shirts when I was digging around there.' She gave him the number and then asked what they would do. 'Maybe she'd know something.'

'We'll find out her full name and run a check on her. If she's been hooking, she might very well have a record.'

'If you talk to her, don't mention me.'

'Why not?' Towne asked, watching her as she ran a finger down the side of her coffee cup.

'I don't want her to know I'm Tricia's sister. I don't even want her to know that Tricia had a sister. I just want to stay out of it.'

'That's fine.'

'I would like to know what you find out about her.' Amy finished her coffee.

'So when's the funeral?' Towne asked.

'There's going to be a memorial service at our church tomorrow and the burial will be right afterward.'

'Could you give me directions on how to get there?'

'You're going to come?' Amy asked.

'I try go to the funeral,' Towne told her. 'It's almost standard procedure.'

Chapter 16

When she swung her leg out of her car, Amy winced. It hurt, there was no getting around it. But pain was all right as long as the leg wasn't damaged, no muscles or ligaments torn, no bones broken. Maybe she should have gone to the hospital when Towne offered. But she was sure it was just sore, a little bruised.

She hobbled up the marigold-strewn path. The plants were so large and heavy with flowers that they leaned over the cement walkway, and she had to gently push her way through them. Some of the heads had been knocked off and were lying on the ground. If her leg hadn't hurt so much, she would have picked them up for a bouquet. She stiff-legged it up the stairs to the front door and went inside.

It felt immediately cooler in the stairwell, shaded from the sun. She took a firm hold on the stair railing and slowly climbed up. She tried bending her leg, and although it felt all right, she only did it for one step. All she wanted to do was get into the tub and then take care of her leg. But she should probably check in with her parents. After limping over to the phone, Amy called home.

'Hi, honey. Molly and I are just sitting here talking.' Her mother's voice sounded lower than usual, rather monotone.

'I'm so glad she's here. How long is she going to stay?'

'She's going to stay through the weekend. I don't know what I'd do without her.' There was a catch in her voice.

'You doing all right, Mom?'

182

'Not really. I have moments when I can't stand to think anymore. I just don't want it to be like this. Why couldn't it have been me? Your children aren't supposed to die before you.'

'I know, Mom. It should never happen.' Amy looked down and didn't say anything. No one should die, she thought.

'How are you?' her mother asked.

Amy examined her leg, which was scabbing over. She needed to do something about it. 'Just all right. I banged my leg up pretty bad.'

'Did you do it dancing?'

Amy lied. 'Yeah, tried to do something that I wasn't quite ready for.'

'Put cold on it for a while. Not too long. That should take the swelling down. Oh, before I forget, Luke called.'

Amy asked, 'He did? What did he want?'

'He didn't say. Just said to tell you he called.'

'Thanks, Mom.'

'Are you coming home tonight?'

'No, I think I'll take care of this leg. But I'll see you tomorrow before the funeral.'

When Amy got off the phone, she filled a plastic bag with ice and sat at the kitchen table with her sore leg propped up on another chair. Thinking about her audition, she suddenly decided on what song she would dance to, the song Tricia had sung for her audition, Tracy Nelson's 'Down So Low.' She hopped over to the record player and put it on.

> It's not losing you, that's got me down so low,
> I just can't find another man to take your place.

Over the throaty voice of Tracy Nelson, Amy could hear the unsung harmony of Tricia. The overlay was in

183

her mind, would probably always be there when she heard the song. She sat back down in the chair and reapplied the ice to her leg. Her body sagged, resigning itself to a loss. She had softened and was vulnerable in a way that her mind hadn't accepted yet. She missed Tricia physically. In her bones and muscles there was an ache for her.

Amy hadn't turned any lights on in her apartment, and as she looked out the kitchen window she could see the last glow of the sun. The warm air was still soft and luminous. Almost alive. So Luke had called. She wondered if she should call him. He might have something to tell her about Hank. Maybe Hank had gone over to Tricia's that night and knew something.

She still remembered Luke's number. Once or twice, when it had been real bad, and she had missed him too much, she had called him. Just to hear his voice answer the phone. He would say hello a few times, then get angry and hang up. It left her feeling worse than before. The last time she had done it, more than a year ago, a woman had answered. She was sure it was Angela, and that had cured her.

But this was different. She was calling him to talk to him. He had called her first. Staring at the phone, she took a couple of deep breaths. It really was all right for her to call him. Nothing was starting all over again. So she dialed his number and listened to the shrill ring go unanswered five times before she hung up. The kitchen clock showed it was eight-fifteen. If he was playing tonight, he would have left already.

Now she really wanted to talk to him. She was sure he had something important to tell her. She picked up the weekly entertainment newspaper that listed all the music around town and found that his band, the Privates, were playing down at the Flash Club.

She had thought she'd stay in for the night, but she

decided to go down and see the band, not for long, just until they took a break and she could talk to Luke. She wanted to see him again.

As the sky dropped into a deep blackness, Amy dug through her closet looking for something to wear. It had been a long time since she had been to the Flash Club. Located right on Hennepin Avenue, the one really seedy street in downtown, it had a reputation as a tough bar. The rumor had even floated around for a while that it was the connection in Minnesota for the young farm girls who ended up on the streets of New York.

Tight black spandex pants that she danced in would be good, and she'd wear a loose red top. Right in keeping with the club. High heels and red lipstick. She went to the bathroom and, wetting her comb with a mixture of oil and water, slicked back her hair.

When she looked in her full-length mirror, she decided she looked like a dancer. Her body was more than revealed in her flashy outfit, it was provocative. Her tones and muscled legs looked longer than ever in the skintight pants. At the moment her bruised leg was numb from the cold compresses and felt fine. She wondered how long it would last.

The one other time Amy had been in the Flash Club was with a group of dancers. They had gone directly to the dance floor and taken over a part of it for themselves, danced for a couple hours, and then left. She had not noticed much else about the club.

The outer room, the one she walked into, had a horseshoe bar with several pool tables around it. Hanging over the pool tables were light fixtures that resembed a tacky whorehouse's with the customary red lights in them. Amy wondered how the players could tell which ball was red and which was white. The men standing around playing were a mixed group, from polyester suits to cowboy shirts.

She walked up to the bar and ordered a club soda with a twist. A solidly built man in corduroys and a paisley shirt turned to her at the bar and asked her what she was doing in a place like this all alone. He appeared to be in his late thirties and looked like he probably made money. All his clothes were neat and fit him perfectly, looked like they had been custom made.

'Looking for somebody.'

'Large, dark, and reasonably good looking?' He smiled and revealed a set of perfect teeth, nestled within a dark beard.

He seemed so confident she said, 'To tell you the truth, I go more for the blonds.'

Running a hand through his stick-brown hair, he sighed. 'God, don't tell me that. Let me buy you a drink.'

The bartender picked that moment to set down her drink.

'I've taken care of myself.'

Appraising her, he smiled, and it looked good on him. 'I don't doubt that. You seem more than able. Do you lift weights?'

'Just my own.'

'I wouldn't mind giving that a whirl.'

She laughed nervously, not knowing how to answer him.

'Do you want to go dance?' he asked her.

'Actually, I'm supposed to be meeting someone here,' she improvised, hoping he'd take the hint and leave her alone. 'I'm not sure they're going to show, but I'm going to go look around. Maybe later.'

'Yeah, make it sooner if you can.'

Leaving him at the bar, she went into the main room, which had a dance floor and the band. The dance floor was crowded and most of the tables were taken. Looking up onstage, she saw Luke. He was tapping his hand on his jeans in time to the song. His saxophone was hanging in front of him and he was staring into space. He looked like a statue, out of place onstage, separate. She knew she was still in love with him, that she had never stopped loving him. She wondered if it were too late, or if she could do anything about it. He seemed so far away.

Suddenly across the floor she saw Sandra dancing. Her long blond hair was down and she was swinging it from side to side in time to the music. The man she was dancing with looked slick and slightly weaselly. He grabbed Sandra around the waist and rubbed up against her.

The man from the bar walked past her into the room. Amy reached out and grabbed his arm and was amazed at the rock solidness of it. When he turned to look at her, she smiled and said, 'You know, I didn't introduce myself. My name is Amy.'

'Amy, glad to meet you. Just call me Ace.' He swallowed her hand up in his and then stood there holding it and looking down her blouse.

She wanted to get out on the dance floor, and this was her chance. 'I think I've changed my mind about dancing,' she told him. 'The music's too good to waste waiting for somebody who might not even show.'

'All right,' he said.

She led the way out on to the dance floor and maneuvered them fairly close to Sandra. Amy kept her back to her, as she didn't want Sandra to see her before the song was over. She wanted to get a chance to say a few words to her.

Ace was showing himself to be a moderately nimble dancer. He was one of those large people who have learned how to move their weight around so that it seems to float above their legs. Amy wondered what he did to keep himself in such good shape. As she studied the way he moved, it seemed familiar to her. Then she realized he moved like a boxer, with his hands, unconsciously, making little punching movements in time to the music.

'You're an incredible dancer,' Ace said.

Amy toned it down a little. Her leg was starting to ache. She wanted to get off it. She smiled at him and said, 'Thanks.'

'Are you like a professional?' he asked.

At first she was flattered, assuming he saw her talent and recognized a good modern dancer when he saw one, but then, when she saw he was staring at her body, she realized that he was talking about another caliber of dancer, one that often wore even less clothing than she had on at the moment. It was her own fault for wearing what she had worn. 'Just an amateur,' she said.

The song wound down and she moved in on Sandra. As it ended she managed to be right next to her. When Sandra turned, Amy was already facing her.

'Sandra, can I talk to you?'

Sandra grabbed the hand of the man she had been dancing with and pulled him close. 'Ted, this is Amy. Amy, this is Ted. I told you about him – the bartender at the IDS.'

'Nice to meet you. Sandra, could we talk for just a second?' Amy realized Ace was still standing there, next to her. 'Ace, could you excuse me?'

The two men moved off the dance floor as the next song started. Sandra and Amy stood near the edge and looked at each other. Sandra wound her long hair around her hand, raising it up off her back. She wouldn't look at Amy. Finally she said, 'Amy, it wasn't my fault. I just couldn't talk about it with the police. Listen, I'm in this pretty deep too. I was afraid he was going to arrest me. So I said I didn't know anything. I'm sorry.'

Amy knew the only way to get her to talk was to be understanding. 'I don't blame you. But I really wish you'd talk to Detective Towne. You could be a big help.'

Sandra was distracted, she kept looking at Ted. 'I should go. I don't want Ted to know I've had anything to do with the police.'

'Do you know that woman's name, the one you said would set Tricia up sometimes?'

'I really can't talk. Listen, call me at home. Or stop by at the IDS. I gotta go.' Sandra walked away.

Ace joined Amy just as the band was taking a break. Amy's leg was throbbing and she knew she should go home, but she wanted to talk to Luke before she did. She didn't think he had seen her, so as he came off the stage, she walked over to him. Ace followed. Luke was headed toward the bar and she called out to him. 'Luke!'

He turned and smiled when he saw her. 'Hey, what are you doing down here?'

'Mom said you called.'

As Luke came walking up, Ace put his arm around Amy's waist. She tried to move away, but before she could, Luke saw the casual embrace. He stopped a few feet away from them. Then he smiled again, but this time it was his professional smile, cold and empty. 'Hi,' he said and thrust his hand out to shake Ace's. 'Glad you could stop down.'

Amy introduced them, then asked, 'Why did you call?'

'No special reason, just wanted to see how you were doing.'

'I'm all right.' She didn't know what to say to him. She wanted to get rid of Ace, but didn't know how to do it without being rude. 'The band sounds good tonight.'

'Thanks. Well, I'm going to go get a drink. Catch you later.' And he walked away.

Disappointed, Amy watched him step back up to the

189

bar. Then she saw Hank coming toward her. He walked right up to her and gave her a big bear hug. 'Heard the news about your sister. It's a shame.'

'Hank, did you go over there Saturday night?'

'I did, but nothing was going on. She didn't seem to be home. Then I split for my folks.'

'I just wondered.'

Hank shook his head. 'I've been thinking a lot about her. Especially tonight. This is where I met her for the first time.'

'You met her here?'

'Yeah. That's how she happened to audition for the band. She was down here a few nights and we got to talking. Luke introduced us and I told her we were looking for a singer.'

'I didn't know she met you down here.'

'It's kind of a weird bar, isn't it? Some folks that hang out here have some strange sexual habits, if you catch my drift.'

Amy wondered if that was why Tricia had been hanging around this bar and, if so, how involved in the scene she had been. It would also explain why Sandra was here.

'Well, I gotta go. Luke runs a tight ship and I gotta make a visit to the john before we start up again.'

Ace was still hanging over her like a shadow. She saw Luke up at the bar talking to some woman with a very short leather skirt on. As she was watching, the woman reached out and touched Luke on the arm. Amy turned away.

Ace asked her, 'What happened to your sister?'

Amy thought quickly. She didn't want to tell him the truth, as she had a strange feeling about him. Maybe he had even known Tricia. She thought back over her conversation with Hank and was relieved they hadn't mentioned her name. 'She broke her arm. Nothing serious.' She looked around the bar one last time. 'You know, I'm going to go.'

Ace offered to walk Amy to her car. It was after midnight and Amy decided to take him up on his offer.

'Was that the blond you were waiting for?'

'Who?'

'That guy you were just talking to?'

'Hank? No.'

'So your guy didn't show up?'

She thought of Luke. He had been there but she hadn't really talked to him. 'That's right.'

'Are you upset?'

'Maybe.'

'You want to go get some coffee?' he asked hopefully.

'That's the last thing I need right now. I'm so wired I can hardly stand it.'

'I know something that would take care of that.'

She wondered what he was offering – sex or drugs. For a second she imagined what it would be like to be in bed with this huge mountain of a man. More for the wonder of it than anything else. But then she looked at him and shook her head.

'You're a very beautiful woman. And smart, I can tell that. I like smart women. Some men don't.' He moved closer to her and rubbed a hand on her shoulder.

He eased her up against the side of the car. 'We could have a good time together. I'd get you a little high, just to loosen you up a little, and then I know you'd catch on.'

'What are you talking about?'

He moved his hand down to the upper part of her arm and grabbed it, slowly applying pressure until it started to hurt. 'New ways of doing things. You're smart, you'd pick it up quick. I can tell by the way you dress that you want to. You're asking for it.'

'You're crazy.'

He laughed and let go of her. 'Maybe, but you are too.'

'I gotta go.' She opened her car door and slipped in.

He didn't seem upset that she was going. Bending down so he could look in the car window, he said, 'If you want to get in touch with me, talk to Suzanne. She knows how to get a hold of me. She's the woman who runs this place. Just tell her to get in touch with the Ace of Hearts. There's something in it for you too.'

As Amy drove away she wondered if Ace's Suzanne was the same woman whose telephone number had been left in Tricia's pocket. After all, Tricia had met Hank at the Flash Club. Maybe everything was tied in together.

When Amy reached the top of the stairs, she wasn't watching where she was going. Instead she was concentrating on her leg, which was throbbing. When she straightened up and looked at the door to the apartment, she saw a pocket knife stuck into the wood. Carved in the wood of the door were the letters *T*, *R*, and then *I*. The knife was dotting the *I*. It was a message she didn't want to read. It made her remember the knife handle sticking out of Tricia's body.

Amy had her key in her hand, so she went for the door, but the key stuck in the lock. She couldn't seem to turn it. There was a scuffling noise behind her and she tried to force the lock to turn. Her breath caught in her throat as she heard a low moan close by. As she was turning to run, a hand went around her neck. She jabbed her elbow into whoever was grabbing her, but she hit nothing, and the hand tightened to the point where she couldn't breathe. She was gasping for a breath that wouldn't come. Another hand slipped around her waist and she was caught in a tight grip. The man who was holding her smelled bad, like old socks and rotten food. She twisted in his arms to get a look at him.

'I told you not to do that.'

Even though it was a whisper, she recognized Chuck's voice. Her legs gave out and he was holding her. She gasped out, 'Chuck, let go off me.'

'You told the police and they hassled me. I might lose my job now.'

She had to keep him talking. His grip loosened slightly when he talked. 'Why?'

'It wasn't my fault about Tricia. I didn't do it. It was those other men that would come by all the time. I could see in their eyes what they were thinking about her.'

Amy started to try to slide out of his grip, but when she moved he tightened his hold. The hand around her throat was again cutting off her breath. She felt herself gowing faint, but she couldn't let herself pass out. She had to keep talking, reassuring him, fighting him in the one way that she could. Tricia hadn't fought and she had died. 'Chuck, I'm sure they believed you. I'll tell them that you had nothing to do with it.'

'You will?'

Again she felt him loosen his hold for a moment. 'Yes, just let go of me.'

'Amy, I never had such a good job before. Nobody better try and take it away from me. I mean it. It's all I've got right now.'

'Let go of me, Chuck.'

He let go and she fell against the wall by the door. He was staring at her with anger and resentment in his eyes. 'You're just like them. You never give a person a chance. Tricia never gave me a chance.'

All she wanted to do was run, but she stayed still and asked him, 'Where did the knife come from?'

'I didn't have anything to write with. I wanted you to know I was here. I always carry it around in my pocket.'

He reached up and pulled it out of the door. He was staring at it, not paying attention to her.

Amy stepped closer to the door and starting turning the key again. This time it moved easily in the lock and the door swung open. He reached out to grab her and she ducked under his arm and slid through the doorway. She slammed the door in his face and locked it.

'Amy,' he screamed outside the door. 'Come out here, I'll get you.'

'Chuck, leave now. Or I will call the police.'

'I have something to tell you.' He pounded on the door and she watched it jiggle in the frame. She had to stop him or he would break in.

'I'm calling the police. You'd better go or they'll take you away.' The threat scared him and she heard him lumbering down the stairs.

Knowing there was no way she could get in touch with Towne at this late hour, Amy dialed 911 and reported an assault. About fifteen minutes later two policemen stopped by and took a description of Chuck. She explained, without going into great details, about her sister's death and they checked around the building.

The younger one of them, who looked as if he might be her age, said, 'We'll keep our eye on this place tonight. Kind of make rounds and be sure no one's lurking around.'

'Thank you,' Amy said. 'I'll talk to Towne right away in the morning. I appreciate your help.'

The phone rang later that night as Amy was falling asleep. She sat up at the first ring and tried to shake the sleep away. At the second ring she stumbled out of bed and, without taking the time to turn on a light or put on any clothes, ran to answer it.

After she said hello, a woman's voice she had never

heard before spoke. 'Hi, I tried to call earlier and you were out and I figured if you were anything like me, you were out partying and a good time to call you would be late at night. I always stay up late.'

Amy could feel her mind working slowly, pulling itself out of the first stage of sleep, but she was not able to place the voice. She decided to admit her confusion. 'I'm sorry. Who is this?'

The husky voice started up again. 'You know, you called me. I got your message a few days ago, but sometimes I'm too busy to get right back to people. But I always write all my messages down. I don't forget about people. It's my business to keep track of all of that stuff. I'm Suzanne.'

Amy gasped and then turned it into a cough. Forcing herself to wake up, to sound energetic, she exclaimed, 'Oh, Suzanne, well thanks for calling me back. Yes, I called you a few days ago.'

'What can I do for you?'

'I heard you knew what was what in this town.'

'Well, I like to think that.'

Amy thought quickly about what to say next. 'I'm short of cash and could use some work. I wondered if you might know of anything.'

'If you're looking for some work, I might be able to line some up for you. How'd you get my name?'

Amy had known this would come up and decided to be vague and see if she could get away with it. 'A friend.'

'I'd like to meet you before I do any business with you. You understand. See what you look like. Talk over what you're willing to do. This all involves a certain amount of risk, and if I'm going to be putting myself out on the line for you, I want to know what you're all about.'

'You want references?'

A burst of laughter came over the line. 'That's a good

one. I can see you've got a sense of humor. Few people realize how important that is in this line of work. When do you want to meet?'

'How about tomorrow night?'

'Sounds good. Not too late, though, that's when it starts to get busy for me. How about eight o'clock at the Flash Club? You know that place.'

'Of course.'

Another gravelly laugh erupted. 'I've probably seen you before there, huh?'

'Who knows?' Amy wondered if Suzanne had been down at the Flash Club that night, if they had danced next to each other on the dance floor.

'OK. Tomorrow at nine.'

'Yeah, and I wanted to ask you, do you know Sandra?'

There was a silence on the end of the line. Then Suzanne asked, 'Is she the one who recommended me?'

Amy was caught. She didn't know what to say and she didn't want to alienate this woman in any way. 'She might have mentioned you, but that isn't where I got your name.'

'Where did you get my name?'

Amy decided to take a risk. 'The Ace of Hearts.'

There was a pause on the other end of the phone line, then Suzanne said, 'OK, that's good by me.'

In chest-deep water we play a game we call 'buckin' bronco.' One person is the rider and the other is the wild horse. The rider wraps her legs right around the horse's waist and then the horse dives underwater and thrashes and twists as hard and crazy as she can to get the rider off.

I am the rider and Tricia is the horse. She can never get me off, but I still let her try. We go under the water and I'm holding my breath while she wriggles between my legs. Then something grabs me from behind, a hand nips at my shoulder. Without thinking I let go of Tricia and turn. Peering through the stirred-up water, I see nothing, only murkiness.

Chapter 17

Todd and Amy sat in his car at the edge of the cemetery. They had been third in the procession that had driven from the church to the grounds. First the hearse with the casket, then her mother and father and Aunt Molly, and then Todd and Amy. Their neighbors and relatives had followed behind.

'This is worse than I thought it would be,' Amy said softly.

'Why?'

'Because everyone's here. It's such a public event. For some reason I didn't think of that.' Amy turned on the radio and then switched it off again. All she wanted to do was lay her head back and listen to the blues for an hour. She wondered who funerals were for and hoped her parents were feeling some relief from it. She wasn't. She didn't want to see her sister's body lowered into the ground.

'This is how us Americans mourn, with plastic flowers and false emotions,' Todd said, and turned to look out the car window.

'I don't know if the emotions are false, but I feel everyone watching me. You know, to see if I'm going to cry. I wish I knew where Tricia was. It sure makes you think about life after death. Wondering if I'll ever see her again, talk to her about anything. I don't think there is anything. I think we just get mixed back into the universe and diffused throughout. I've even wanted to believe in ghosts lately, just to get another chance to say a few things.'

'It looks like they're ready up there,' Todd said to Amy, and opened the car door.

'OK, you go up. I'll follow in a second.'

Todd got out of the car and climbed up the hill to the grave site. Amy stared at the dark-figured people circled around the grave, a huge wood-and-brass casket raised up on some kind of hoist. The pastor was standing at the head of the casket. Amy knew she had to get out of the car. They might even be waiting for her.

As she opened the door, she smelled falling leaves. It was late August, and although it was a very warm day, in the eighties, there was a sense of winter coming. A few dried leaves had fallen from the oak trees that shaded much of the cemetery.

She could remember riding her bike past here and sometimes stopping and walking among the graves for a while. There was something romantic about the old gravestones, the little burst of history chiseled into each one. The last story that would be told about many of these people. She wondered how many people would stop at Tricia's grave and wonder about her, why she had died so young, if she had had family, if she had married, what her life had been like.

Amy walked up the hill and stood on the outskirts of the gathering. The pastor was reading a passage from the Bible, an Old Testament passage, one of the Psalms. Her father had picked it out.

'The Lord is your keeper; the Lord is your shade on your right hand. The sun shall not smite you by day, nor the moon by night. The Lord will keep you from all evil; he will keep your life. The Lord will keep your going out and your coming in from this time forth and for evermore.' The pastor paused, then lifted up his head and spoke to the assembled group. 'Tricia was taken from us early and we will miss her, but we must remember that

199

the Lord is watching over her and she is with Him now. Amen.'

She looked around at the people gathered together. Many of them were friends of her parents and she didn't know them. But Dot had come and some of the dancers from the Dance Studio. Luke and Hank had come too. Luke's hair was slicked back and he was wearing a suit. He looked slightly uncomfortable in the outfit and younger than usual. She had noticed him in the church but hadn't had a chance to say anything to him.

She looked past the grave and saw that Detective Towne had made it, as he'd said he would. He was standing unobtrusively on the other side of the grave from her. Dark suit, dark tie, his hands folded, he looked more like an undertaker than a homicide detective.

Amy heard the pastor say something about 'ashes to ashes, dust to dust,' and believed it when she looked at the casket and thought how little of her sister it contained.

Her mother walked up to the casket and put a large bouquet of dark red roses on it. They seemed to make up for something, sprawled dark and beautiful across the gleaming wood. Everyone bowed their heads in silent prayer, except Amy. She had heard footsteps behind her. When she turned, she saw Danny and her first instinct was to yell out to Towne, but she kept quiet and let Danny walk toward her.

He had thrown a suit coat over a T-shirt and jeans. His face was marred by weeping. He had a fifth of something sticking out of the top of his suit-coat pocket. When he saw Amy, he began crying and walked up to her and put his arms around her. She wanted to pull away but didn't. He smelled like a bar. Patting his back, she looked to see if Towne had noticed.

He had. He was making his way around the periphery of the crowd. The pastor said 'Amen,' and people lifted their heads. As the crowd broke, she held on to Danny. When Towne was standing in front of them, she gave Danny a large cloth handkerchief she had brought for herself and made him dry his face.

'Danny, this is Detective Towne. He'd like to talk to you.'

Panic spread across Danny's face. 'I didn't kill Tricia. You can't put me in jail.' He broke away from Amy's embrace and went running toward the grave. Towne went after him, trying to cut him off before he got to the grave site. Somehow Danny managed to rush past him and get on the other side of the grave. Then he stopped and looked wildly around. Towne pulled out his gun and pointed it at him. 'Don't move.'

Someone screamed and Amy looked around for her parents.

'Danny, I have to take you in,' Towne told him.

Sobbing, Danny collapsed on the ground next to the casket. Towne rushed up to him and frisked him. Then he grabbed Danny under the arms and made him stand up.

'Give me one second.' Danny reached out and picked a bud flower off of the bouquet and put it in his pocket. He straightened up and stood for a moment in front of the casket. Towne walked up behind him and locked a pair of handcuffs on his wrists. He let Danny stand there for a moment longer, then he put a hand on his arm and said, 'Let's go.'

Amy felt her mother link her arm through hers. 'God's will be done,' Edna said.

There was a small gathering at Edna and Red's that afternoon. Todd and Amy went over and helped set up the food and beverages. People would walk up to Amy, take her hand, pat her shoulder, and tell her they were sorry and she would thank them. She found it ironic that she was thanking people when they said they felt sorry for her.

Todd and Aunt Molly hit it off. They started showing each other card tricks in the living room. Amy went in and sat by them and watched. Once she heard her mother laugh in the kitchen and Aunt Molly looked at Amy and said, 'It's going to get better now. The worst is over.'

But Amy knew the worst wasn't over. When they found Tricia's murderer her death would explode all over again. She wondered about Danny, what they were finding out from him.

She watched Todd shuffle the cards. His hands moved as gracefully as his feet moved on the dance floor. He had worn a light gray summer suit and a short-sleeve shirt. Once they were at her parents' house, he stripped down to the shirt and then opened it at the neck. He looked comfortable and seemed to be having a good time.

When he felt her eyes watching him, he looked up and winked. 'Watch out, we're going to start playing poker next and then I'll clean your aunt out of all her money.'

'You will, will you?' responded Aunt Molly. 'Cut the cards.'

Looking out the picture window, Amy saw Luke and Hank pull up in front of the house in his old Buick. Amy went into the kitchen to greet them.

'Hi, are you two hungry? We've got a ton of food.'

Luke looked a little embarrassed. He was sweating, and looked uncomfortable in his suitcoat.

'Let me take your jackets,' Amy said, and went to the refrigerator and grabbed them two beers. They handed her their coats and she gave them the beers.

When she came back out of her parents' room, where she had deposited the jackets, they were loading up their plates at the buffet. Standing by the kitchen door, watching Luke from the back, Amy found it so strange that he should be back at her parents' house on the occasion of her sister's death.

There was a pounding at the door, and when Amy went to see who it was, she saw Dot standing on the front steps.

'Hi, you coming in?'

'No, actually I've got to go back to the restaurant. I just wanted to stop by and tell you something.'

Since Dot didn't seem to want to come in, Amy went outside and stood next to her on the steps.

'You know, you've been trying to figure out who stopped down to see Tricia that one night. Well, it wasn't Danny. He was the guy the police dragged away, right? It was another guy who was at the funeral.'

'Who?'

'Young, blond.' Dot looked into the kitchen. 'Him,' she said, and pointed at Hank, who was still putting food on his plate.

Amy knocked her arm down. 'You mean Hank?'

'Yeah, he was the one who came in that night and Tricia left with him.'

'He's the guy in the band she was trying out for. It probably doesn't mean anything. Maybe they were just going to go over some songs. But thanks for telling me.'

'Just thought you might like to know. I'll see you later.'

When Amy walked back in, she found that Luke and Hank had gone into the living room. Hank was eating a sandwich, which he held in one hand while holding a poker hand in the other. She wanted to ask him about that night when he had gone to the Burger Delight and picked up Tricia, but not with everyone else around. Anyway, she decided, it was probably nothing.

Hank looked over at Amy and said, 'Well, I'm sure glad they caught that Danny. Luke was filling me in a little on their past history. Do you think he did it, Amy?'

For some reason it really bothered her that Luke should be telling Hank about Tricia and Danny; not so much that Luke had told something he shouldn't, but just that Hank would know more about Tricia than she wanted him to. 'Innocent until proven guilty. I guess I'll stick to that. Actually, there's a woman, Sandra, who mentioned some other guy to me. So who knows?' She turned away from Hank and asked Luke, 'You're not going to play cards?'

Luke looked at her. 'To tell you the truth, I don't think I know what you're supposed to do at a funeral.'

'No one does. I guess reminisce. Drink.' Amy held up her beer bottle and they clicked rims.

Luke gave a little laugh. 'Tricia would appreciate the drinking.'

'God, I guess so. She couldn't seem to live without it and it killed her in the end.' Amy heard her voice start to quaver at the end of the sentence. She stopped talking and took another swig of her beer. She had already had two and she was feeling a little muddled. It was the middle of the afternoon and she hadn't eaten anything. Her stomach closed down whenever she tried to introduce food into it.

'How are you doing?' Luke looked concerned.

'Just all right,' she said. 'I'd kind of like to get out of here.'

'Let's take a walk,' Luke suggested.

Outside, the air was thick with humidity. Amy kicked off her shoes and ran her feet through the grass. It felt cool on the bottoms of her feet.

'Where to?' Luke asked.

'Let's go down to the lake.'

The lake was about four blocks away. It was where she and Tricia had taken their swimming lessons while they were growing up. They had spent most of their summer days lazing around on the grass and sand and in the water.

204

Watching boys and reading magazines, comparing tan marks and listening to the top forty radio stations, that had been heaven for them as teenagers.

Some warm summer nights, she and Tricia would return and do another kind of swimming. They'd do a fast crawl out to the raft and then, diving under it, hang their suits on the supporting struts.

The slippery feel of the lake would shake up their already awakening bodies. Water touching every part of them was illicit and tender at the same time. Amy thought there could be no wrong in something so clean. But once Tricia's suit fell from the strut and sank to the bottom of the lake. She had to walk home in the moonlight with only a towel wrapped around her. They went in the basement door to avoid explanations.

Amy remembered floating on the water's surface in the moonlight before the fall of the bathing suit, offering her slight body up to the sky, and hearing the beat of the lake, as if it were pulsing with the two of them in it, a huge rhythmical organ that they were a part of; but, looking back, she wasn't sure if it were only the gentle lapping of the waves on the shore, or maybe, lesser still, her own small heart pounding in her water-filled ears.

'Did you go skinny-dipping when you were a kid?' Amy asked Luke as they kicked rocks, walking down the tarred street.

'Not when I was a kid. I think I did it for the first time when I went away to school.'

The lake appeared in front of them. It was late afternoon, so the beach was almost empty. Only one mother reading a magazine and her child playing in the water close by. Luke and Amy walked out to the end of the wooden dock, took off their shoes, and hung their feet in the water. The lake had turned silver gray and the sun glinted off it like pieces of broken glass.

'Dog days,' Amy said, breathing in the slightly swampy air that rose off the lake at the end of a hot sunny day.

'What does that mean anyway?' Luke asked.

'See that scum over there? It's only algae, but it starts to really grow in August and can sometimes turn a whole lake green. I always figured it meant that only a dog would be stupid enough to swim in the lake when it's like this.'

'Like mad dogs and Englishmen.'

'I don't know if that's where it comes from.'

Luke tickled her feet with his toes, then he screamed, 'Ouch.'

'What happened?'

'I think a fish bit me.'

'Probably. I remember one incredibly hot day Tricia and I came down here to escape the heat. I bet it was almost a hundred degrees. Well, when we stayed out of the water, the deerflies and horseflies bit us, and when we got in the water the fish bit us. It was pretty miserable. I guess everyone feels like biting when it gets that hot.'

Luke kicked up a huge spray of water. 'You're really missing her, aren't you?'

'Yeah. It hits me every once in a while. Hard.' She stared at the water and noticed that, as the sun lowered itself in the sky and took on a pink tinge near the horizon, the water was turning a rose color, like a white sheet with a trail of blood pouring over it.

Luke patted her hand and said, 'Don't forget you've always got your old pal.'

Amy closed her eyes and wished he would hold her again, put his arms around her and squeeze as tight as he could. As much as she wanted it, she was afraid to move toward him. She couldn't stand him not wanting to hold her.

Luke took his hand away and said, 'I've gotta go play tonight.'

Amy thought of her meeting with Suzanne. If Luke were going to be down there, it would make her feel so much safer. She realized she could hardly think about that meeting. She wanted to find out what Suzanne knew about Tricia, but didn't even know how she could ask the right questions. 'Where are you playing, at the Flash Club?'

'No, not tonight. We're back at the Times. Why don't you and Ace stop down?'

'Luke, I don't even know that guy. I came down to see you that night and he just asked me to dance.'

Luke looked off across the lake and smiled. 'I wondered. He didn't seem your type.'

'Oh? What is my type?'

Luke looked at her, then answered, 'I don't know if I've figured that out yet.'

Chapter 18

'You can just drop me off,' Amy told Todd as they neared her apartment. The sky had sunk into mourning and Amy shivered at the crisp air blowing through the car. They both had rolled their windows down to enjoy the cool air as night came on.

'Why don't you invite me in for a cup of tea or something?' Todd asked quietly.

'I don't have time. I'm meeting someone at eight and I'm going to be late if I don't hurry.'

'I'll make my own tea.' Todd parked the car in front of her house.

'You don't even like tea,' Amy pointed out, hoping he would get the hint and not come up; but she watched him turn off the car and open the door to get out. She didn't want to talk to him about Suzanne. She didn't want to try to explain to him why it was important to go see her. All she had left of her sister were little scraps of her life, shreds of evidence that she had lived, clues to how she had died, and Amy wanted to hoard all of them.

Now that Tricia was dead, it seemed even more important to Amy that she understand her. While she had been alive, there had always been the possibility of change, that she would turn over a new leaf, really quit drinking and getting into trouble, but there would be no more changes now. Tricia was frozen in time, and Amy realized that although she had seen hints of danger, for the most part she had only been aware of the surface of Tricia's life. The need to understand Tricia's life was about herself also. Who she was. What she might do. How far she would go. They were alike and she needed to know what made them the same and, maybe more importantly, how they were different. She didn't want to die like Tricia. She wanted to live and really live, fall in love with someone, not be caught up in the past.

'Thanks, don't mind if I do.' Todd was standing, waiting for her to get out of the car.

'OK, come on.'

'I don't imagine you want company wherever you're going.' Todd settled himself down on her bed.

'Want it but can't have it. I need to do this alone. Anyway, what happened to your new sweetheart? You haven't mentioned her lately. I mean, at least not today.'

'We broke up.'

'Well, that was one of the shortest relationships in history.'

'She thought I was just going to use her.'

'Were you?'

'I hadn't given it that much thought.' Todd laughed, then grew serious. 'I would like to fall in love with someone. It's been a long time. Speaking of which, how was your walk with Luke?'

Amy thought of Luke's toes tickling her foot, his hand resting on top of hers, nothing more, simple touching. 'I don't know if I want to talk about it.'

'Why not?'

'Because I don't know what's going on.'

'So why should that stop you trying to figure it out with your old buddy, Mr Relationship, who has somehow managed to avoid having an affair last longer than two weeks for about four years now?'

'I don't know. If he were just a guy I met, I'd feel more comfortable, but it's Luke. I feel so vulnerable around him.'

He stood up and walked to the window. Amy went into her closet and pulled on an outfit that wasn't too outrageous, a short skirt and a tight top, high-heeled sandals. She could put lipstick on in the car before she went into the bar. Todd had his back to her when she walked out of the closet. His shirt was wet along his spine in a kind of Rorschach print. The print looked like a huge hand to Amy.

She realized she hadn't told him about her decision to go ahead with the audition. 'I've decided to try out on Saturday. I even picked a piece of music for my improv. Maybe I'll be lousy. I haven't done more than warm-up exercises all week, but I'll give it a try.'

'Actually, not having worked out for a while might work in your favor.' Todd turned around and faced her.

Just then the phone rang and Amy rushed into the kitchen to answer it.

'Towne here.'

'Yes, this is Amy.'

'Well, I think we've got our man. Danny hasn't actually confessed but his alibi, a guy named Eddy, turned around and told us that Danny had in fact gone over to Tricia's house that night. I'm hoping he'll admit to it soon.'

'Oh.' Amy didn't know what to say. This was it. She knew who had killed her sister and it didn't make it any better.

'And I thought you'd like to know that we caught up with Chuck and threw him in detox, and after that he's going back into some kind of halfway house if I can arrange it.'

'Good.'

'I just wanted you to know.'

'Fine.'

'You'll tell your folks.'

'Yes.' She wondered if there was something more she

should say, like 'Good work, Detective.' It seemed like horrible work to her. He seemed to be waiting for her to react, but she couldn't.

'OK. Good-bye.'

Amy sat down on the floor. She felt too tired to cry, too distant from this new event. She stared at the linoleum tiles and remembered when she was a kid how she had loved to figure out the stories locked in the green swirls on the white background, the dragons she would imagine, the princesses, the castles, never had she imagined such a story of love and lust and death. Now the tiles seemed blank, only clouds sadly drifting away. Then she saw Todd's feet right next to the tiles she was staring at.

'What are you doing?'

'Shit, Todd. It looks like Danny killed my sister.'

Todd sat down on the floor next to her. 'At least you know.'

'Yeah.'

The phone rang again and Amy just looked up at it. 'Would you get that, Todd?'

'Hello,' Todd said, listened for a moment, nodded his head, and then said to Amy, 'She says it's an emergency.'

Amy hoped it wasn't Suzanne canceling their appointment. She still wanted to meet with her and find out a little about the life Tricia had been living. But it wasn't Suzanne on the phone, it was Sandra.

'Amy, I have to talk to you.'

'What's the matter?'

'I just need to talk to you, but I can't do it over the phone. Can you come over?'

'I can't right away.' Amy thought for a moment. She wanted to try to get down to see Luke tonight. The meeting with Suzanne shouldn't take very long, she decided. 'But I could be there by ten. Is that soon enough?'

'I hope so. Yes, that'll be fine.'

Amy took her address and said she'd see her later. She didn't let herself sit down again. It was nearly time for her to meet Suzanne. 'I gotta go.'

'I'll walk you to your car.'

The Flash Club was a different place early in the evening. The back room was empty and the front room was quiet. Without the crowd it looked tackier, shabbier. People rimmed the bar, talking and smoking and steadily drinking. The balls on the pool table bumped against the felt sides with a soft thudding noise. Amy stood in the doorway for a few moments, hoping someone would look up from the bar and wave. No one did, so she walked up to the bar and glanced at the people circling it.

She had an image of Suzanne in her mind. Bosomy, tall, black hair, long fingernails. No one resembled the witchlike creature she had fantasized, so Amy reevaluated the possibilities and looked around the bar again. Most of the women were talking to men and she thought Suzanne would be alone, waiting for her. Most of the women were really only girls, young, blond, and thin.

One, who was standing close to Amy, wore a halter top and her ribs showed through her skin in the back. She was wearing heavy makeup, but it didn't hide the fact that she was too young to be drinking in a bar. The man she was talking to was carrying about thirty extra pounds in a tight little wad on his stomach, restrained by a huge brown belt. From time to time he would try to fit a hand between the belt and his flesh, but would invariably have to give up. When he reached out and ran a pudgy finger down the jawline of the young girl, Amy wanted to reach out and yank his hand away. But the girl wiggled and closed her eyes.

'What's your pleasure?'

Amy jumped, then saw the bartender leaning closer to her, about to repeat his question, so she quickly ordered a gin and tonic. A summer drink, she thought. Then she turned to watch the door. A heavyset woman in a flowered dress came in and stopped for a moment, filling the doorway with her bulk. The bartender glanced over and shouted, 'Hey there, Suzanne. What's with you today?'

'Tony, give me a beer. I'm thirsty as they come or thirsty 'cause they come. Whatever.' Suzanne roared with laughter at her own joke and Tony giggled behind the bar.

Suzanne settled at the bar a few people away from Amy, so Amy walked over to her and said, 'Hi, Suzanne, I'm Emma. We talked on the phone.'

'I like that, punctual. It's a good sign. You're reliable. I can tell by looking.' Suzanne gave her a hard once-over. 'You got a clean look about you.'

'Is that a compliment?'

That set Suzanne off. She lifted her head back, laughing. 'Let's go sit at a table.'

Amy looked around the room and saw no tables. 'Where?'

'In the back. It's a little more private.'

Amy followed her into the back room. It was empty and dark. Suzanne switched on a light in a booth and they sat down. Looking closely at Suzanne's face, Amy saw she wasn't bad looking; even weighing too much, her bones showed through. Her hair looked as if it had been dyed about four months ago, as the band of dark-rooted hair was a couple inches long, tipped with golden straw.

'So what can I do for you?' Suzanne asked.

Amy took a sip of her drink, wanting to appear casual. 'Well, to tell you the truth, I was kind of hoping you could help me out. I'm new in town. I mean, I used to live here, but I went away for a while. I need some new connections and all, and I've heard good things about you. That you know what's going on.'

'I try.'

'Well, I could use some help.' Amy left it at that. She didn't want to explain too much.

Suzanne lit a cigarette and sucked on it hard. When she pulled it away from her mouth, the end was circled in red. 'Like what?'

Amy had been afraid of that. She didn't want to be too specific, but she didn't want to come off dumb either. Thinking about it on the way over she'd decided she would be daring and use Tricia's name. See what kind of reaction that evoked and find out what Suzanne knew about her. 'Actually, it was Tricia Curtis who mentioned you to me a few months ago. I called her from LA.' Amy watched Suzanne's face tighten up.

'Don't you read the papers?' Suzanne asked.

'I guess not. Why?'

'She died a few days ago.'

'God, that's awful. I can't believe it. How?'

'I'm not sure.'

'Did you know her well?' Amy forced herself to keep talking. Tricia's death must appear important, but not devastating.

Suzanne took a long sip of beer. 'I wouldn't say that. She did some work for me. I liked her, she could be a kick when she was laying off the brew. I have a feeling she did herself in.'

'Suicide?'

'Maybe not so thought out as that. I think she drank herself to death. Alcohol gets them all in the end.'

'I can't believe this. We were pretty good friends. She's one of the reasons I came out here. She said she'd be

214

around, and I couldn't figure out why I couldn't get hold of her.'

'I hadn't seen her in a week, but we had talked on the phone. Actually, I had just set her up with a guy who's a real good client. You know she's got family in town.'

Amy turned her head away. 'Oh, I don't think I'd want to talk to her family. It might be a pretty weird thing to do at a time like this.'

'So are you looking for some action?'

'Yeah. Can you find me some? I don't like to work the streets. The money's no good and you just can't be sure.'

'I'm not sure I've got anything for you.'

Amy had known this might happen. She consciously tilted herself forward so she was closer to Suzanne. 'I'm a good worker.'

Suzanne looked her over again, nodding slowly. 'You know, it takes a special kind of woman. A little warped, outside the world, the norm. Tricia was like that. She was so scared someone would see she was actually a pretty nice kid. She never wanted any of her clients to like her. Except this latest guy. I think she had a crush on him.' Suzanne pronounced the word crush as if it were a disease.

Amy took a large sip of her drink, realizing she had been holding her breath as Suzanne talked about Tricia, her sister, a pretty nice kid. Who had the guy been, Amy wondered. If Danny had known about him and how Tricia felt about him, it might explain why he had killed Tricia. Jealousy, not just rejection.

Suzanne put a hand on her knee. 'Do you do couples?'

Amy forced herself to smile. 'They're not my specialty, but I'd give them a try.'

'How kinky are you?' Suzanne placed a hand on Amy's wrist. The hand was enormous, the skin on the fingers

215

indenting for the knuckles, then bulging out like little sausages.

'I'll do bondage and moderate S and M. Fantasy stuff, I'm good at. Beggars can't be choosers.' Amy was watching Suzanne closely. She seemed to be buying it. She decided to push it again. 'How about that guy that used to hang out with Tricia?'

Smiling, Suzanne circled Amy's wrist with her hand and, slowly, as she was talking she started to squeeze and twist. 'Mmm. That's an idea. But he's kind of a special deal. He has quite specific tastes. You'd have to dress up. You got any leather outfits?'

'Boots, leather corset. I can make do.' Amy was trying to concentrate on her words, as her wrist was burning and she didn't dare look at it. Somehow she knew she wasn't supposed to show any pain. Suzanne was testing her and Amy wanted to pass the test, if for no other reason than to make it out of the room with nothing more than a sore wrist.

'I bet you'd look real cute in an outfit like that.' Suzanne released her wrist and patted it.

Amy let her hand rest where it was, feeling the blood rushing back into it. Her strongest urge was to stand up and run out of the room, but she fought it down and finished her drink. She wondered if the man Suzanne was talking about was Ace; for some reason she could picture him in the role of dominator.

'Might work out. I'll have to talk to him. See if he can work a clean-cut girl into his fantasies. Actually, that might just do the trick.'

'You probably shouldn't mention I knew Tricia. It might put him off.'

'I know how to handle my customers,' Suzanne snapped, then asked politely, 'Can I reach you at that same number?'

'Yeah, anytime. And I am like you, so call as late as you like.'

Suzanne pulled her hair back and took on an almost mannish look. 'How about going to work tonight?'

Amy looked at her watch. 'You know, I'd like to, but I actually have an appointment. I wasn't sure things would work out so well.'

'That's a shame. You know, sometimes you don't get another chance.'

Amy stood up. She wondered what it would be like, who Suzanne was thinking of setting her up with. In a way it made her scared and excited to think about it. She didn't want to leave Suzanne antagonistic, but she knew she couldn't do what she would have to do. 'I hope you'll give me another chance, because I know I'm going to enjoy doing business with you.'

Suddenly Suzanne wrapped an arm around Amy's neck and pulled her close. Turning her head toward Amy's, she kissed her. Without flinching, Amy felt wet lips, then a tongue lick her face. 'I'll be giving you a call.'

'That's fine. Anytime. Sorry about tonight.' Amy was horribly aware of how large Suzanne was and who would win in a tussle. Slowly she extracted herself from Suzanne's embrace, trying not to appear repulsed.

'You know' – Suzanne looked at Amy and then lowered her eyelids as if she were staring at the sun – 'you remind me of Tricia, and I can't figure out why.'

Sitting in her car, Amy found a Kleenex in the glove compartment and wiped her face. Finally, she looked down at her wrist and was almost sick. There was a raw red stripe circling it, just as there had been on Tricia's wrist when they were at the beach. What kind of relationship had Tricia had with Suzanne?

Sickened by this glimpse of what Tricia had been

involved in, Amy knew she never wanted to be alone in a room with Suzanne again. Amy couldn't believe she had been so blind to all that had been going on in Tricia's life. Thinking back, she could remember small incidents. A bruise on Tricia's neck. A tie left in her bedroom. Tricia had claimed it was Danny's, but Amy knew now it hadn't been. Tricia going from being short on cash, to buying a television set two weeks later. Amy had just figured she was doing really well at the Club.

Amy had gone through a promiscuous period in her own life, sleeping with men she hardly knew. She would find herself in a situation where it seemed easier to go to bed with them than to create a scene. Once she had even demanded that a guy call her a cab in the middle of the night so she wouldn't have to wake up next to him in the morning.

What made her behavior so different from Tricia's? Because she didn't accept money for her favors? Maybe she had been an idiot not to have taken anything, not even pleasure.

Amy wasn't sure what she would do if Suzanne called. She never wanted to go back to the Flash Club. She had a feeling if she did, she might not be the same woman when she left.

She looked down at her watch. It was almost ten-thirty. She needed to stop by Sandra's and tell her not to worry about talking to the police, that the chase was over and it looked like Danny had killed Tricia. That would make Sandra feel better, reassure her. She had sounded so anxious on the phone.

After that she would go and see Luke. She would sit quietly at the bar, out of his range of view, and watch him play. Have a couple drinks. Maybe something would happen between them tonight.

We watch the moon grow from a turned smile to a wide-open throat. When it is perfect, we know we must go. I have my favorite scarf wrapped around my hand. Tricia is clutching the turquoise ring that Dad bought her last summer in the Black Hills. We are sitting up straight at the foot of our beds with our bathing suits on under our pajamas. The TV blares until after midnight. Then the house goes still. We wait a little longer.

The night air slips against us like a wet rag. The grass in the front yard is covered with dew. Mosquitoes whine in our ears. We hold hands and run down the road. Ahead of us the lake glistens like a wavering moon. We leave our pajamas on the beach and walk out to the end of the dock.

Chapter 19

When Amy was driving over to Sandra's house, she saw
an auburned-haired woman walking down the sidewalk
ahead of her. For an instant she was sure it was Tricia.
She thought, we've made a mistake, that wasn't Tricia I
found dead after all, it was someone else. Tricia went on
a trip and now she's back and I don't have to worry
anymore. She sped up the car to get closer to the woman.
She'd stop the car, Tricia would turn around and smile,
then start laughing. Amy could hear the laughter, liquid
with a slight edge to it. But it only lasted a second, this
fleeting impression of the impossible manifesting itself in
the dark red hair and wide hips of a woman walking into
a grocery store.

Amy thought of going in after her, just to see what her
face looked like, but she didn't have time. It was ten
forty-five and she didn't want to be late; Sandra had
sounded upset.

Sandra lived on Oakland Avenue in a run-down house
that had once been a stately mansion in an upper-class
neighborhood, but as the rich families moved out to the
suburbs, south Minneapolis had declined, and the house
had been subdivided. Amy wasn't sure if Sandra lived in
the upper or lower duplex, but when she pulled up across
the street from the house, she noticed the lights were on
in the bottom floor.

Amy saw Sandra's name on the bottom mailbox and
assumed that meant she did live in the lower duplex. The
front door opened into a hallway and Amy walked up to

the large oak door off the hall. She knocked but as the door was already open a crack she stuck her head in the living rom. She looked around for a doorbell, thinking that would attract more attention than just yelling in, but there didn't seem to be one, or it was hidden so well she couldn't find it. She was surprised that Sandra would leave the door unlocked, because the neighborhood wasn't that safe.

'Sandra, hello?' When there was no answer, Amy grew anxious and thought of stepping back outside, but she knew she was being ridiculous. Sandra probably couldn't hear her in the back. That might be why she had left the door open.

Stepping into the living room, she ran into something. She let out a small shriek, then felt stupid when she saw it was just a floor lamp. The room was decorated much as it must have been in its heyday. Tasseled lamp shades, velvet couch, old wood buffet, Persian carpet. Very somber but effective. She wished Sandra would come bustling out from the kitchen or someplace. Music was playing in the back of the house.

'Sandra, I'm here,' Amy yelled, and then walked into the kitchen, where a coffeepot was being kept warm on the stove. That proved Sandra was around. Maybe she had gone downstairs to do her laundry. Amy reached out and touched the pot. It was hot. Amy thought of the open door of Tricia's apartment, then pushed the thought away. She poked her head into the hallway that led to the bedroom and bathroom and yelled again, 'Sandra?'

When there was no answer, Amy stood still in the kitchen and felt awkward. She didn't know this woman very well, and here she had walked right into her house. After hollering out Sandra's name again, she went down the hallway to the bedroom.

This time the room seemed to darken, then to shimmer.

221

In the naked glare of the overhead light there was no way to deny what she saw, a naked woman, tied up and gagged. This time there had been a struggle. Her eyes were open and the wrists were bleeding. She walked quietly up and touched Sandra's neck. Nothing moved in the room. No blood moved through her veins. The music was coming from a brown, squat radio right next to the bed. A woman was singing about a love that knew no bounds.

Sandra's brow was wrinkled and she looked as though she wanted to say something, but there was a gag in her mouth. No, Amy decided she didn't want to talk, she wanted to scream, and again within herself Amy felt a scream well up so large that it threatened to choke her unless she let it out. She opened her mouth and a noise as huge as an ocean swell roared into the room. It kept coming out of her mouth and then she drowned in it.

When Amy came to, she was staring up at the ceiling. Out of the corner of her eye she could see a hand dangling over the edge of the bed. Her head was nearly under the bed and it hurt as if she had cracked it on something as she fell. She got on her knees and crawled out of the room. She didn't want to stand up for fear she'd faint again and she didn't want to see Sandra. Dead Sandra. All she wanted to do was call Towne. She prayed he would still be down at his office.

Amy was sitting in the kitchen when the police arrived. Not wanting to touch the front door, she had just left it open. She was so relieved to see Towne when he came into the kitchen that she almost hugged him. But the look on his face stopped her. This was serious, it said, very serious.

He just looked at her and asked, 'Where?'

'Back in the bedroom.'

When he came out of the bedroom, leaving a crew of policemen at work, and sat down with her at the kitchen table, he was visibly shaken. 'OK, tell me, what are you doing here?'

'Sandra called me tonight. About two hours ago. Said she wanted to talk to me. Urgent. I had something else to do, so I didn't get here until about fifteen minutes ago. I found her exactly like that. I didn't touch anything except her neck. The door was open.'

'Amy, do you realize how serious this is?'

Amy could tell he was trying not to explode at her. 'Yes. I think so.'

'Well, in case you don't realize the implications, somehow you've managed to find another brutally murdered woman,' Towne said to her. 'How have you happened to be so lucky?'

The words jarred in Amy's stomach. She stood up to go to the bathroom, but realized that the policemen were swarming in the hallway and bedroom. 'Excuse me,' she said to Towne, and went outside.

A policeman stopped her at the door and she explained, 'I'm with Towne, but I need some fresh air.'

He nodded and she continued outside. She walked around the side of the house and found some rhododendron bushes. Bending over next to them, she threw up. She felt tears coming and wished she were six years old and someone would come and put her to bed. She straightened up and wiped her mouth with a leaf from the bush.

There was no question about this one, Amy thought. She had found another dead woman. Sandra had been killed in the same way as Tricia, although there was no knife this time. Sandra had been afraid when she had talked to Amy on the phone that night; maybe she'd known that this might happen.

Suddenly Amy sensed that someone was watching her, and in her mind she conjured up a tall man with black gloves and black eyes, standing in the shadow of the house. She felt defeated by him. When she had found Tricia, even though she knew someone else was responsible for Tricia's death, it still seemed that her sister had willed it on herself. That she had somehow given up on living and that the man had only played a minor part.

But Amy had seen that Sandra had fought her killer. She had not wanted to die. And now Amy felt something hovering around her. If there were a man standing under the shade of the eaves, she didn't know what she would do. She turned and saw the policemen, who had been standing guard at the door, looking around the corner of the house.

'Are you all right?' he asked.

She stifled a gasp, and said she was fine. Walking past him into the house, she felt as if she had left something behind her in the bushes.

Just as Amy was about to enter the kitchen, she heard Towne talking about her to another policeman and stood quietly outside the door, listening.

'I'm getting concerned about her. She seems to know more than she's letting on or else her intuitions are awfully good. This guy, whoever he is, isn't messing around. And we don't know if he knows that Amy exists. What do you think?' Towne asked the cop.

'Think there's any chance she could be involved with the murders?'

'No, it wouldn't make any sense. Why would she stay at the scene of the crime?'

'Maybe she's nuts,' the policeman suggested, then walked back toward the bedroom.

Amy backed away from the kitchen and thought of leaving, but that might really make them suspect her of something. She made some noise in the living room and then walked back to the kitchen. Towne was sitting right where she had left him. She looked at Towne and asked, 'What about Danny? He obviously couldn't have had anything to do with this.'

'We have no evidence that the two murders were done by the same person.'

'You couldn't get Sandra to talk and now look at where she is. I think she knew something and she was killed so she wouldn't have the chance to tell anybody.'

'Maybe. I'm just pointing out that this might have been done by someone else and not be connected to your sister's murder at all.'

'I don't think so, and I don't think you do either. When I talked to Sandra the other night, she was scared from the moment she heard that Tricia had been murdered. I think she might have known who it was and didn't want to say, because she didn't want anything to happen to her?'

'But wouldn't telling us have safeguarded her?'

'Not if there were more than one person involved.'

'I wish she'd talked to us. You might be right. Maybe Danny was working with someone else.' Towne rubbed his gray hair back. 'This one is going to hit the news hard. We've been able to keep back some of the info on Tricia's case, but now it's all going to have to come out.'

'Would you let me in to see Danny?' Amy asked.

'Why?'

'I want to ask him some questions about Tricia. Did you ask him if he knew Sandra?'

'No, I didn't know how important she was.' Towne thought for a moment. 'Come tomorrow and I'll let you in to see him for a few minutes.'

'Thanks.'

'Oh, we got some information on that Suzanne. She was picked up for soliciting once. That was a number of years ago. The charges didn't stick. She's now the owner of the Flash Club. She appears to do things on the up and up. Did Tricia ever waitress for her?'

'No but she hung out at the Flash Club a lot.'

'It's quite a scene. A lot of the pros hang out there and take their customers to the hotel next door.'

'Could you talk to Suzanne?'

'Why?'

Amy touched her wrist. It was very tender and sore. She wanted to see Suzanne scared. 'I think both Sandra and Tricia might have worked for her. Not as waitresses.' Amy looked down at the floor. She was finding it hard to say what she had to say. 'I think they were tricking for her.'

She left shortly after telling Towne about Suzanne, but didn't want to go home, then remembered she had promised Luke she'd stop by. The thought struck her that there was a chance the killer knew she had been planning on stopping over at Sandra's. She drove over to the Times Bar and sat outside, watching couples walk in and out, arms around each other, drinking, laughing, partying.

She slipped into the Times while the band was playing and went and sat at the bar, where she could see the band but they would probably not notice her. Even though her stomach felt queasy, she ordered a Scotch and soda, a clean drink, she thought. All she knew was she needed something. She watched Luke and tried to relax, clear her mind of distorted faces, Sandra's and Tricia's, death masks, and the one face she couldn't see, just felt watching her, maybe even now. The bar was close by Sandra's; maybe the killer needed a drink too. Stop it, she said to herself, listen to the music. The last song of the set wound down, the saxophone growling at the end, and then the band went on break.

Luke sat down at a small table right next to the stage. He was drinking coffee and reading a book when she walked up.

'Hi,' Amy said, and sat down at the table with him. 'It's not too dark in here to read?'

Luke looked over at her and smiled. 'All right. I was about to give up on you.'

'Don't do that, Luke.'

'Well, I'm glad to see you.'

Amy looked at him and said, 'I'm glad to see you too.'

'Can I get you a drink?'

'Actually, I would like a Scotch.'

'I'll be right back.' He walked up to the bar.

Hank came up to the table and put a hand on her shoulder. 'Well, this is a surprise. Twice in one day. So what happened with Danny? They put him in jail?'

'Yeah, they're booking him on suspicion of murder.' Amy didn't mention that she had her own suspicions. It did look like Danny killed Tricia, but then who killed Sandra?

'That's great that they finally caught him. I never trusted the guy.'

Amy was surprised. 'I didn't know that you knew Danny.'

'Oh, I don't really. Just some of the things Tricia told me about him. He sounded like a real weasel.'

Luke walked up and asked, 'Who's a weasel?' He handed Amy her drink.

She told him. 'Danny. The police think he murdered Tricia.'

'God, that's really unbelievable, isn't it? I can't conceive of someone doing that. I guess when you read it in

227

the paper it's just words on a page, a flat story, but knowing Danny, it means it can really happen. How does that make you feel?' Luke asked Amy.

'I don't quite believe it. Somehow I can't accept that Danny did it, although I guess I'll have to.'

Hank seemed interested. 'Why?'

'Maybe it's just like Luke was saying, you read about stuff and you know that people kill people, but this was the man who went out with my sister and supposedly loved her for years. How could he turn around and murder her?'

'Maybe things just got out of control for him,' Hank said. 'I'm going to step outside and smoke a little reefer. You care to partake?'

'No, thanks,' Luke answered for both of them. When Hank left, he turned to Amy. 'I'm glad you stopped down. You must not feel too much like going out these days.'

'It depends. Sometimes I just need to get out and stop thinking about Tricia. I wanted to thank you for coming to the funeral. It meant a lot to me that you were there.'

'Sure. So how are you?'

'God, I don't know, Luke. I could really stand to talk to you for a while. You're not going to believe this, but another woman was murdered tonight, and I found her too.'

'Shit, Amy, what are you talking about?'

'A friend of Tricia's. She called me to come over and talk to her, and when I got to her apartment, I found her dead. Like Tricia. Same setup, bound and gagged.'

'What is going on? I can't believe it. Is there a connection?'

'The police aren't sure. They do think Danny killed Tricia. They don't have any ideas about this one yet, at least not that I know of.'

'I've got one more set to play. Will you wait for me?'

'Yes.'

He got up to play and Amy sat and stared at him. The sleeves of his shirt were rolled up and she could see the soft skin on the inside of his arm. When he played, the muscles of his arm and in his neck flexed.

Once she got up and went into the bathroom to make sure that she looked all right. She brushed her hair back and looked at her face. She opened her mouth and looked at her teeth. They were slightly crooked. She put some lipstick on and then didn't like the way it looked, so grabbed a paper towel and wiped it off. She touched her lips and wondered if Luke would kiss her.

When the set was over and Luke was packing up his horn, Hank walked over and asked Amy, 'Do you need a ride home?'

'No, thanks. Luke and I are going to get some coffee or something.'

He lifted his eyebrows, 'Or something. Huh? Sounds good.'

She didn't like the way he said that, but she just nodded. Luke came up and they walked outside. Out in the parking lot he turned to her and asked, 'So where do you want to go?'

'Well, actually, I'd rather go to your place than a restaurant. I'd feel more comfortable talking there, than out in public.'

'OK, you know where it is. I'll be right behind you.' He walked her to her car and then followed her to his place.

When they walked up the stairs to his apartment, Amy recognized the smell of the entryway. It had always reminded her of her old apartment building, a little moldy smell mixed with dust and smoke.

They walked into the kitchen and she sat down at the

229

table while he made the coffee. It had changed a little. There were red-and-white curtains in the window, probably Angela's doing. Amy didn't like seeing the traces of another woman in his life, but she had to face them. For two years she hadn't been in his apartment, and now she was. Whatever it meant. Whatever she wanted it to mean. She wanted to be here with him. It seemed right and natural. Drinking coffee late at night.

'So what happened tonight?' he asked her, sitting down next to her at the table.

'Do you know Sandra? I saw her down at the Flash Club when you played there.'

'Blonde. I think I know who you're talking about. She used to hang out with Tricia?'

'Yeah, that's her. Well, she called me tonight when I got back to my place. Wanted to see me. She sounded anxious, scared. But I didn't know what was going on. I didn't know why she was afraid. When I got over there, I found her naked, bound and gagged.' Amy was staring at the windowpane, which was reflecting her own face, over which she was seeing Sandra's. 'Maybe she was strangled, maybe she just choked on the gag, but she was dead. I knew right away. Her eyes were open and it was horrible. Luke, I'm afraid. What if the guy knows about me?'

Luke put an arm around her. 'Don't worry about it right now. You're all right. The police will find him. Do you want to stay here tonight?'

She nodded her head. Luke reached out his hand and ran it across her face, touching her as if he were blind and he needed to feel her to really see her again. Then he lifted her chin up and kissed her. Time was blurring. They had done this before. She remembered and felt it happen again. It was the same, even with a layer of time in between. It was happening twice, in her mind and in the kitchen with the coffee on the stove. They were kissing each other and his arms were around her. She wanted him to be so close to her.

'Amy,' he said, and she shivered as if someone were calling her from a long way away. He pulled her up out of the chair and they were standing, locked together, rubbing against each other. His hands were up under her shirt and she pulled his shirt out from his jeans. An image of Sandra shot through her mind, so she opened her eyes and looked at Luke. It was all right. She was safe in his arms.

Then, as if he were blessing her, Luke's hands cupped her head and he pulled her close, kissing her face, her eyes. He took her shirt off and kissed her shoulder. They shed the rest of their clothes quickly. He pushed her against the kitchen table, then lifted her up and set her on it.

Whispering in her ear, he said, 'I want to make love to you.'

'Yes, please.' She sighed, and wrapped her arms around him more tightly.

He took his time. He always had. Making sure she was ready. It had been a contest between them. He loved to hear her ask for it. She would try to stay quiet, hold off, make him wait too. But then a moan would rise out of her like a bubble, she would feel all fizzy inside, her legs growing weak, and she would say, please.

For a moment, they stayed locked together, not moving. All that moved was the kitchen around them, the air swirling. It was dancing. He led, she followed, and when he stopped, sucking in air, she grabbed his waist and pulled him onward. She was saying, yes, yes, and he was humming low. Then the world expanded and contracted, she felt him grab her, and she saw her toes were pointed, a sign, Luke had figured out years ago, that she had come. Luke let out a long, soft sigh in her ear and held her tight.

They stayed up late, drinking coffee, talking more about Tricia's and Sandra's murders. She told him about Suzanne and he told her to stay away from that woman. He told her a little about Angela, but said it was really over. He said he'd known it was when she came and destroyed her avocado plant. She had grown it from a seed in the kitchen window and he had thought she might leave it for him, but she had come back once when he wasn't there and uprooted it and thrown it in the trash.

They slept with their arms around each other, and once Amy woke in the night and watched him breathe. It seemed a miracle that he was living on an invisible substance drawn from the air. She matched her breathing to his and went back to sleep.

Chapter 20

In the morning a bright light shining in her face woke
Amy and she sat up to find the sun streaming in through
the window. Luke was sprawled over two-thirds of the
bed and had pulled a pillow over his face to block the
light. The sheet wound around his body, leaving one leg
and most of his chest uncovered.

'Luke, I've gotta go,' she whispered, not really wanting
to wake him, but not wanting to leave him without saying
something.

He struggled out from under the pillow. 'Where can I
reach you later?'

'I'm going down to the police station now, but I should
be at the Dance Studio around five.'

'OK, maybe I'll stop by there.'

She leaned down and kissed him good-bye. Rubbing
her face against his, she wanted his smell to stay with her,
hair and dirt and rain.

'When you get down there, they'll have to call up here to
be sure I said it was OK. You'll only be allowed fifteen
minutes.' Towne was sitting at his desk, a tie dangling
loosely around his neck, his shirt-sleeves haphazardly
pushed up to his elbows. He wasn't looking at her as he
was speaking.

'Thank you.'

'Don't mention it.' Towne said the words as if he really
meant them.

Amy stood looking down at him, but instead of noticing
her, he started to shuffle some papers on his desk, 'Listen,
I had no idea what was going on with Sandra. I hardly

knew her at all. She was a friend of Tricia's. She called me, not the other way around.'

'Sure.' Finally he looked up at her and she saw that he wasn't mad, his eyes were sorrowful. 'Amy, get out of this. I don't want to find another young woman killed on her bed. Especially not you.'

'I will. But I want you to know that I had nothing to do with Sandra's death. Tricia was my sister and I do feel somewhat responsible for what happened to her. Maybe I didn't do enough to help her. All I know for sure is I don't ever want to see another dead person as long as I live.'

Amy turned to leave, but before she could go Towne asked her, 'Why do you want to talk to Danny?'

'I want to ask him a few things about Tricia. I want to know what was going on with her.'

Towne's voice dropped as if he were telling her a secret. 'You know, he hasn't confessed to anything yet. He claims he's innocent, that he's being framed.'

'Is he?'

Towne looked blank, then said, 'I'm not ruling it out, but I doubt it.'

The Hennepin County Adult Detention Center was down two floors from the homicide division, which meant it was actually located below the streets of the city. There was a waiting room outside a huge steel door, and a number of people were filling the chairs. It was almost one o'clock, and the sign posted on the door gave the visiting hours from one to three P.M. Another sign said, NO PURSES, HANDBAGS, PACKAGES, CONTAINERS WILL BE ALLOWED. It almost looked like a doctor's office, except instead of the friendly smile of a nurse, there was an armed police officer watching the waiting room.

Amy walked up to the window, which looked like a

drive-in banking window: the thick plastic glass, the space under the window to slide information through, and a grill. A blond woman in a police uniform glanced up at her.

'I'm here to see Danny Swenson.'

The woman checked a list of names. 'He's only allowed to see family members and his lawyer. Are you a member of his family?'

'No, but I have special permission from Detective Towne in homicide. You're to call him.'

The woman turned away, picked up a phone, and dialed a number. She spoke for a second, nodded her head. Then she turned back and said, 'You're Amy Curtis?'

'Yes.'

'Can I see a photo ID?'

Amy slid her driver's license under the window and waited. The woman looked from the picture to Amy.

Amy felt self-conscious and explained, 'I had longer hair then.'

The woman said, 'Step up to the door.'

Amy waited at the door until a loud, grating buzzer went off and stirred everyone in the waiting room. She walked through the door and found herself in another lounge area. She didn't know what she would say to Danny. All the questions she should ask him seemed futile.

Another police officer asked her, 'Who are you here to see?'

'Danny Swenson.'

'You don't have a purse?'

'No. I didn't bring it with me.'

'May I check your pockets?'

Surprised at the question, Amy just looked at him. She felt as if it were a violation of some part of the constitution, but she had placed herself in this position and she had to let him pat her down. 'Of course.' Amy lifted her hands up and the officer slapped his hands down her sides.

Then he waved her to a table. 'Have a seat and I'll bring him right in.'

When Danny walked into the room, he didn't look good: his skin was pasty gray and his eyes were watery. He sat down in a chair across a table from her and looked at her. She stared back at him. She guessed the guard would stop her if she reached across the table and started shaking Danny. There was so much she wanted to know, and she had the urge to beat it out of him. 'Why did you do it?' she finally asked.

'Amy, I didn't do it. No one will believe me, but I didn't.' His voice was a whisper, as if he had used it up talking.

Somehow, looking at Danny, she wanted to believe him. He looked worn away, bone showing through, pushed to a point where it would be hard to lie anymore. But maybe he was just better at it than she could imagine. Maybe it was his desperation that was making him look so truthful. He could be so scared of what he had done and what might happen to him, that he actually believed he didn't do it.

Finally she said, 'Then why did Eddy say you did?'

'I can't quite figure it out. I thought we were friends. I knew he didn't like the police, but I didn't think he'd do this to me. I wish I could talk to him. I think I could get the truth out of him.'

'You don't look so good.'

'I need a drink. I haven't had one in twenty-four hours and I had been hitting the bottle pretty hard before that. I've never been in detox.' He looked around the room and then started cracking his fingers, one after another. The noise made Amy think of small twigs cracking, someone walking through a forest, lost. 'I guess this is what it's like. Going on the wagon. Tricia sure hated it. Now I can see why.'

'Yeah. Danny, I'd like to ask you a few questions about Tricia. I've figured a few things out and I want to know how Tricia started being a prostitute. How did it all happen?'

'Oh, God, she wasn't a prostitute exactly,' Danny said, turning around and looking back at the door he had just walked through as if he wanted to leave already.

'What was she exactly?'

'All right, she took money for sex, but she wasn't a real prostitute.'

'Why don't you want to admit what she was? Would that make you her pimp?'

Danny looked straight at her and spit out the words. 'Why didn't you want to see what she was? I loved her, too, you know.'

'OK, I'm sorry. How did she get involved in whatever she was doing?'

Danny shook his head and Amy waited, unsure whether he was signaling he couldn't talk about it or was trying to clear his head. Then he looked at the ceiling and began talking. 'I just keep thinking about it. Like I could have stopped it. Especially at the beginning.'

'When was the beginning?'

Danny shook out his hands. 'You don't want to know this stuff. She's dead.'

'Yes, I do, Danny. I've gotta know it. I'm her sister. I suppose you've told a lot of this to Towne, because I know they've been questioning you, but I want to hear it from you. Please. It would help me. I've got to understand what happened to her. Even if it's really bad. Please, Danny.'

When Danny didn't say anything, Amy asked, 'Tell me how it all started.'

Danny licked his chapped lips and said slowly, 'She started doing it when we were out in LA. God, when I think back. I encouraged her, because we were really low on money. She had lost a gig singing, because she was getting too damned drunk. I didn't know how to stop her. The band loved her, but they finally got sick of having to prop her up onstage. So one night she went to a bar and when the guy sitting next to her started buying her drinks, she asked him if he was interested in a little action. He was, so I guess they went to his hotel room. We actually had a good laugh about it. I didn't think it would go any further. It seemed like such a good trick at the time. Brought in a little money, didn't hurt anyone.' Danny sunk into his chair and stopped talking.

While Amy was listening to him, she was staring at the large round clock that was right in the middle of the wall behind him. The second hand smoothly ticked away the seconds while she heard the story of Tricia's other career. If only time would stop for a moment, she might be able to absorb what she was hearing. But she had already been here five minutes, so she had to keep Danny talking. There was a lot more she needed to know. 'Then what happened?'

'I don't know. She just kept doing it. We needed money bad. She was drinking all the time. She'd go to bars and guys'd buy her drinks and then she'd bring them home.'

Danny cleared his voice, which was growing stronger as he remembered more. 'At first she would call ahead and tell me to leave for a few hours, but then she started to just bring them home. I would go get a drink or sometimes just watch TV in the other room. One night I left and she got roughed up. She blamed me for not being there, and that's when she came back here.'

'Yeah, I remember picking her up from the airport, but she didn't tell us any of that.'

'It wasn't my fault. I should have stopped her, but we needed the money. For a while it was a game and seemed to make things between us better, you know what I mean. We weren't so worried about money, we got along. But then she started to turn on me. She didn't want to share the money. She claimed she was doing all the work. She would go out and blow it in one night, drinking, buying clothes, tipping cab drivers twenty dollars and then pro-positioning them. That was in LA.'

'Then you followed her back here?'

'Yeah, and it changed when I got back here. Tricia settled down. She swore she wouldn't do it anymore. That's when she was working at the Club. She was good for a while.' Danny sighed, remembering. 'But she seemed to miss it. She said it was exciting, a kind of drug. She said she never knew what was going to happen.'

'So she started up again?'

'Yeah.'

Amy wanted to crack off the hands of the clock or, better yet, Danny's hands. Why hadn't he stopped her? How could he have slept with her after all those other men? One thing Amy knew for sure was how much she had loved Tricia, and no matter what she had done, nothing would change that. It just meant that she hurt more and more for her sister and couldn't do anything about it. It was so much too late.

She didn't want to hear anything more about her starting up again, so Amy asked him some of the questions she had thought of beforehand. 'Did you know Sandra or Suzanne?'

'I met Sandra once at the IDS. She and Tricia were pretty good friends.'

'What about Suzanne?'

'You mean the woman who owned the Flash Club,

right? Oh, I knew Suzanne. Tricia started hanging out there and through someone, I think Suzanne, got introduced to this guy. She told me at first he was a date. What she meant was he was a *date*. Once a month or so she'd spend the night with him. I think he was rough on her, she wouldn't talk about what they did. She said it had nothing to do with her and me. I believed her. Sometimes Suzanne would call her up and arrange the dates. But when Tricia got fired from the Club, she cooled out for a while. I thought she wasn't seeing him anymore. Then all the trouble between us started up. There was no pleasing her.'

'That's when she wanted to break up?'

'Yeah.'

'So when was the last time you saw Suzanne?'

'Not very recently. In fact, I think she and Tricia had a falling out. She started to call and threaten Tricia.'

'Why?'

'The only thing I could make out was that Tricia was going behind her back seeing some guy.'

'Did you ever meet the guy, or do you know his name?'

'She wouldn't tell me much. She just called him some crazy fairy-tale name. Said he was a real prince.'

Amy was quiet, thinking of the woman she had never known and how this woman had been her sister.

'I should have made her stop. I knew how crazy she could get. But I was getting tired of fighting. She would provoke me, oh, God, how she could do that. The things she would throw in my face.' Danny cracked his fingers again and then planted his hands on his knees. 'I loved her, you know, I really loved her.'

'I know you did. You did what you could. I did too. We both loved her and it didn't help.' Amy glanced up at the clock again. She had only a few minutes left. 'Tell me about Sandra, what did you think of her?'

240

'She was all right.'

'Were she and Tricia friends?'

'I guess so. She seemed like a real tease to me. She and Tricia partied a lot together. They'd go out drinking after work. But when Tricia was fired from the Club, Sandra didn't seem to want to hang around with her much. I think it hurt Tricia.'

'Well, she was killed this morning.'

'Shit. Was it connected to Tricia's death?'

'I think so. It was done the same way.'

'Listen, Amy. Doesn't that prove I'm innocent? You know I asked you to meet me the other day at the bridge. Well, I had a feeling about Eddy and I was right. Somehow I was worried he would do this to me. Would you go talk to him?'

'God, Danny, what good could that do? The police have already taken a statement from him. Why would he lie about you going over to Tricia's that night?'

Danny laced his fingers together and told her, 'Because we were doing a cocaine deal together. He doesn't want to have to split the money with me. It's a real easy way to get rid of me. The police did his dirty work for him. I bet he's laughing all the way to the bank.'

'How much are you talking about?'

'Twenty thousand at least. Please, go see him. Listen, tell him I'm going to implicate him if he doesn't come clean. That'll scare the shit out of him. He lives at Two-twelve Smith in St Paul. It's about three blocks from the Cathedral.'

'I don't know, Danny. I really don't like the idea of going to see him.'

'Amy, I didn't kill Sandra and I didn't kill Tricia. If you believe me at all, even a little, that I didn't kill Tricia, then you've gotta see that someone else did. And that someone else is walking around free while I'm sweating and stinking behind bars. The police won't look any further. They think I did it. If Eddy would just come clean, maybe they would find out who did do it.' Danny put his hands out, palms up. 'I know you never liked me very much. I know it. But do it for Tricia, for God's sake.'

I'm shivering partly from the cold air and water, but also from the night. But I did it, I jumped off the dock and swam down to the bottom of the lake and left my scarf on the sand for them. Now it's Tricia's turn. 'I don't wanta, Amy.' 'Chicken, chicken. Bock-bock.' 'I'm scared they'll get me.' 'No, they won't. They're waiting for you. This is your chance to do it. If you don't then they'll get you. But you're safe now.' 'I can't.'

'Do you want me to push you in?' I put a hand behind her. 'No, Amy, don't.' I start to walk away. 'Well, OK, I'm going home.' I take a few more steps down the dock. 'I'll do it. Come back. I'll do it.' Tricia screams. 'Would you be quiet, dummy. Just do it.' So she jumps in and I wait. The night spins around quietly. The lake dimples and sways. She doesn't appear. It's taking too long. She isn't coming out of the water.

Chapter 21

Smith Avenue was being renovated, but somehow the block that Eddy lived on had been overlooked in the process. A small pharmacy and a derelict building framed his house. Amy parked the car across the street and sat in it for a while. She hadn't promised Danny she would talk to Eddy. She could still leave if she wanted to. But Eddy had known Tricia and maybe he would tell her something that would let her know what had happened. It was worth a try.

She knocked on the door and got no response. Knocking harder, she waited and listened to see if she could hear anyone moving around inside. She thought she heard footsteps, but she wasn't sure. Taking a few steps back, she looked at the front window. It was covered with a black curtain. A shadow image appeared behind it, a face with no features. It reminded her of her nightmare, the face she couldn't make out. Before she could turn away, a thin face stared out at her, then let the curtain drop. The door was opened by a man with a polyester shirt unbuttoned to the belly and a meager chest with a few hairs showing through. Amy smiled at him and he opened the door wider.

'Who sent you?' he asked.

'Are you Eddy?' she inquired.

'Yeah.'

He was staring at her, waiting for her to give the password. She grabbed a name and used it. 'Suzanne gave me your name,' she said, and waited for him to motion her inside.

He stared at her for a second, then moved aside, saying, 'Suzanne, yeah, she's all right.'

The room she stepped into was a combination living room-bedroom. A futon on the floor served as both bed and couch, and the TV was on.

'I'm watching my favorite soap opera. You like the soaps?' he asked.

'Yeah, but I don't have a favorite.'

He reached up and turned the set off. 'So what can I help you with?'

She remembered what Danny had told her about their drug deal. 'Cocaine?'

He flashed a smile. 'Come on and sit down. Just got a new shipment in. How 'bout a little toot? Then we can talk business.' He reached under the futon and brought out a small vial and a mirror with a hundred-dollar bill rolled up on it. He dumped out a small mound of white powder and began cutting it with a razor. 'This is good stuff.'

Amy had done cocaine a couple times before at parties. It was the last thing she wanted to do with Eddy, but she decided to play along. She sat down next to him on the lumpy futon. Maybe it would make him get loose and tell her a little more. So when he held out the mirror, she bent her head and sniffed up a line of the cocaine. He did the remaining three lines and then looked over at her.

She tasted a metallic bite in the back of her throat and stifled a sneeze.

'Good blow, huh?' Eddy asked.

'Yeah, how much for a lid?'

'What you talking? Coke doesn't come in lids. You're not a fucking narc, are you?' He pushed her down on the futon and held her there.

'Get away from me.' Amy tried to twist out of his arms.

'What the hell are you doing here? It was obvious that

245

was the first time you've ever snorted cocaine. I don't like this one bit.' When she didn't say anything, he grabbed her wrist. It was her sore one and she screamed.

'Shut up.' He slapped her.

She decided she couldn't do it, even if it would help out Danny. She had to get out of Eddy's house. She tried to scramble up and he pulled her back down.

'Who sent you here? I don't believe it was Suzanne.'

'Let me go.'

He slapped her again and repeated, 'Tell me who sent you here.' His hand was raised and ready.

Amy realized that she was only making Eddy more nervous than he already was by avoiding his questions. She decided to tell the truth. 'I just saw Danny.'

His beady eyes showed white all around the pupils. 'They let him out?'

'No, they let me in to see him.'

'Why?' He gave her wrist another twist.

'I'm Tricia's sister. He told me he didn't kill Tricia and I believe him. What did happen that night?'

Suddenly Eddy let go of her wrist. 'I've heard more than I want to hear. You're wasting your time.'

'I hope not. I think you know that Danny didn't kill Tricia. I want the police to know that so they'll concentrate on finding the person who did it. Do you understand me?'

'Listen baby, you gotta understand me. I don't get involved. Danny made a mistake. I can't be jumping in to rescue him. What good would it do me?'

'What good is having him in jail doing you? Maybe I could help you out.'

'So what do you have to offer?'

'Well, I know you'd be going out on the limb for Danny. Especially in your line of business. I understand that and I wouldn't want you to do anything that would jeopardize your own affairs. So I'd like to offer you some financial assistance to help you minimize the risk.'

'You're offering me money? You know, babes, I make a lot of money in my line of work. More in a week or two than you've probably ever had your whole life.' He wet a finger and wiped up the white residue on the mirror and then rubbed it on his gums. Then he smiled and Amy found it impossible to smile back.

Amy didn't know what to say. But he was still grinning at her, so she remained silent.

'You know, I used to know your sister pretty well. In fact, let me offer you my condolences. She was a fine woman.' Eddy slicked back his hair. 'Very generous, you know what I mean. She had a lot to offer. So let's you and I try to come to an agreement. I'd like to see them catch the person who murdered her, too. I really would.'

He had so much as admitted that Danny hadn't done it. If she pushed him gently, maybe he would tell her a little more. 'What kind of an agreement?'

'You know, I have certain needs. Do a little coke and it makes me horny.' He reached over and grabbed her shoulder.

Amy tried to pull away, but Eddy held on to her and continued talking. 'I could use a little loving just like everyone else. Why don't you and I both do another line of coke and see if we can make each other feel better. Then I'd be pretty apt to call up the police and tell them I just remembered something they might be interested in. It could happen that way. You could make it happen.'

Amy didn't want to blow it. She couldn't stand his touching her, but she didn't want him to start slapping her again, or worse. If he knew how afraid she was of him, he might not even be asking so nicely. Maybe she could reason with him, appeal to his friendship with Tricia. It was worth a try. 'Eddy, I've been pretty shook up by what

247

happened to my sister. I know she liked you, and under other circumstances I'd think about it, but I just don't feel up to anything these days. I'm so obsessed about my sister's death. You can understand that, can't you?'

His hand trailed down from her neck to her breast and Amy couldn't help herself, she jerked away.

He grabbed her by the back of her neck and pulled her closer. She could no longer hide her fear, she was shaking in his hands.

Eddy reached out and pulled her shirt down. 'Nice. I like what I see. You're skinnier than Tricia, but I can see a resemblance.'

'Eddy, please don't.' Amy's voice broke into a sob.

'Oh, I like to hear that. You're going to beg a little now.' When she tried to pull away from him, he pushed her down on the futon. 'What do you think you're doing? You come over here with that skimpy little shirt on and those tight pants and then you're surprised when I do something about it. You came over here asking for help and I offer it to you. Now you better be willing to do something for that help. I knew your sister. You can't be so different. You're going to like it, just like she did.' He straddled her.

Amy went limp for a moment. He was on top of her, but he was little and thin. She could smell his sweat, acidic like rusted iron. He leaned over her and she twisted around and jabbed him in the groin with her knee. When he doubled up, she scrambled out from under him and went for the door.

He raised himself up to his knees on the futon. 'You cunt.'

'I'm not like Tricia. She was my sister but we're not the same.'

He staggered up and lunged for her, but she slipped out the door. As she ran to the car, he shouted after her, 'I'll

248

get you, and when I'm done with you, Tricia will look like a saint compared to what I'll make you do.'

Amy started up the car and drove a few blocks away. Then she stopped and cried. The tears were hot and painful. She felt as if someone had whipped her body inside and the tears were springing out of the wounds.

Amy stood at the door of the studio and looked at the empty room. The late-afternoon light was streaming in the window and fell across the floor like keys on a piano, the white from the sun, then streaks of the dark floor. She had promised herself she would work on her improv today, and yet, after what had happened to her with Eddy, she had no desire. She wanted to curl up in a ball in a corner of the room and sleep. Eddy would never find her there.

Eddy's face kept appearing, leering, his teeth with white powder on the gums. His hands on her breast. She tried not to think about what would have happened if she hadn't gotten away. She didn't want to dance. She had to open herself up when she did, and she didn't seem to want to do that anymore.

Lowering her head to the foot-worn floor, Amy realized she could hardly bring herself to think about the audition. It was lost to her in a way, simply because she didn't think it was possible anymore. In many ways Eddy had defeated her. He, even more than Suzanne, had shown her the world Tricia had lived in, and she didn't know her sister anymore. She thought of Tricia's singing the blues, how she would bend her head to the beat of the music, how she would bend her head as if submitting to the music. In that way they were alike, how music could move them.

Then something in her said, do what you like to do, stop trying to figure everything out, you like to dance, dance, do it. Before she could change her mind, she ran into the dressing room and slipped into her leotard. Staring into the mirror, she looked at her body as if it were someone else's. She was losing weight, and it didn't look good on her. It was a clear example of how she wasn't taking care of herself, and she didn't like to see it. It wouldn't help her dancing at all.

Amy went through her warm-ups. Her body felt stiff but then surprised her and warmed up quickly. After a slight hesitation the muscles gave the way they should. She lay on her back and kicked her legs up toward her face until they almost touched her nose and then the spring in them pulled them back to the ground.

Dancers had to have an intimate knowledge of gravity, how it helped and hindered them. It wasn't a scientific learning, it was a sense of body and earth. Amy swung over on to her side and started doing leg lifts. She smelled the sweat in the room and felt at home. This life demanded work, and she was not afraid of that. She was afraid of the something extra it asked for, the unknown quality that must be present to make it an art.

She hadn't brought the music with her for her improv, but she could hear it in her mind. Slowly, she started doing bits for it. Little actions from life, slowed down, sped up, out of context, with extra movements stuck in, swinging a swing, bending to hang up the wash, pulling in a rope, twirling around. She used to grab Tricia by the ankles and twirl her around on the grass and then wished Tricia could do it back to her, but Amy had been too big. This wasn't her dance, this was her life.

After she finished trying out a few more actions and linking them together into a dance sentence, she stretched out on the floor and then heard someone walk into the room. She scrambled to her feet with a scream caught inside her mouth, ready to explode out if necessary. Turning to look at the door, she saw Luke.

'Hey,' he said, 'I didn't mean to scare you. You look like you've seen a ghost.'

'I was pretty absorbed in what I was doing, I guess.'

'I said I'd stop by.'

'Yeah, I remember. I'm glad you did. Give me a few more minutes and I'll be done.'

'Can I watch?'

Amy felt shy. This was another way of being seen naked. In many ways it was scarier than just peeling her clothes off. 'Sure.'

Amy tipped her head back and drained it of thought. She could never try to think out what she had to do. Her body learned it, her body did it, she kept her mind out of it as much as she could. She began and maneuvered through the new tongue she was creating, dancing the strange sounds through her body.

When she was done, she turned to see Luke's reaction. He was smiling, and then he started to laugh.

'It's not funny,' Amy said quietly, but meaning it. 'I haven't danced in a week. I'll never dance for you again.'

'Amy, I loved it.' He pulled himself together and walked over to her. 'You were wonderful. You were great. The dance just reminded me so much of you and some of your quirks. You seemed like a little girl in it.'

Amy tried to calm herself down, but found she couldn't. She was shaking. Luke put an arm around her and kissed her cheek. She jerked away.

'Amy, what's the matter?' Luke didn't move away but looked down at her.

'Don't touch me.'

Luke tried to pull her closer, but when she resisted, he asked, 'What's going on?'

'I don't want anyone to ever touch me again. I hate myself. I hate my sister.' She looked at Luke as if he could stop her from saying what she was saying. He

251

reached out and put his hands on her shoulders and she yelled louder, 'I hate her. I hate my sister.'

She tried to struggle out of his hold, but when he wouldn't let go she hit him with her fists and screamed. 'Do you know what she was? She was a whore. Men made her do things and she let them. Maybe she enjoyed it. I was almost raped because of her. She would have liked that.'

'Stop it, Amy. Don't say that.' Luke was shaking her.

Amy was hysterical, unable to stop herself. 'I'm glad she's dead. I never want to see her again. She's not my sister. I don't have a sister.'

'Amy, you don't mean that.' Luke wrapped his arms around her so she couldn't hit him anymore.

Suddenly she stopped struggling and went limp. Luke let her slip to the floor, then knelt down next to her and pulled her into his lap. She tasted the salt of his sweat and the salt of her tears. He held her and rocked her, crooning, 'It's all right. It's going to be all right.'

Chapter 22

Amy stopped over at her house, turned on the phone-answering machine she had borrowed from Todd, and went to stay at Luke's. After her explosion she didn't want to be left alone, and she was afraid to stay at her apartment. Eddy might track her down.

The next morning she drove down to the police station to tell Towne about her encounter with Eddy. As she was going in the main entrance, she looked down the street and saw Towne walking away from the building. She started running after him. When she got close enough so he would hear her, she yelled, 'Towne.'

He turned around and looked to see who was calling his name and she waved her hand. He didn't walk back toward her, but waited for her to catch up with him.

'Listen, I have to talk to you for a second. It's about Danny.'

'He's being arraigned tomorrow, Amy. What do you want?'

'Well, that's why I want to talk to you. I don't think he did it. After talking to him, I went and saw Eddy. They were doing a cocaine deal together and he just wants to cut Danny out of his share.'

Towne shifted his weight from foot to foot before he answered her. 'Danny told us that too. But I don't buy it. His fingerprints are on a glass that was found in the sink, he was seen fighting and threatening Tricia in public, he was known to be over at Tricia's that night. He even acts guilty. He'd say anything to get out of the murder rap.

I've gotten to the point where I don't believe anything he says. He's a con man.'

Amy had to convince Towne. 'He didn't kill Tricia. I know it. Eddy let it slip yesterday.'

'We have a signed statement from Eddy.' Towne looked over his shoulder, down the street in the direction he had been walking when she stopped him. 'I've got a few things to do. If you recall, another woman was murdered.'

'Couldn't you at least talk to Eddy again?'

'Amy, I want you to drop this, all of this. I want you to go home and do whatever you do when you're not being a little detective. I'm tired of you snooping, and I don't want to have to worry about you. You go sniffing around Eddy, and I'd say you're liable to get your nose pinched.'

She couldn't believe what was happening. He wasn't even listening to her. She didn't know what she could say that would convince him.

'I've gotta go, Amy.' He started walking away.

'When you find out who killed Sandra, you'll find out who killed Tricia,' Amy said to his back. He didn't turn around, but just kept walking.

That afternoon she worked out long and hard at the studio. Only one more day before auditions. Luke and she had dinner, and then he went to play and gave her the key to his apartment. She went back to her place to get some clean clothes. When she got there, the light was blinking on her answering machine. She rewound it and listened to the first message, which was a hang-up.

Then came a familiar low voice. 'Hey, Emma. This is Suzanne. It's a little after six and I have someone down here who would like to meet you. If you can come down in the next hour or so, please do. Otherwise I'll talk to you later.'

254

Amy looked at her watch. It was after eight o'clock. She didn't want to go down to the Flash Club, but she knew this might be the man who had killed her sister. It was all fitting together. Eddy had as much as told her Danny didn't do it. The Flash Club was where Tricia had hung out, where she had met a man she liked, a man whom she would have trusted enough not to struggle when he tied her up. Amy had to know who the man was, she couldn't let him get away. She thought of trying to get hold of Towne, but remembered what he had said to her that day. She couldn't take the chance – he might even try to stop her from meeting with this man.

Amy decided she had to go down. It could no longer be a question of wanting to or not. But she could also take the precaution of having her gun with her. She took it out of her top drawer, where it was hidden under her nylons, and loaded it. She put it in her purse and hung the purse on the doorknob so she couldn't forget it. She ran to the bathroom and put on eye-liner and lipstick. Then ran to her room and threw on a pair of white pants and a pair of high heels. It would have to do.

On her way down to the Flash Club she realized that this person might not be the guy Tricia had had dealings with. He could be anyone. Just because she had asked Suzanne to set it up with Tricia's old john didn't mean it would ever happen. What would she do if it wasn't?

What would she do if it were the man Suzanne had set Tricia up with? The prince of a guy, as Tricia had called him. Ask him if he murdered her sister and then get his home phone number so the police could get in touch with him later? And then, as she was asking him how he happened to know her sister, he would be tying her hands to the bedposts.

She was crazy for going down to meet him, but some-how she couldn't turn back. This was a man who had killed two women, and if he had any idea who she was or what she knew, he wouldn't hesitate to do the same to her. However, she did have the gun, loaded and ready. She hoped she wouldn't have to use it but was glad it was there.

When she walked into the Flash Club, she started to shiver as a wave of air-conditioning hit her. The darkness of the bar after the glaring sun of late August was a relief, and when her eyes adjusted to it she saw Suzanne sitting on a barstool talking to a small dark man. A man who in no way fit her preconception of Tricia's man. Amy considered turning around and walking out. She should have thought this through more carefully. But then Suzanne turned around and saw her. With a big smile on her face she motioned Amy over.

'Hi, Emma.'

'Suzanne, I got your message and came as soon as I could.'

Suzanne was dressed in a muumuu with bright tropical flowers splashed all over. Amy commented, 'What a nice dress.'

Suzanne fanned it out to show Amy its full glory. 'You like it? Believe it or not, I really got it in Hawaii. They know how to dress us big girls there.'

Amy was surprised she wasn't being introduced to her 'date.' She sat down on the stool next to Suzanne and watched as Suzanne motioned over the bartender.

'Let me get you a drink, since you've come all this way for nothing,' Suzanne offered.

Amy looked quickly at the small dark guy. Suzanne followed her glance and then laughed. 'This is Pierre, Emma. He doesn't really like girls too much. Only if they can sing cabaret or make him laugh. I can't sing worth beans, so I assume it's the other reason he hangs around here.'

'*Enchanté*,' Pierre said, then looked the other way.

'He speaks French a little better than me, but I can swear better in it than him,' Suzanne said while the bartender waited for her to finish talking. 'What would you like?'

Amy felt this drink was in the line of duty. And she badly needed it. 'I'll have a gin-and-tonic.'

'A nice summer drink. You're obviously not a real drinker if you still care about such things.'

'Oh, yeah?' Amy wanted her to continue talking so she would have time to calm down.

Suzanne needed little encouragement. 'The real drinkers have one habitual drink and it does for all occasions. Usually something like a shot of bourbon or Scotch, anything straight, or on the rocks if they want to feel like they're cutting down. I've learned a lot running this place. Believe it or not, this is a serious drinking bar. My regulars don't even know I've got a back room where you can dance. They just sit up at the bar and swill it down.'

'Do you drink much?'

Suzanne seemed surprised by the question. 'Actually, I've been noticing that lately I've been picking up the pace. I've gotta watch that. There are a lot of calories in a drink. Course, you don't have to worry about that. How much do you weigh?'

Amy took a sip of her drink and answered, 'Around a hundred and five.'

'God, I remember seeing that number on the scale when I was twelve. Sure won't ever see it again.'

After another sip Amy felt brave enough to venture a few questions of her own. 'So what happened to the guy that you called me about? I came as soon as I got the message.'

'He waited an hour or so, but he's a busy guy. He had something to do tonight.'

'Like the type that frequent the Club in the IDS?'

'You've been up to that bar? Yeah, I think he hangs out up there, although he's really kind of a hick. You know Tricia used to work up there.'

'I think she did mention that once.'

'That was a plush gig, but she came down here one night and really tied one on. I guess she didn't make it in the next day. She really started going down hill after that.'

'So will I get another chance with this guy?'

Suzanne looked at her. 'Yeah, I think so. But could you dress a little more kinky? He likes black. He likes drama. That's what he comes here for. He likes the sense of danger.'

'Just the sense?'

'Well, who's to say? One man's pain is another man's pleasure.'

Amy let that one stand. Suzanne stood up and shook out her muumuu.

'Enjoy your drink. I'll be in touch.'

Amy thanked her and then asked. 'So who is this guy? What's his name?'

Suzanne looked a little surprised, then smiled and said, 'I don't give out the customers' names or phone numbers. Just like I don't give out yours. But we've kind of developed code names for them, so they're not totally anonymous. This guy likes to be called Peter Pan.'

The name entered her stomach like a blow and then, just to keep it light, she said. 'Wasn't that the guy who came and took little girls out of their beds in the middle of the night?'

Suzanne laughed. 'You got it, sweetheart, you got it.'

Chapter 23

She dreamed she was in a dark, warm, red room like a harem tent and Tricia was there, lying among the pillows, smiling at her as if she had been expecting to see her for quite a while. Amy didn't remember the words, but Tricia told her everything was all right, she was comfortable where she was. And then the tent flew up into the air, transformed into some kind of mythical bird. Amy was left behind. The land around her was flat and empty. Amy was standing in the middle of it and Tricia was gone. Her heart ached. Her sister had left her again. This time in the middle of a desert. And she hadn't even had time to ask her who had murdered her. Now she might never know. She picked up a handful of sand and threw it hard.

Lying as still as she could, she woke up and felt the dream leave her. Next to her Luke slept, an arm thrown across her stomach. When she moved slightly, he cupped his hand around her waist, without waking. She lay quietly in bed, thinking about the audition.

Up until a week and a half ago she had worked single-mindedly for this day. She would give it as good a try as she could. There was no way to cram for a dance audition. The lessons had to be disciplined and steady, years of practice. She hoped she was ready. By the end of the day she'd either be in or she'd be out of the Dance Studio.

Stretched out flat on her back, she started to tense and relax her muscles, first the forehead, then the jaw and back of the neck, moving downward until she finally reached her toes. When she was as relaxed as she could be, her mind turned to Tricia. Her solo dance, she knew now, would be dedicated to her sister. It wasn't the dream so much as the lingering of it, the mood that would carry over into the day. It was reassuring to know that she would be able to see Tricia in dreams.

Amy rolled over to look at Luke and watched as one of his eyes cracked open. Then he smiled and said, 'Today's the day.'

'Oh, God, don't say that.'

'You're gonna do good. I know it. Why don't you take a shower and I'll make us some breakfast?'

Just as she was rinsing the shampoo out of her hair, Luke slipped into the shower with her. He hugged her, then washed her back, and told her she had a nice ass.

He finished drying himself first, and after he left, she stood in the steam-filled bathroom and felt how unreal love made the rest of the world seem. It scared her; moments in the shower, hugging, didn't last. She couldn't hold on long enough or tight enough. There was always an end to the embrace.

The audition started at noon and went until three – grueling, but then it would be over. There were ten of them auditioning; only two would make it. Amy knew that Dara, who was the youngest dancer auditioning, had the best chance. She had taken ballet all her life, and only in the last two years had switched to modern, but she danced with a lightness and precision that Amy envied.

Then there was Mark. She had worked and danced with him for the last few years. She admired him, but she didn't think he was necessarily any better than she was. And today, just this once, she hoped he was worse. He was almost her age, so he didn't have an advantage there, but he had remarkable flexibility for a man.

* * *

Once inside the rehearsal space, her confidence left her. She was the last one to arrive. The other nine dancers were stretching, bending, massaging muscles, and, she knew, as she was doing it herself, praying. It was not a religious prayer to any namable god, more a calling to all her powers.

At twelve exactly the judges came in and sat at a table at the far end of the room. There were four of them. Two were from the Dance Studio, one was the choreographer from the Guthrie, and one was a visiting choreographer from New York. Amy bent over her outstretched legs and took long, deep breaths. She couldn't look at them. She wanted to stay bent over, staring at the floor, as it gave her a sense of incredible stability.

After twenty minutes of stretching and doing positions they lined up to do runs across the floor. Now they were being divided and singled out. The runs started out simply, turns, jumps, hops, easy rhythms. Slowly, they became more complex. After each run she finished successfully, she rewarded herself by shaking out her body. It was going all right. She was hanging in there. She was doing as well as she could. Mark also looked good, while Dara looked perfect. Then on the second to the last run, Amy faltered. It came right at the end of the run. Maybe no one had seen, but she had felt it. When she came back into line, she avoided everyone's eyes. She did not want to see recognition in them, or sympathy. She couldn't give in.

When the runs were over they were given a five-minute break, during which time they were also told the order in which they would be performing their improvisational dance solos. Amy's number was seven. Her hands broke out in a sweat. How could she stand to wait that long?

Mark walked up to her and handed her a glass of water. 'How you doing?'

'This is no fun.'

'You look great to me,' he said.

'So do you,' she answered. There had never been an acknowledgement between them of their competition, and they certainly couldn't afford to do it now. She looked around the lobby and, not seeing Dara, asked, 'How do you think Dara's doing?'

'She dances like an angel, but you know, sometimes I think she's unsuited for the style that the Dance Studio professes to do. She's a little too floaty.'

'I know what you mean.' Amy felt a bubble of a giggle rise in her. She said quickly, 'Our cattiness is coming out.'

'Survival techniques.'

Mark was the second person to perform. He danced to a Herbie Hancock jazz-funk tune, and his piece was exciting and flashy. In spite of herself Amy felt carried away by it. When he was done and sank down on the floor next to her, sweating and breathing heavily, she whispered, 'You were great.'

His eyes rolled back and she saw his panic. It had danced with him, chasing him all the way through.

Dara went sixth, and to forget that her own piece was next, Amy paid close attention to it. It was a languorous and beautiful piece done to a women's vocal choir, and Dara floated her way through it.

Then the head of the Dance Studio called Amy's name. Somehow she got her legs under her body and walked forward. Amy took the position on the floor of someone about to rise from bed. She closed her eyes for a moment and tried to forget the room and its watchful eyes. Only Tricia was watching her. The music started.

When you went away, I cried for so long.
I wanted you to stay, but that was all wrong.
The pain you left behind has become, has become part of me.
And it's burning out a hole where my heart used to be.

She rose up slowly, as if she were unwinding from some spool of thread. The song was smooth on the surface, the pain was underneath, where it belonged, but it broke through the surface as the singer's voice cracked, and so her dance started to rip. Where she had wanted it to be liquid and flowing, it began to jar and jolt.

I've learned how to give now, but what good, what good does it do?
When no one can touch me the way you used to do.

It had never been like this in her imagination or in her sketchy practices. It had been private and intimate pain, controlled and held in check, but somehow it was spilling out of her. Tricia's contorted body on the bed, her dad throwing the grill on the floor, her mother's hunched shoulders, Danny's shuffling walk, they were being translated into dance. And her own loss, she had never known how great it was before she tried to dance it. It was filling everything, the voice and her feet were following it, she had on the red shoes and she had to keep dancing.

This coldness inside me, well, it's starting to melt.
A woman can't be a woman, unless she's fulfilled.

She thought of Luke and slowed down. There was another side and she was coming through. There were arms for her to fall into and hold her. She saw her mother hanging out sheets and she remembered swimming in a lake with her sister.

But it's not losing you, that's got me down so low.
I just can't find another man to take your place, there's no one can.

The song wound down and Amy wound into herself. She was like a twisted tree as the last notes sounded.

She didn't stay to watch the last three, but went right up to the locker room and put on her clothes. Suddenly, she felt fiercely hungry. No more yogurt and carrot sticks for her. She wanted a hamburger and a malt. She decided to go to the Burger Delight and wait there until the results were posted.

Dot seated her in the booth by the kitchen door. 'I got a call from Chuck. Said he would be in a halfway house for a while. Said you had something to do with it.'

'He waylaid me at my door one night, with a knife.'

'Lord. Don't you have enough excitement in your life? I'm sorry about that. I do feel partly responsible. This social worker asked me to give him a job, said it would be good rehabilitation. What do you want to eat?'

Raising her eyebrows when Amy ordered her hamburger, Dot cracked, 'I thought you were a vegetarian.'

'I told you I wasn't. I just don't like to eat meat. Or not usually.'

In little time, as the restaurant was not crowded, Dot set a hamburger down in front of Amy and watched her take the first bite. 'How's the burger?'

'Good and greasy.'

'How are you?'

'Just about as fried. I did my audition.'

Dot waited and Amy shrugged her shoulders.

'That bad?' Dot asked.

'I can't tell. I really don't know. Usually I know. I have a sense of how I did. But this dance could have either been great or totally off the wall. I don't want to talk about it.'

'Fine,' Dot said, but stood waiting for more. When Amy said nothing more, Dot asked, 'Why?'

'Because I'm so nervous. I'll find out in about an hour if I made it.'

'You going to hang out here?'

Amy nodded yes.

'You want to read the paper. It's yesterday's.'

Amy read it cover to cover. There was a review of a dance piece by the visiting choreographer from New York that was not too bad, given the reviewer's traditional approach to dance. 'Complicated pauses, bursts of energy – this choreographer's work is uneven at best.' She hoped he wasn't taking it too hard. She was glad the reviewer had not seen her latest piece.

Then she saw a news item with the headline WAITRESS STRANGLED, NO SUSPECTS. She was surprised at how vague it was, 'a woman found dead in her bedroom. No evidence of a break-in.' It didn't say anything about the fact that she had been naked, that she'd been found by another waitress.

When she put down the paper, Dot came back over. 'So what's going on with you lately?'

Amy really didn't want to give her the rundown on Tricia, so she simply said, 'They think Danny, her boy-friend, might have killed her. They're not sure.'

'What about that other guy?'

'Hank? I don't think he was ever really considered.' Amy handed the paper back to Dot. 'I think I'd like to come back to work next week, if you can fit me into the schedule.'

'Are you kidding? Guess who's been doing your shift. The worst waitress on the force. Me.'

'You're not so bad.'

'I'm impatient as hell. I've been averaging about three dollars in tips a shift.'

Amy laughed. 'That is pretty bad.'

'We'll be real glad to have you back.'

Amy waited until five-thirty to go look at the results, which were pinned up on the bulletin board in the lobby. No one else was around. She guessed they had all come and gone. She walked up close enough to see the two names. She read them and that was it. She turned and walked out of the Dance Studio.

Amy sat at the kitchen table, stirring her herbal tea, and stared at the window. Her gaze was stopped by the windowpane. She was really looking inside of herself and assessing the damage. It was very simple. She had tried to help her sister and, in some minimal way, save her, and she had lost her to death. She had tried to dance her way into a company and she had failed. She was sleeping with Luke and she didn't know what it meant.

Looking down at the Formica top of the kitchen table, she waved her hand over it as if she were spraying the gold flecks across the whiteness. When she was a child she had been fascinated with Formica and had even once connected the dots to see what drawings were hidden there. Maybe her kitchen counter's flecks were like the swirlings of tea leaves stuck to the cup when the beverage was gone. Maybe she could read what was in store for her on its slick surface.

Where was the real Peter Pan? Where was the magic? She wanted a second chance at everything. She finished her tea and looked at the inside of the cup. Nothing. There was not a speck of tea left. It was a huge whiteness that she wanted to be rid of, so she turned it lightly into her hand and felt the heft of it and then pulled her arm back and swung it forward, the cup leaving her hand, as it should, tilting through the air until it hit the wall below the window and crashed into a fistful of fragments that went tumbling to the floor and skidded around on it.

Having done that, she bent and hid her face in her hands, wanting to see no more, surprised at the calmness of her action. She had always thought that people hit and punched and threw things out of an uncontrollable rage, and now she knew that it could come out of a wish for there not to be only nothing. For there to be, at least, some noise and pain, some feeling and reaction.

The phone rang and she pulled her hands away from her face. It rang again and she looked at it. At the third ring she stood up and answered it.

'Hello?'

'Suzanne here. How are you?'

'Fine, Suzanne. What can I do for you?'

'Well, our friend Peter Pan is coming by in an hour. Can you make it? If not, I'll get someone else.'

Amy knew she had to say yes, and then she could think about it. 'Sure, I'm free. I'll be right down.'

'Fine. We'll talk particulars when you get here. Remember what I said about the way you dress.'

'I remember.'

Amy hung up the phone and walked over to the remains of the teacup. She picked up the largest shard of porcelain and ran it along the back of her hand. It broke the skin and she bled and she felt the gentle whisper of pain.

Tricia's leather corset was hung up in the back of her clothes closet and she hadn't looked at it since she had found Suzanne's number tucked inside the pocket. She pulled it out now and tried it on. Her breasts only half filled the cups of the corset. Readjusting it so it sat higher, her breasts plumped up a little. She had a pair of black silk underpants that Tricia had given her for her birthday. Turning, she caught a vision of herself in the mirror and was surprised at the titillation she felt. With heels on she could pass for what she needed to be. She put a red silk blouse over the corset so she wouldn't feel indecent driving downtown in it and pulled on a pair of black strapped pants.

In the bathroom she sniffed her armpits. She hadn't taken a shower since the audition, and she smelled like it.

She took some musk oil and applied it to her armpits, her wrists, and her throat. She darkened her eyes with black mascara and dark gray eyeshadow. He'd get drama if that's what he wanted.

After slicking her hair back, she put on long, dangling black jet earrings. She even rubbed a drop of oil into each eyebrow to make it gleam. She smiled at herself in the mirror and thought, I'm just getting ready for a date. I wonder if we'll go all the way. Her face in the mirror looked scared, and she closed her eyes so she couldn't see the fear imbedded in them.

She chose the darkest lipstick she had and put it on with exaggerated care. They must be perfect; her lips must invite kissing, but not allow it.

Amy picked up her purse and walked to the full-length mirror by the door. She took the gun out and felt the weight of it in her hand. It was heavy and black. It might explode in her hand. She didn't know what she was capable of. Pointing it at the mirror, she looked at herself again and saw someone else. Someone who could point a gun at another person and go all the way. A blink made that person disappear and Amy was left alone with herself and she was scared.

She tucked the gun back into her purse and walked out the door.

Her car was an oven, as she had left it sitting in the sun with the windows rolled up. As she started the car, she left the door open to air it out. As she was closing the door, she saw Todd walking toward her.

'Where are you going?' he yelled.

'Out.'

'Has he gotten in touch with you yet?' He had a knowing grin on his face.

'What and who are you talking about?'

'That choreographer from New York disagreed with

the other judges. He thought you were the best dancer there.'

'You're kidding.'

'He described your dancing as imagistic and beyond avant-garde, whatever that means. But in simple terms he thought you were terrific.'

Amy felt something surge through her body; relief, confidence, maybe even a hint of joy. 'Oh, God, I can't believe he liked me.'

'Amy, you're good. I'm really sorry you didn't make the company, but I don't think you should give up. You are a dancer.'

She wanted to stay with Todd and talk about dance and how she had felt when she had done her improv and what she might do next.

'That's great, but I've gotta go do something.' She got back into the car.

'Do what? Where are you going dressed up like that?'

'Something came up. I have to take care of it. I won't be long. I'll call you when I get home.' She didn't want Todd to worry. Everything was going to be all right. She had to believe that.

The water is a glove around me, a black glove that fits tight around me, but I can't see, only feel. I dive in right where I last saw Tricia. I swim down to the bottom and begin to feel along it. She must be near the dock. My eyes are open but they are filled with black liquid. Then I feel her close to the legs of the dock. I touch her foot and then her hands. She grabs on to me. So she's still alive, but why isn't she swimming out? I try to pull her up. But somehow she's caught. Her small hands are around my neck. She's trying to climb me. Then they go slack. She's going to die, I think. I can't let it happen. I yank at her again, but it does no good. I have to find out what's holding on to her. Maybe it is them, maybe they are real. I think I see them in the water. Shapes swimming behind her. I want to scream. I need air, but I can't leave her. I feel along her back and find it is her hair that is caught on the dock leg. I tug but it doesn't come loose. Then I know that I have to rip it out or she'll die. I tear at the hair and it begins to give. Another pull and she's free. I wrap an arm around her waist and swim toward shore. When it is shallow enough, I lift her out. She is like wet clothes in my arms. No movement. I lay her in the water at the shore and start to breathe into her mouth like I have seen on TV. I slap her face and water gushes out of her mouth. I turn her over and hit her back. She coughs. Then she sucks in air and starts to cry.

Chapter 24

Amy parked the car in a downtown parking lot and sat for a minute, watching the attendant coming toward her. He was a tall, thin man and his coveralls hung off his body so he looked like a scarecrow trying to shoo away the birds. She felt an enormous tiredness. All she wanted to do was remain sitting in the car. She wondered what Tricia would have thought of what she was doing. Amy got out of her car and handed her keys to the attendant.

'How long you going to be?'

Amy thought about how long it might take her to do what she was about to do. 'Not too long, I hope.'

'I leave at nine, so try to be back before then. If you're not, the keys will be with the guy in the next lot over. He stays on until twelve.'

'OK. Thanks.'

As she turned to go, she heard him give a low wolf whistle and she shivered at the sound of it.

Before she walked into the Flash Club, she stood outside the door and unbuttoned her blouse. But she couldn't bring herself to take it off. Rather than being revealing, she'd be suggestive. That was more sexy anyway.

Inside it was quiet. Three businessmen arguing over a real-estate deal and two flannel-shirted men playing pool. A couple of women were drinking and smoking at the end of the bar and laughing as if they wanted someone to ask them what the joke was. Amy walked up to the bar and asked where Suzanne was.

The bartender said, 'She was here a minute ago. She's around. What can I do for you?'

'Nothing. Thanks.'

She perched on one of the stools and turned her back to the bar and watched the pool game. The men were unevenly matched. The short stocky one, Pete the other guy was calling him, was a top-notch player. The taller one, Sam, hit the balls straight in, if he had such a setup. Otherwise he could do nothing. Pete did the opposite. Even if he were given a straight shot in, he would bump it off of something. She watched him hit the white ball, which hit a blue ball and then lightly tapped the orange ball, which dropped down a hole. She wondered what was down that hole.

Someone tapped her on the shoulder and she jumped.

'Got the jitters?' Suzanne asked, sliding on to the stool next to her.

'No, just engrossed in the game.'

'You play pool?'

'I only watch.'

'You look good.'

Amy wished she could say the same for Suzanne, but she looked awful, her makeup was smeared and she had a lime-green bruise on her cheekbone. Amy automatically asked, 'What happened to you?'

'Nothing really. This just hasn't been my week. The police came to talk to me the other day. It was weird. They were asking me about Tricia. And then there was a fight in here the other day and for some reason I got in the middle of it. Thought I could talk some sense into the guys.' She pointed at the bruise. 'This is the medal I got for that act of bravery.'

'What did they want to know about Tricia?'

'If I knew her. If she hung out with any guys I knew. I told them nothing. That's my policy with the police.'

'Oh,' Amy said, but what she wanted to know was how much the police had told her. They couldn't have told her about Emma, as they didn't know about her. Had they mentioned Tricia's sister, Amy? Had they asked about Peter Pan? Amy doubted it. She wished she had talked to Towne more recently. Maybe he would have mentioned the visit. But there was no way she could do it now.

'He's waiting upstairs – Peter Pan.'

'OK.' Amy felt her mouth go dry and asked a question just to stall for time. 'So how does this work?'

'He pays me. I pay you. That's how it works the first time.' Suzanne looked serious. 'And you pay for the room. Do you have enough money?'

'I have twenty dollars.'

'OK. It's ten for a room. And you'll get it back.'

'How much do I get?'

'Depends on how long and how far. Basically it's fifty bucks an hour. If he gets into heavy S and M, it goes up to, say, seventy-five. Actually, you can negotiate that a little. Maybe give him a good deal the first time.'

Amy didn't say anything. She didn't want to know how far it could go, and she certainly didn't want to think of this as a first time with the possibility of other times following. To take money for sex, she realized you had to think of your body as a commodity, only worth as much as it could take. Thinking about how much Tricia's body had suffered under the hands of men, she shuddered.

Suzanne patted her shoulder. 'You're going to do fine. Just do what he asks. You ready?'

Amy nodded and slid off her stool, hoping her legs would support her. She looked around the bar and wondered if any of these men would help her if she started to scream. After looking them over, she thought not. She was on her own. Clutching her purse, she looked at Suzanne.

'OK, follow me. I'll introduce you two.'

Suzanne led the way out the back door. The sun was setting and a breeze had just picked up. Amy stopped for a second to stare at the pool of red on the horizon. Then they went into the back entrance of the Hennepin Hotel. She should have guessed it would be where they would go. Once inside the hotel, Suzanne let her take the lead until they got to the desk.

The desk clerk just nodded and handed her a key. She slipped him a ten.

'It's two flights up,' he said, chewing on something that had turned his lips brown.

'Thank you,' Amy said, then wanted to take it back. He had watched too many women climb these steps to ever be thanked for anything in his life.

Once again she took the lead and was aware of Suzanne walking closely behind her, watching her climb up the stairs. Her hands were shaking and she clenched one into a fist and with the other held on to the stair railing.

Stopping outside of the door of the room, Amy fitted the key into the lock. Suzanne slapped her ass and said, 'Good luck, sweetie. Give him your all, so to speak.' Suzanne laughed her low, harsh laugh and pushed Amy through the doorway.

Before Amy had time to say anything back to Suzanne, she was in the room with the door locked behind her and a man sitting in a chair with a floor lamp on behind him. It was the only light on in the room. He was wearing a baggy suit, dark sunglasses, a broad-brimmed hat, and gloves. She couldn't see much of his face, but a glimmer of blond hair showed under the hat. The room was small and dingy. A picture of a girl with large sad eyes standing out in the pouring rain hung above the bed. The bedspread was dark maroon chenille, and rumpled looking as though someone had been lying on it. Black blinds were drawn down, so it was impossible to tell what time of day it was. The man was not moving, but she could tell he was looking at her. Even though he was wearing sunglasses, she could feel his gaze cutting into her.

She took a couple steps closer to him and said, 'Hi, I'm Emma.'

He nodded, then spun his finger around, and she decided he was motioning her to turn around. She turned, self-conscious in her heels, and then stood still again.

'Take off the shirt,' he said to her in a gravelly whisper.

She slipped it off and hung it over the back of a chair that was sitting by the door. Amy held her purse tight against the black corset. She had to set it down, so she walked over and put it down on a nightstand next to the bed.

'Nice,' he said. 'I like what I see.'

Amy felt icy sweat on her bare arms.

'Come here,' he said. She came and stood in front of him and he touched her gently on the open skin above her breasts.

'Lie down on the bed.' He said it as if she were a waitress and he wanted more coffee.

Amy stood still. Not being able to see his face was making the situation seem very unreal. Somehow she had to find out if this was the man who had murdered her sister. She had thought just seeing him she would know. But she couldn't see him, and she probably wouldn't have known even if she could. He would have to tell her, and she hadn't any idea how she would get him to do that. So she said, 'Let's talk for a minute or two. I'd like to get to know a few things about what you like first.'

'There's nothing to know about me. My life is separate from all this. Don't get any ideas.' For the first time she saw him reveal some emotion. There was something he was afraid of – exposure.

275

'Oh, no, you misunderstand.' She moved in closer and reached a hand out toward him. 'I don't want to know who you are. I want to know about what you do here. What you've done and what you like to do. There are any of a number of games we can play together, you and I.'

He leaned back in the chair, as if to move away from her, and pulled the brim of his hat down. 'Like what?'

'Just relax.' She took off her tights so she was just in her black silk pants, corset, and high heels. She turned around so he could see her from all sides and pretended to be busy folding her tights. Then she walked over and knelt in front of him. She held up her wrists and said, 'What would you like to do with me?'

'I brought some things along,' he said, and reached into his pocket and pulled out two leather straps.

Amy felt her knees weaken but fought the feeling. 'What would you like to do with those?'

'You'll see.'

She tried to see his face – it seemed familiar to her. But the voice was hard to recognize, it was so low. She had to keep him talking. 'No, tell me. I want to know first. It excites me. Are you going to tie me up?'

'Yes.'

'Why?'

'Because then I have you in my control?'

'Why do you need to be in control?'

'Because women don't know what they want. But I do. I show them all the possibilities.'

'How do you do that?'

'I give them what they ask for.'

'Do you beat them?'

He seemed shocked. 'No, never do that. Nothing so unimaginative.' Shaking his head back and forth, he said, 'What I do goes a little deeper than that.'

'What do you mean?' she asked, following his lead, pushing him with her questions.

'You'll see.'

'Are you going to do it to me?'

'I don't know. I don't know what will happen between us.'

'How will you find out?'

'When you tell me what you want me to do.'

Amy took a breath and began to tell him what he could do to her. She didn't know where it was coming from. She had never spoken in such a way before. It was as if she gave herself over to his imaginings. 'You can do anything to me. I will take your cock anyplace, in my mouth, in my asshole.'

He stood up suddenly and grabbed her. Covering her mouth with his hand, he spit out, 'Don't talk like that. I hate it when women talk dirty like that.'

Amy couldn't breathe. She shook her head and tried to break away from him, but the more she struggled the tighter he clamped down on her mouth. This was happening too fast. Then she relaxed and he let go of her. She fell to the floor.

'I won't talk like that anymore,' she promised, and got to her knees.

'I'll tell you what to do,' he yelled at her. He hit her across the mouth. 'Keep your mouth shut. You don't know what that can do to me. You don't understand me.' He pushed her back down on the floor and strode across the room.

'Of course,' she whispered. She didn't want to get him any more riled up than he was already.

'I don't want to talk anymore. Let's get this over with.'

She walked over to the bed and sat down on it. He came toward her and pushed her down on the bed. 'It's time for you to get ready. Take your clothes off.'

He was standing over her, waiting. When she tried to sit up, he pushed her down again. She closed her eyes for a moment and knew she couldn't fight him. She would never win that way. He was rubbing up against her. She smiled and opened her eyes.

He reached down and unzipped her corset. It came open and her breasts were exposed. She had to stop herself from covering them with her hands.

'Nice,' he said, and put out a hand to touch them. 'I thought you would have nice tits, Amy.'

She froze. He had said her name, her real name. Something was horribly wrong. There was no way he should know her real name. She tried to run, but he pushed her down on the bed. She kicked him and he slugged her in the stomach. The air whooshed out of her lungs and she folded up. While she was struggling for breath, he took off the glasses and the hat and Amy saw it was Hank she was fighting. Hank, the country boy from Willmar, Hank, the murderer of her sister. She saw it all now that it was too late.

She had to think fast. She could breathe again, but she acted as if she were still incapacitated. He took a step back from the bed and she saw her purse on the far side. She had to get to it, but she couldn't let him know what she was trying to do. It was her only chance. Because if she didn't get it, he would rape her, then he would kill her. By the third time it had to be getting easier for him to do.

Amy decided she would have to try to attack him again, get off the bed, and try to grab the purse as he sent her sailing back. So she rushed him and he cracked her in the jaw. Drawing on her dancing abilities, as she flung herself across the bed she grabbed the purse and then sprawled on top of it. She had done it, she could feel the purse beneath her on the bed. But he had hurt her. She was tasting blood inside her mouth and it was making her sick. She had to ignore it.

Groaning, and not a fake groan, she moved her hand toward her stomach. He laughed at her and said, 'Let's try it again, I'm kind of enjoying myself. You've really got a knack for this S and M stuff, Amy.'

She felt for the purse, and when she had located it, she opened the purse latch and inched the gun out. When she sneaked a look at him, he winked back at her. 'You done, sweetie?' he asked.

She groaned again to cover the noise of her cocking the gun, and then sat up, pointing the gun right at Hank.

'Fuck you, Hank. This gun is loaded and I know how to use it. So now it's your turn to sit on the bed. I want you to answer a few questions before I take care of you.' Slowly and carefully, Amy stood up and walked around Hank, so she was between him and the door.

'What the hell?'

'Sit, I said, sit. And don't move. Not an inch, or I'll blow you away.'

Hank sat down on the edge of the bed. He moved slowly, as if he were trying to believe what was happening to him.

'So tell me about you and Tricia.' Amy found herself speaking clearly. The gun was such a welcome weight in her hand.

'Amy,' he said, holding up his hand to stop her from doing something, 'it's not the way you think it is.'

'What way is that?' She was just going to let him talk.

'Tricia and I were friends. I knew her through Suzanne. I didn't have anything to do with her murder.'

'How did you get to know Suzanne?'

'I got a couple of young girls from around my home-town to work for her. She taught them the ropes, then

279

sent them to New York. That's why she calls me Peter Pan.'

'Oh,' Amy said, and took a step closer. She stretched out into her shooting position, legs spread to right below each shoulder, her right hand wrapped around the grip and her right elbow locked, her left hand wrapped around her right. Finally she lowered her chin to her shoulder and sighted right at his chest. After hours of target practice she was comfortable in this position and could maintain it for a long time. However long it took Hank to tell his story. 'Keep talking. If you stop talking, I'm going to start shooting.'

'Amy, this isn't the way this should be handled. Put the gun down and we can talk. I wasn't serious about coming on to you. I just heard that you were working for Suzanne and thought I'd pull a trick on you.'

She could see sweat working up around his neck. His hands were clutching the sheet on the bed. Some trick. He's lying so deep and so thick, he's going to choke on his words, she thought. 'Keep talking.'

'OK, I met Tricia through Suzanne and, yeah, we did fool around a bit, you know, but we really liked each other. Suzanne and she started to have some trouble over that, in fact. Tricia was seeing me for nothing and Suzanne started to get pissed.'

'Then how come you and Suzanne are so buddy-buddy now?'

'Just worked out that way. Anyhow, it was Danny who killed Tricia, he's the one who's in jail. Put the gun away, Amy,' he started to plead.

'Let me ask you a few questions. What did you do that night?'

'Like I told you, I went over there, but nothing was going on. Tricia wasn't there. So I left and went home. The police know I was in Willmar that night. Ask them.'

She was starting to feel uncertain. Maybe he was telling the truth. But then, why was he here? 'So how did you find out I was working for Suzanne?'

'She started to describe you to me. Telling me about the new girl. Sounded familiar, so I asked a few more questions and then she tells me you knew Tricia. Then I was pretty sure. I've had my eye on you, Amy. I could tell you were hot. Thought I'd try you out.'

She slightly lowered the gun, although she kept it pointed at him, and asked him one more question. 'Why do you think Danny killed her? Because of you? Was he jealous of you?'

'I doubt it. It was probably her own fault. She always liked to be tied up. Maybe he just got carried away.'

With his last words Amy knew for sure who had gotten carried away. Hank had told on himself. Only the killer could know that Tricia had been tied up. It hadn't been mentioned in any of the media coverage, and Amy had told only Todd. Amy stepped closer to him, the gun starting to shake in her hands, screaming. 'You did it, you killed my sister. That's the only way you could know what you just told me.'

Before Amy could do anything, Hank had whipped the bedspread up in the air and wrapped it around her. She fell to the floor and he was on top of her, pinning her down. He pulled the spread off her face and started punching her. She heard her nose crack and felt a numbing pain.

Then he clamped a hand over her mouth and she bit down on it as hard as she could. He screamed and punched her. For a moment she was lost in a world of swirling mist. Then she felt his hands move under her body and grab the gun. He wrenched it out of her hand and stood up.

'Get up,' he said.

She lay on the floor in a heap. The carpet beneath her face was the color of dried blood. Sweat broke out across her chest and she was sure she was going to be sick. It didn't seem possible that she could even sit up. He would kill her. That had been his plan all along, and now she couldn't even stop him. She thought of Luke and wished she had told him that she loved him. But most of all she wished someone knew where she was. She hadn't thought of anything but finding out who had killed her sister.

'Get up and get on the bed. We're not finished.'

She lay still, groggy on the floor. He kicked her in the ribs. She saw it more than she felt it. She knew she had gone too far. She would never come back from this. And he might even get away with killing her.

Holding her head in both hands, she slowly sat up. He grabbed her elbow and pulled her up, then threw her at the bed.

She clutched the sheets and pulled herself on to it. 'What do you want?'

'I'm going to fuck you, you bitch.'

'What did you do to Sandra?'

'I had to kill her because I knew she was going to talk to you. I thought I saw you talking to her down at the Flash Club and then you mentioned her out at your folks'. We were playing pretty close to her apartment that night, so I went over between sets. It even gave me a good alibi. The guys just thought I was out smoking a joint.'

'Why did you kill Tricia?'

'That's her own fault. She would get so fucking drunk. We were doing our game. I put the straps on her and then the phone rang. She wanted to answer it and I wouldn't let her. She started calling me names. I tried to make her be quiet. But she wouldn't stop. So I gagged her. Then I left the room. When I came back, she was lying nice and quiet. It was good, the way it's supposed to be. I thought she had passed out, but she wouldn't wake up. I didn't mean to do it. It just happened. I remembered seeing Danny's knife around there, so I stabbed her with it. Then I left and drove all the way home.' After telling her that in a low voice, he turned the gun around and slammed it in to her head.

When she came to, he had taken her stockings and pants off and was strapping her left hand to the bedstead with a leather thong. Amy pretended she was still unconscious and bunched her right hand up into a fist, a trick she had learned when she and Tricia had played cowboys and Indians; so that when he tied it and she relaxed her hand, it would be loose.

Through slitted eyes she saw him stand up after he had finished tying her other hand, and pull down his pants and then step out of them. His penis was erect and he held one hand around it. As he climbed on top of her, she had to swallow to keep from screaming. He was hurting her, bruising the inside of her legs, crushing her. She turned her head away and saw that he had left the gun sitting on the table next to the bed, almost within her reach if her hand were free.

He was squeezing her breasts like they were made of rubber, digging his fingers into them. When he started prodding his penis between her legs, she felt as if she were going to faint again. His smell was covering her, a bitter sweat like metal. Nausea and fear were crawling over her.

She tried to wriggle her hand free but the leather wasn't slippery, it grabbed at her hand. Reaching down, Hank separated her legs, then he stopped himself for a moment and looked up at her face.

Laughing, he slapped her lightly on the face. 'Come on, Amy. I want you here for this. Wake up.'

When she wouldn't open her eyes, he started pinching her on the cheeks, the shoulders, the breasts; mean tearing bursts of pain. She opened her eyes and screamed.

He slapped a hand over her mouth, and said, 'They don't pay a lot of attention to noise in this place, but might be a good idea to shut you up.' He took a corner of the sheet and started stuffing it into her mouth. Amy started to gag and tried to relax so she wouldn't throw up.

This was how it must have been for Tricia. Amy could hardly stand to think that anyone had done this to her. Something was dying in her and she had to fight to keep it alive. She was giving up, she was giving in to death.

When Amy closed her eyes, she saw red. The world was turning red around her. She could hardly breathe. She went limp and Hank stopped trying to force more cloth into her mouth. 'Now keep those eyes open. I want you to enjoy your last fuck.'

He bent down to his work, and as he tried to thrust into her, she pulled away from him. She stared at the top of his straw-colored head, hating it, and decided she would get him before he could kill her. With all her might she yanked at her hand. It slipped partway out. She felt him enter her and, pushing as hard as she could against him, she jerked at her hand again and it came loose. Hank had his head bent down and was pushing inside of her.

Quickly, she pulled the sheet out of her mouth and took a deep breath. Then she hoisted her legs up in the air. He was surprised at her movement and looked up. As his head came up, she wrapped her legs around his neck. Both his hands went to his throat and he tried to pull her legs away. She pushed against him and reached her free hand out to the gun, feeling it with her fingertips. Hank tried to stand, and that movement shoved her forward enough that she could grab the gun.

She brought the gun down and shoved it into his belly.

'OK, pull out nice and easy. If you want anything left of that stump of yours, don't try anything.'

His hands automatically went down to protect his penis, but when she shoved the gun farther into his gut, he raised them up.

She knew she had to get away from him, but she couldn't get off the bed while one hand was still tied to it. 'Now, real slow, I want you to untie my hand.' She lowered the gun to his groin and said slowly, 'Don't try anything or you'll be even less of a man.'

After he had untied her hands, she slipped off the bed. Her head was pounding and her legs were starting to cramp. Touching her jawline by her ear, she felt it was wet, and when she looked at her hand it was covered with blood. The room tilted slightly. She stretched out her hand with the gun in it and it wobbled. She had to sit down. Slowly backing across the room, she found the chair that Hank had been sitting in earlier.

'Stretch out on the bed.'

He stared at her.

She said it again, 'Stretch' and then fired the first shot. It hit the picture of the young girl, which fell off the wall behind the bed.

He stretched out on the bed and his chin quivered, while tears poured from his eyes. 'What are you going to do to me?' he asked.

He lay shaking and quivering on the bed, his arms held out as if he were about to embrace something. A wave of hatred broke over her, and it felt worse than any sickness she had ever known – it was a poison so strong, she wondered what the antidote could be. Amy didn't know what she was going to do with him. He had his eyes closed and was breathing, in gulps, through his mouth.

She took careful aim and fired, the bullet plunging into the mattress. He shrieked and she shot again. She imagined the bullet ripping up the white stuffing, the flesh of the mattress. Once more she aimed very close to him, she had been very good at target practice, and pulled the trigger.

Hank was muttering something under his breath and she had to listen closely to hear him whimper, like a small child would in the middle of the night when the darkness is closing in like the worst of fears, 'Mama, mama.'

She looked at the mess of a man on the bed and wondered how Tricia had looked, how scared she had been, if she had fought or if she had just slipped away. Amy knew it was all over and she would never know any more than she knew now. Tricia was still dead. Tricia would always be dead. Amy placed the gun in her lap and sat still, watching the blond man cry.

Five years have gone by. I left Minnesota shortly after the trial, after the man who murdered my sister was found guilty and I found out how little difference it made. All I wanted was my sister back.

Luke came with me out to New York, and somehow we've managed out here. It all seems so long ago, and the lakes of Minnesota are so far away. Yet I'm often surprised how little I've changed. A small softness has come into my life, and I can smile when I think of words Tricia would twist to say what she meant, like 'wondy,' she would say, 'that's just wondy,' when she meant wonderful.

I wish she had had more wonder in her life. I wish she were with me to see what is to come. I want her with me when it rains and I walk down the street under my umbrella to get a cup of coffee, I want a sister to talk with about babies and boyfriends and bathing suits. I think of her on her birthday and even have a free drink in a bar for her, I think of her on Christmas and buy myself the present that she would have bought me, I think about her at Thanksgiving when I wash the dishes, and I think of her on the day she died. It comes around once a year and I think of a gravestone, familiar handwriting, curled red hair. I wonder where she's gone and I miss her more than I can put down in words although I have tried. At least I've tried.